PRAI

A GRIM REA
TO CATCHI

"I'd follow this grim reaper anywhere. Wildly creative and impossible to put down, sure to induce both belly laughs and tears, *A Grim Reaper's Guide to Catching a Killer* is full of heart and soul(s)."
—Laura Hankin, author of *One-Star Romance*

"Witty, moving, and with a mystery that'll keep you turning pages late into the night, Dara's debut is a creative, laugh-out-loud novel about the business of death, and what it can teach us about family, love, and the best parts of being alive."
—Claudia Lux, author of *Sign Here*

"I was hooked right away by the inventive premise of Maxie Dara's *A Grim Reaper's Guide to Catching a Killer*, but it was the relationships that really did me in. I loved watching Kathy bond with Conner, a dead teenager, and work through her relationship with recent-almost-ex-husband Simon, all set against the backdrop of a surprisingly corporate job in human soul logistics. Funny and warm and full of little moments that kept me guessing, *A Grim Reaper's Guide to Catching a Killer* is a delightfully fresh mystery!"
—Alicia Thompson, *USA Today* bestselling author of
Love in the Time of Serial Killers

"Sure to lighten the darkest mood. Come for the mystery, stay for the punched-up pairing. This new series is one to watch."
—*Kirkus Reviews*

"Fun and lighthearted despite the presence of death, the characters are relatable and funny, and the paranormal aspects are balanced with the ordinariness of Kathy's messy life. The ending fleshes out this creative premise and sets the book up for the next in a heartwarming series."

—*Booklist*

"This debut paranormal mystery offers humor, love, and a strong cast of characters who form a found family."

—*Library Journal* (starred review)

BERKLEY TITLES BY MAXIE DARA

A GRIM REAPER'S GUIDE TO CATCHING A KILLER

A GRIM REAPER'S GUIDE TO CHEATING DEATH

– A –
GRIM REAPER'S GUIDE TO CHEATING DEATH

Maxie Dara

BERKLEY
NEW YORK

BERKLEY

An imprint of Penguin Random House LLC
1745 Broadway, New York, NY 10019
penguinrandomhouse.com

Book design by Jenni Surasky
Title page art: Stars © intueri / Shutterstock

Library of Congress Cataloging-in-Publication Data

Names: Dara, Maxie, author.
Title: A grim reaper's guide to cheating death / Maxie Dara.
Description: First edition. | New York: Berkley, 2025.
Identifiers: LCCN 2025009524 (print) | LCCN 2025009525 (ebook) |
ISBN 9780593815816 (trade paperback) | ISBN 9780593815823 (ebook)
Subjects: LCGFT: Paranormal fiction. | Cozy mysteries. | Novels.
Classification: LCC PR9199.4.D368 G76 2025 (print) |
LCC PR9199.4.D368 (ebook) | DDC 813/.6—dc23/eng/20250303
LC record available at https://lccn.loc.gov/2025009524
LC ebook record available at https://lccn.loc.gov/2025009525

First Edition: December 2025

Printed in the United States of America
1st Printing

The authorized representative in the EU for product safety and compliance is
Penguin Random House Ireland, Morrison Chambers, 32 Nassau Street,
Dublin D02 YH68, Ireland, https://eu-contact.penguin.ie.

To the P Girls.

A GRIM REAPER'S GUIDE TO CHEATING DEATH

1

Statistically speaking, you're more likely to die on your birthday than any other day of the year. Unfortunately for Nora Bird, her parents beat the odds and died on *her* birthday instead. Eighteen years later and that gray mid-November air still weighed heavy as she shut the day behind her with the swing of a pigeon-graffitied glass door and began the daily trek up the stairs to her office.

It was just after seven a.m., and the corporate-beige halls of S.C.Y.T.H.E.—Secure Collection, Yielding, and Transportation of Human Essences—were still holding their breath between shifts. Nora liked this part of the day best, when the world was empty and belonged to no one in particular. She tucked herself into her office on the top floor of the building. It was a room with no windows, which had served its previous occupants just fine since they were mostly mops, brooms, and the odd bucket. It served Nora just as well. No natural light meant no sun exposure, and no sun exposure meant less risk of skin cancer, something the fluorescent bulbs that buzzed from their rectangular homes on the ceiling never threatened.

In the middle of Nora's desk sat a cupcake frosted with bright blue icing. She cocked her head at it. Ran a finger through the icing and examined it with narrowed eyes. The food dye Blue No. 2 had been found to contribute to brain tumors in rats. She wiped the icing on the rim of the garbage can under her desk, wrapped the cupcake in tissues, and threw it away too, making a mental note to thank Larry, janitor extraordinaire, for the gesture.

Then she got to work.

It always felt fitting for Nora to work on her birthday. It had long been a day marked by death, and after all, that was the nature of her business. Beside the now-vacant spot where the deadly cupcake had just sat rested a pile of manila folders that reached to Nora's chin. The day's cases were patiently waiting to be sorted into their designated department—Natural Causes, Murder, Accidental Deaths—and assigned to specific agents. It was an easy job for Nora, almost mindless at times. Each file needed to be matched with the most appropriate person to collect the soul and bring it to the next stage of its journey. And Nora had studied the agents' files thoroughly enough to matchmake with the prowess of her bubbie.

Moira from Accidental Deaths had studied proctology before coming to S.C.Y.T.H.E., which made her disconcertingly comfortable with nudity, so Moira got the shower falls and toilet mishaps. Ricky from Murder went to school with the kids in most of the major mob families in town, so he got the mob hits and a chance for a quick class reunion to boot. It was easy. Routine. Almost formulaic. Sometimes all Nora had to do was glimpse a single word in a file—"peanut" meant she was dealing with anaphylaxis, which would go to Jorge, who had an unexplained vendetta against legumes and would be the most likely to empathize with anyone who fell victim to one.

Nora skimmed the file of an essence who would definitely be handled by Heart Attack Harpreet in Natural Causes and let her mind drift beyond the four walls of the former broom closet. Nora had been working as an administrative coordinator at S.C.Y.T.H.E. for nearly two and a half years and was finally content with her life. Not happy, exactly. That felt too high stakes. But her dream of pursuing architecture was fading nicely, and the loneliness that came from losing her parents at eight and the grandmother who raised her a few years back didn't sting as sharply as it once had. Her apartment was fine—nice, even, now that she had some art on the walls and a few plants that hadn't yet died despite their best efforts.

She hadn't texted Charlie yet. That was something she should do, probably. Maybe. Unfortunately. It was his birthday too. Though he hadn't texted either, and it didn't seem fair that she had to be the one to send the first text every year.

She opened her phone to Charlie's contact profile. The dumb picture of him with a Fruit Roll-Up hanging out of his mouth like an endless tongue. Their last text exchange, one year ago to the day.

Nora: Happy birthday!
Charlie: HBD butthead

Then silence. She scrolled up to find a similar exchange from the year before that, and the one before that, and several prior, and nothing in between. She closed her phone and returned to her files. Charlie had always been a mystery to Nora, which in and of itself was a mystery to her. Twins were supposed to have something in common, weren't they? And yet, despite sharing a womb and half of their genomes, they couldn't have been less alike. Nora liked facts and statistics and a world that made sense, while Charlie . . . Charlie Bird . . . Charles Ezra Bird was . . . written on the file in Nora's hands.

Nora stopped her daydreaming and sank back into reality, hard. She stopped skimming the page and read it properly, certain she must have mentally inserted her brother's name since he was on her mind. And yet, no matter how many times she reread the name at the top of the file, it never morphed into something different and unconnected to her. The ink was stark and confident.

```
Case # 73588
Charles Ezra Bird
Age: 26
Cause of Death: Struck by Vehicle
Time to Collect: 11:15 a.m.
Location: Calton Avenue
```

The walls of the dark, windowless office marched towards one another, trapping Nora inside. She could almost hear them stepping forward to suffocate her, which wouldn't do much good since she'd stopped breathing all by herself.

Statistically speaking, you're more likely to die on your birthday than any other day of the year. But Nora couldn't let that happen. Not again.

Without thinking, without breathing, Nora stuffed Charlie's file under her arm and fled the broom closet.

2

Case # 36658
Mary-Beth Duke
Age: 83
Cause of Death: Struck by Vehicle

It was the third case Nora had sorted after joining S.C.Y.T.H.E., and she'd thought Mary-Beth's death was an easy enough one to avoid. The octogenarian had been on her way home from a farmers' market when one of her freshly acquired peaches tumbled from the top of her bag onto the road. Mary-Beth chased after it, and within seconds both were asphalt cobbler. Nora was still under a probationary period, with her supervisor, the ever-disinterested Janice, sitting beside her at the already-cramped desk. It wasn't until Nora sorted the file into the "Natural Causes" pile that Janice perked up enough to tut at the new hire. Mary-Beth's case, she explained, belonged in "Accidental Deaths." But to Nora, there was nothing accidental about it. You cross the road without looking both ways and then both ways again, well, you experience the natural consequences.

Everyone knew that. Someone would have to be pretty careless to ignore the cause and effect in a situation like this. Someone like Charlie.

"YOU NEED TO GET IN THE CAR. RIGHT NOW."

By 8:20 a.m. Nora had crossed town at a safe but rapid pace, trudged through the heaps of rusting, tetanus-encrusted car parts on the lawn, and summoned Charlie to the peeling front door of the little clapboard house he shared with four roommates who seemed less than pleased to be woken up before noon. Charlie, for his part, wore a crooked smile beneath a layer of grogginess. His yellow-blond hair, brassy from years of bleach and various dyes, leapt from his head in no less than six different directions. He ran a hand through his red-tinged goatee, currently accompanied by specks of morning stubble on his cheeks. His white T-shirt was stretched out of shape, and his flannel pajama pants had holes in unfortunate places. He smelled of weed and pepperoni pizza. And he was all Nora had left.

"Uh?" Charlie mustered at last.

"You. Car. Now," Nora tried again, her relief at seeing him alive wrestling with her annoyance at his general existence. It wasn't just his death she needed to protect him from; by going against company protocol, she would very shortly need to protect him from an inevitable pursuit by S.C.Y.T.H.E. as well.

"So weird to actually see you here. Is this, like, a birthday thing?"

"No, Charlie," Nora said. "This is not like a birthday thing. This is like a life-or-death thing. This is like a 'you're going to get hit by a car at eleven fifteen a.m. and die' thing. Just. Please. I don't have time to explain it right now, I just need you to trust me."

Charlie let out a laugh that would have been a snort from anyone else. "This morning, huh? Nor, you need to cool it with the 'everyone's going to die all the time' schtick, man. Or at least wait until the birds are up."

He turned to shut the door, then added, "Oh, right. Happy birthday, butthead," before he disappeared behind chipped seafoam paint.

Nora stood on the porch for a moment, hands balled so tightly into fists that her fingernails left little half-moons in her palms. She could feel two and a half decades' worth of sibling rage crawling through her like those little green army men Charlie used to play with at Bubbie's, the ones he'd throw at her while she was drawing to get her attention. Their plastic faces were always poised for battle. But so were her crayons.

Nora unclenched and dug a package of vitamin lozenges from the purse on her shoulder. She loosened one and hurled it at Charlie's window to the left of the front door, at the top of the house, the blinds shut. She threw another and another, their taps growing louder with her increasing force. Finally the blinds separated and Charlie poked an eye out. Nora threw another lozenge for good measure. Charlie reappeared at the door a moment later.

"Dude."

"Charlie." Nora forced her frustration down, just like she always did with Charlie, and went for a different tactic. It was tricky. S.C.Y.T.H.E. policy meant she couldn't share the nature of her job with anyone. But then, S.C.Y.T.H.E. policy also strictly forbade employees from taking any documents off the premises, much less preventing an upcoming death, so one more breach wouldn't make a difference at this point. Besides, she was running out of time. The day shift started at nine a.m., and when none of the Collections Agents had cases on their desks, someone would visit her office and alert her boss, who would inevitably cross-reference the files on her desk with the master spreadsheet, only to find the pile one case short. From there it was only a matter of time until S.C.Y.T.H.E. tracked her down. She was breaking not only the most critical company rules but the very laws of life and death. It wouldn't be easy to get away with. Her head spun at the gravity of the situation.

"Charlie, I need you to listen to me. My job . . . I . . ." *I work for a company of modern-day grim reapers, and according to Death itself, you're slated to die today,* was what Nora wanted to say. Instead she said, "Yes, actually, this is a birthday thing. Happy birthday. We're going away for a while. Starting right now."

Charlie examined his sister for a long moment. They hadn't seen each other in roughly six months, spoke rarely and had even less to say. Nora braced for a very warranted refusal, or at least some mild scrutiny, but instead Charlie's inspection face softened into an oversized smile.

"Cool."

"Wait, what?"

"Like a road trip or something?"

"Uh, sure," said Nora, still catching up to the situation. "Yeah, like that. So let's go."

Charlie shrugged. "Sweet, let me just pack a few things. And there's room for Jessica too, right?"

"Jessica?"

"Yeah, you'll love her, she's hilarious."

Before Nora could reply, Charlie had shut the door again.

"Charlie," Nora called through the door, banging a fist against it despite the risk of infectious slivers. This was ridiculous. They needed to be on the road right now to avoid both S.C.Y.T.H.E. and whatever car was going to hit Charlie, and now he was not only taking his time packing for a road trip but also apparently planning to bring his fling of the day along. She knocked again. "Charlie! Charlie! Charl—"

The door opened again and Charlie emerged, still in his pajamas, an unzipped, half-full duffel bag over one shoulder, a cage containing a large gray parrot in his hands.

Nora blanched. "What the hell is that?"

"This is Jessica," Charlie said, with a look that said "duh."

"You can't bring a—" Nora caught herself. "Right. Great. Can we go please?"

"You're not even going to say hi to her?"

"Charlie, we don't have time for this."

"Nor, it's, like, dawn, what could you possibly be in such a rush for? Come on, you're an aunt now, won't you at least—"

"Hi," Nora said tightly, bending down to the cage from a safe distance. "Hi, Jessica. Nice to meet you." Then back to Charlie, "Let's go now, please."

Charlie closed his eyes contemplatively and held a finger up to Nora—whether to tell her to wait or shut up she couldn't tell.

"Fucking hell, Char—"

Charlie shoved his held-up finger directly into Nora's face. Nora had to swallow down the urge to bite it.

After a beat, a high-pitched squawk emerged from the cage. "Hi. Hi. Fucking hell."

Charlie burst out into his snort-laugh.

"It talks." Nora blinked at the bird. "Perfect. Okay, can we go now?"

Charlie shrugged, but before he could open his mouth, Nora had hooked an arm under his and was hauling him and Jessica towards the car, the open road, and safety.

"So why the kidnapping?" Charlie turned in the passenger seat to face his sister as they crossed through town towards the highway.

Nora kept her eyes on the road. "What are you talking about?"

"I'm talking about how the last time we celebrated a birthday together we had an Elmo cake and you cried because I ate the piece with the balloons on it. So what's up? Like, actually up."

Nora let her eyes slip momentarily to her brother. Then to the clock on her dashboard. It was just after nine; only two hours before Charlie Bird was meant to die.

"You wouldn't believe me."

"Try me."

"Charlie."

"Nora. C'mon. What, you on the run from the law or something?"

A swarm of black-clad S.C.Y.T.H.E. operatives filled Nora's mind's eye, their glistening onyx SUVs practically materializing in the rearview mirror. She blinked hard to chase them away. Because S.C.Y.T.H.E. operated outside the laws of society, the company had its own enforcement team ready to crack down on anyone in the organization who played too fast and loose with the laws of mortality. They were rarely used, but there were rumors of some kind of soul-abduction scheme that got dismantled at a S.C.Y.T.H.E. office in a different state last year. And if those rumors were anything to go by, Nora dreaded being their next target.

"Well . . ." she said in spite of herself.

Charlie bounced in his seat. "No fuckin' way, dude."

"No fuckin' way," Jessica added from the back seat.

Nora exhaled through her nose. Her hands were clenched so hard on the steering wheel that they were cold from the lessening circulation and sweating from nerves all at once.

"Nor?" Charlie prodded.

"Okay," said Nora. "Okay. Look. If I tell you what's going on, I need you to promise—promise me, Charlie, like, actually promise—that you're just going to shut up and nod along and not ask any questions. And just . . . believe me. Okay?"

"This is bad, huh?"

"Charlie. Promise me."

Charlie sat back in his seat for a moment, contemplating. Finally he swiped his right hand under his left armpit and offered it to Nora. "'Kay. Promise."

"Seriously?" Nora gave the hand a glare.

"Well yeah, duh. It's how we always promised shit."

"I'm not shaking that. We aren't gross kids anymore. I mean, are you even wearing deodorant?"

"Oh sure, I'm supposed to have blind faith in you and you don't even trust me to wear deodorant."

"Well, are you?"

"No."

"Charlie." Something inside of Nora switched on all of a sudden. The siren marked "Hey, you realize everything is very bad and overwhelming, right?" finally sounded. Charlie was set to die. Her job was gone. S.C.Y.T.H.E. would be on her heels at any moment. And worst of all, her brother was so relentlessly, indescribably annoying. And it all caught up with her there, in the car, as they sailed past an empty gas station just before the highway turnoff, the smelly hand still in her face. And so Nora did the only reasonable thing she could do in that moment. She began to cry.

Charlie shifted in his seat. He never could withstand Nora's tears. "All right, jeez, sorry. Here." He offered his untainted left hand.

Nora sniffed, blotting her cheeks with the sleeve of her sensible navy blue winter coat. She took the hand and shook it.

"You're going to die today," she said as the crying bout eased into a mildly wavering voice and the odd sniffle. "And I know that for a fact. Because it's what I do."

She explained her job as best she could, keeping her eyes on the road to avoid any flashes of skepticism in her brother's scruffy face. Finally, she reached over Charlie and pulled his file from the glove compartment. "Here," she said. "I found this on my desk this morning. And I didn't . . . and I couldn't . . . here, just read it."

Charlie flipped the folder open. "Huh. That's my name."

"Yeah, ding-dong, exactly. You're supposed to get hit by a car and die sometime just before eleven fifteen a.m. today. I saw that and I just—"

"No, I'm not," Charlie interrupted.

"What? Yes, you are."

"Am not."

Nora merged onto the highway with clenched teeth. This was infuriating. Charlie was infuriating. They were twenty-six years old—today—and he couldn't even act half that age. But before Nora could help it, her childhood reflexes kicked in.

"Are too."

"Am not."

"For fuck's sake, Charlie—"

"No, I'm serious," Charlie said. He held up the file and jabbed a finger at the section marked "cause of death."

Nora could feel the rush of blood leaving her face, likely on its way to a different body with a life that made sense. Somehow she found herself pulling onto the shoulder despite the fact that 12 percent of all highway deaths occur there. Something inside her decided driving in her current state posed the bigger risk just then. The windshield wipers groaned softly as they swatted away a light drizzle. Nora could barely hear them over the thundering in her ears. She snatched the file from Charlie's hands and squinted at it.

"This is impossible."

Just beneath Charlie's name and basic information were the words:

```
Cause of Death: Choking
Time to Collect: 12:00 p.m.
```

The folder shook in Nora's hands. She looked over at Charlie, who had conjured a snack-sized bag of Doritos from seemingly nowhere and was just prying it open.

"Want one?"

Nora slapped the bag from his hands. "Charlie," she shouted. "Did you not just read the file? According to this you're . . . you're going to die by choking now, somehow. You can't eat those. You can't eat anything until we figure out what the hell is going on. It was supposed to be a car . . ."

"But I haven't eaten breakfast, dude, I'm starving."

"Are you seriously not hearing me? If you eat anything right now, you could die."

"Okay, but, like, isn't that always a risk? Besides, not eating kinda takes the fun out of living."

"Charlie!"

"Okay, okay, no Doritos. Guess I'll just waste away."

Nora glanced at Charlie's hand—the one she'd shaken. "You don't believe me."

"Sure, I believe you," said Charlie. "I've believed weirder. Plus that file thing. Plus, you're my sister."

"Then why the hell aren't you taking this seriously?"

Charlie squared himself to face his sister. He studied her face, his brown eyes shifting back and forth across it as if he was searching for something. When he finally seemed to find it, his own face sobered. "No Doritos," he said. "No food. For now. Got it. I can do that."

Nora nodded. "Just until after twelve, all right? If we can get you past the collection time, we should be in the clear."

"Cool," said Charlie. "So where are we going?"

Nora turned the car back on and set her eyes towards the road. It was 9:20 a.m. and her absence at S.C.Y.T.H.E. would be known by now. She pulled back into traffic.

"Anywhere but here."

3

Case # 77721
Mason Christopher White
Age: 21
Cause of Death: Choking

Nora had learned how to perform the Heimlich maneuver by age eleven. By age eleven and a half, she had practiced on three teddy bears, one Baby-Eats-a-Lot doll, and a coughing man at Pizza Hut who, it turns out, suffered from particularly vocal postnasal drip. No one at Mason's frat party had been quite so diligent, leaving him to choke on a bottle cap after he'd plucked it off with his teeth. The case had come through one particularly rainy morning as Nora sipped on chamomile tea and nibbled at a bran muffin. The muffin promptly hit the rim of the garbage can under Nora's desk and landed with a bounce on a cushion of discarded tissues. Choking cases always made her lose her appetite. Along with learning the Heimlich maneuver, eleven-year-old Nora learned all of the potential complications that came along with it: the broken ribs and gastrointestinal hemorrhaging. Not to mention the number of people who choked to death simply because they were so embarrassed to be choking at all that they left the company of others to asphyxiate without making a whole thing about it. Choking, Nora had long-ago concluded, was something to be wholly avoided at any cost.

CIVILIZATION GAVE WAY TO AN ENDLESS GRAY SKY AND THE ENDLESS gray roads beneath. Neither Nora nor Charlie had spoken in over an hour. Even Jessica held her tongue from her cage in the back seat. Nora's grip on the steering wheel had loosened, her knuckles steadily regaining their color with each passing mile. The farther they'd fled from her branch of S.C.Y.T.H.E., the easier she breathed. Not that they were out of the woods. They wouldn't be that until she had the mental presence to formulate a real plan. S.C.Y.T.H.E.'s national headquarters would eventually hear about the girl who'd stolen a case file, and a soul who wasn't a soul yet. As long as she was in the country, she had a target on her back, and so did Charlie.

Something gave a gurgling roar in the passenger seat. Nora shot a look at Charlie, who gave his soft middle a gentle pat.

"She's hungry."

Nora cocked a brow.

"Señorita Munch Munch," Charlie clarified, indicating his stomach with another pat. "Don't tell me you've forgotten about the señorita."

"Weirdly enough, Charlie, I had," Nora said with an eye roll. "And I'd stop listening to the señorita if I were you. All that processed junk you eat is going to put you in an early grave."

"I thought that was supposed to be choking's job." Charlie's stomach growled again. "You summoned her with all that processed food talk, you know."

Nora just shook her head. "And that's another thing. Choking to death, Charlie, really? You know who chokes? Babies choke. And little kids who don't chew their food properly. And toddlers who suck the plastic eyeballs off their teddy bears. And then you, apparently. It's embarrassing."

"Sorry for not dying cooler, sis. We can't all be Mom and Dad, I guess."

His words hit Nora like a piano falling out a window in a cartoon. She could practically see the little yellow birds flying in a halo around her head from the impact. Their mom and dad had died in an accident of some sort. That was all Nora and Charlie were ever told, in order to spare them the trauma of visualizing the details. What it did instead was leave a void that Nora had spent her life trying to fill by studying death. She could tell you exactly how many people a year died from being struck by lightning (twenty-four thousand), which bodies of water carried the most dangerous predators and bacteria (anything in Florida), and the safest time to cross the street (two p.m. on a Tuesday). But she couldn't tell you how her parents died, and that, more than any accident could, had always killed her.

"Fuck you," she said.

"Fuck you," Jessica agreed.

Charlie's stomach rumbled again, and Nora decided even the señorita was on her side.

"Sorry." Charlie put his hands up, his face soft with genuine remorse. "Sorry. I think I'm hangry. I'm not used to going this long without at least a little snacky snack."

Nora sighed. It was true; Charlie never deprived himself of

anything he wanted. Not the last slice of pizza, not the boy Nora had mooned over their entire junior year of high school, and certainly not a snacky snack. Charlie lived to enjoy living. It wasn't something Nora understood, and it certainly caused her a fair amount of frustration over the years. But that was Charlie, and it had been since the death of their parents. Bubbie always used to say he was a lost soul, but since Nora had started her job and seen real lost souls, she decided he was just kind of an ass.

His tummy gave another pathetic plea.

An ass who also happened to be the only family she had left.

The sign for a rest stop blurred as they cruised past. Nora clocked it and checked the time. They could afford a five-minute diversion. Plus, Nora really had to pee.

"I'll get you a smoothie," she said, and pulled off the highway.

Just past the turnoff sat two rest stops on opposite sides of an otherwise empty road. Nora pulled into the lot of a squat little building with a faded sign reading "Nutrition-2-Go" in a font that wasn't quite, but was definitely a longtime friend of, Comic Sans. She parked the car directly out front, leaving the motor running to stave off the chill of the day, and swung off her seat belt.

"You stay here," she said. "Don't move. And for the love of god, do. Not. Eat. Anything. I'll just be a sec."

Charlie stared at the sign through doubtful eyes. "This place looks like it specializes in kale-flavored spinach."

"Bird food," Jessica added.

"Yeah, probably, but look." Nora jabbed a finger towards the sun-bleached poster in the window displaying an assortment of green smoothies. "Those can't be choked on, so they won't kill you."

"No, but they might make me want to kill myself," Charlie muttered.

Nora's bladder gave a twinge. "Give me two minutes, all right? Got any flavor requests? It looks like they've got avocado with peach and something called Magic-kale Spell."

"Whichever one looks least like Linda Blair regurgitated it, please."

Nora nodded and hustled out of the car, the warmth of the mechanically heated air quickly replaced by a sharp late-autumn chill, which somehow made her have to pee even more. She waddled through the door, a weathered bell above it ushering her in with a defeated sigh, and placed an order for two Divine Detox smoothies. It was getting close to lunchtime, and Nora could use some brain power to figure out the twins' next steps. She shuffled to the bathroom as the blender started whirling and sat down, basking in the first moment of calm she'd experienced all morning. She'd take some relief wherever she could get it at this point.

Nora collected the smoothies in their cardboard holder, sneaking a sip from one of them and wincing as the tart, pulpy sludge settled on her tongue. She shouldered open the door and took a step towards the car before stopping abruptly. Her breath caught as she quickly scanned the lot. It was empty.

"Charlie?" she called into the nothingness around her. Without thinking she let the smoothies drop from her hands, desperately patting down her cargo pants and jacket in search of her phone, a puddle of green forming around her sneakers. Nothing. Her pockets were empty save for hand sanitizer and a stick of aspartame-free gum. She unzipped her purse and rifled through. No phone. She must have left it in the car. The car that was gone.

Could S.C.Y.T.H.E. have caught up with them already? Her stomach sank to her knees at the thought. But what else could possibly have taken her car, and her brother, away? That was actually not a difficult question for Nora to answer. She knew Death, and by extension, in her own way, she knew life. And everything that threatened it. She could have forgotten to put the car in park somehow and left it to roll away. There could have been a carjacker in the area. But the lot was flat and there didn't appear to be anyone around for miles. Nothing made sense. Which seemed very fitting for the day.

Nora's panic flared. Her spindly legs took off at a run before her brain could catch up with them. In a blink, she was at the edge of the parking lot, staring out at a horizon bordered by fields and the odd dot of a farmhouse. She checked her watch. Eleven fifty-five. Five minutes until Charlie Bird was going to die. Was this how it happened? When you stopped someone from dying the way they're supposed to, did they simply disappear?

"Charlie," she shouted again, doubling over, a desperate sob lodging in her throat. "Charlie!"

"Yeah?" Charlie's voice called back.

Nora stood upright, stifled the sob, and tracked the sound of the voice to its scruffy source across the street at the opposite rest stop, just outside a Wendy's.

"You fucking asshole," Nora shouted. She looked both ways and bolted across the empty street and through the Wendy's parking lot, where her car was safely parked, landing a punch on her brother's bare arm just as he took a scoop of the Frosty in his hand.

"Hey," he whined, a lump of icy chocolate slipping from his spoon to land in a heap on the pavement.

"No. No way. You do not get to be the indignant one here. What the fuck were you thinking? I told you to stay put. Do you have any idea the kind of danger you're in?"

"You can't choke on a Frosty," Charlie said, tapping his forehead proudly with the handle of his red plastic spoon.

"This isn't about a stupid Frosty, Charlie," said Nora. "This is about . . . look, the people I work for? They're not going to be too thrilled that I have your file, much less you. I don't know what they're capable of, but I know they're not just going to be okay with this situation. So we need to be careful, and smart, and stick together. Got it?"

"Yeah, right, got it." Charlie scooped another spoonful, but before he could get it into his mouth, Nora grabbed his arm and dragged him back to the car.

Once again in the warmth and security of the little black Honda Civic, Nora let herself breathe. They were on the road again, and Charlie was too busy with his Frosty to annoy her. This was as close to contentment as she could ask for under the circumstances. She checked the time. Noon had come and gone with a buffer of eleven minutes, and Charlie was still alive. She almost allowed herself a smile. They'd done it. Charlie wouldn't die today. Except . . . one thing nibbled at the corner of her brain like a mouse on a cracker.

"Charlie," she said. "Grab the file."

Charlie smeared a dab of chocolate from his cheek onto the sleeve of his T-shirt and leaned forward, popping open the glove compartment. He pulled the file free and looked expectantly at his sister, awaiting instruction.

"What's up?"

"Cause of death," said Nora. "What does it say?"

"Choking," Charlie said without looking at the page. "It's the reason you've got me on a liquid diet, remember?"

"Can you just read it, please?"

Charlie chugged a sip of melted Frosty and put the cup into the cup holder, shifting his position as if he were about to crack open *War and Peace*. He cleared his throat and skimmed down the page with his finger.

"Cause of death," he said, scanning. "Cause of death. Ah. Oh."

"'Oh'? What 'oh'?"

"This doesn't make any sense."

"What 'oh,' Charlie?" Nora demanded, a familiar rush of adrenaline coursing through her.

"You're not gonna like this."

"Charlie."

"'Cause of death: car accident,'" Charlie read.

Nora slammed on the brakes.

"As for example," Charlie said in a shout, a protective arm flung across the Frosty.

"Heavens," Jessica squawked from the back seat.

Nora fell back into herself, realizing in horror what she had done. There were no other cars on this rural stretch of highway, but even still, if a car accident was Charlie's new cause of death, she couldn't be too careful. Hell, even under regular circumstances, there was no such thing. An error like this wasn't in her usual repertoire. An error like this could cost Charlie his life. She drove on.

"Sorry. Jesus. Sorry."

"No harm done," Charlie said.

"Not yet, anyway," Nora said. "The time," she added, frantic. "What's the collection time?"

"Uhhhhhhh," Charlie read back over his file. "There isn't one."

"What?"

"Yeah, it just says 'Collection time,' and then it's blank."

"Okay." Nora sucked in a shuddering breath. "Okay. What's the location? I need to know where to avoid driving."

"Highway 286."

"*Where* on Highway 286, Charlie?"

But Charlie just shrugged. "That's all it says."

"That doesn't make any sense. Again. Why doesn't anything make any sense?" Nora steadied herself with a deep breath. "All right. Well. We broke Death, I guess. So, what do we do now? We get off the road is what we do now. We get off the road and go somewhere safe. A safe house. But not a house. So what? A motel, maybe. There's got to be a motel somewhere around here."

"Do you do this a lot?" Charlie asked.

"Do what?"

"Have entire conversations with yourself."

Nora's mind traveled back to her little apartment and all the lively debates about what to have for dinner or which movie to curl up with that took place therein. To her teens and the crushes she talked herself into or out of. To her hermit's cave of an office at S.C.Y.T.H.E., where all her most complex decisions were puzzled out with only her desk and a dusty filing cabinet there to hear. To the days and years after her parents died, when she would tell herself that this kind of thing happened, but that it would never, ever happen to someone she loved again.

"No."

"Huh," said Charlie. "So, you muttered something about a motel?"

4

The Casa Comfort motel stood at a squat three stories, wrapping snugly around an empty pool that doubled as a museum of shriveled leaves and no less than two dead frogs. Nora wrapped her coat tight around her slender torso, tucking Charlie's file under one arm, convinced she'd sent agents out this way at least once for some unseemly soul collection. She walked around the car to find Charlie squeezing Jessica's cage into his duffel bag.

"Okay, baby girl. I need you to be nice and quiet for Daddy. Can you do that for me?"

"Smells bad," was Jessica's reply as Charlie pulled the zipper and slung the bag over his shoulder.

"Where'd you get that thing anyway?" Nora asked.

"Walmart."

"The parrot?"

"Oh." They passed under the entryway awning just as the wind picked up. "Someone left her on the porch. Crazy, right? A whole-ass bird."

"Do you ever do anything like a normal person?"

"Says the grim reaper."

"Administrative coordinator for grim reapers," Nora corrected. "Wait, no, I mean, they're not—"

But by that point they'd reached the concierge desk and the roughly Gumby-shaped guy of no more than eighteen behind it, scrolling on his phone. Nora left the rest of her sentence at the door and changed tactics, directing her focus towards the motel employee.

"Hey. Hi. Good afternoon," she tried, her nerves too fried for small talk. "We need a room. Like, right now."

"I see," said the young man, stooping his towering torso to meet Nora at eye height. He looked back and forth between the twins with a knowing smirk, clearly stifling a giggle. "A room right now, you say?"

"Oh god." Nora caught up to the teen's tone with horror. "No."

"Dude," Charlie added.

"Not a room like that."

"Dude."

"Two beds, please. As far apart as you've got them."

The teen's face fell slightly. "Oh. Yeah. All right, fine. We've got a few of those available." He tapped at his computer for a second or two, turned to the wall of keys behind him, and plucked one from its hook. "Room 204. You've got a pool view, which is honestly just depressing this time of year. A constant reminder of the many limitations thrust upon us by the weather and her fickle moods. Can't even use the floaties."

"Uh, thanks." Nora took the key from the teen's outstretched hand.

"Enjoy your stay," said the teen. "Or try to, anyway. Enjoyment is a fleeting thing, difficult to conjure and even more challenging to sustain. Checkout is at ten a.m."

"Happiness is temporary," came a squawk from Charlie's duffel. The twins froze, their eyes sliding in synchronicity to meet the other's with a look that said, "Oh fuck, we're screwed."

"The bag gets it," was all the teen said before returning to his phone.

Nora and Charlie simultaneously let out the breath they'd been holding and scurried towards their room.

THE CARPET OF ROOM 204 HAD BEEN A DIFFERENT COLOR ONCE, that much was clear. The mystery of which color was one that would require a crack detective team to solve, and even then it was likely to end up as a cold case. These days it lived its life as a concerning shade of noncommittal beige against the earwax orange of the walls.

Charlie shrugged his bag off his shoulder and onto the bed closest to the window, claiming his territory as he wrangled the birdcage to freedom.

"There's my girl," he cooed as Jessica emerged, her gray head bobbing back and forth in greeting.

Nora flopped heavily onto her own narrow bed, the weight of the day having sunk deep into her bones. She stared sightlessly at the boob-shaped light above her, its glow nearly as orange as the chipped paint on the walls. Her coat rustled against the rough, aggressively floral comforter, and a pang of homesickness struck her. She'd only been away from her cozy little apartment—her sanctuary—for a few hours, but under the circumstances she couldn't imagine when she'd be able to return again. Her fiddle-leaf fig was a goner for sure.

She blinked and the boob light was gone, replaced by Charlie's fuzzy face.

"I'm going exploring," he said. "Wanna come?"

"No."

"Suit yourself, I'll—"

"No, I mean you're not going out there," said Nora. "It's too risky."

"I'm not gonna be in a car, Nor," said Charlie. "Gonna be a bit tricky for me to get into a car accident on foot."

Nora groaned and rolled over, grabbing Charlie's file from where it sat by her scratchy pillow. The cause of death hadn't changed.

"Fine," she relented. "Stay on the premises and, for fuck's sake, be safe."

Charlie gave a salute and disappeared out the door. Nora turned onto her side and found Jessica perched on the pillow, waiting for her. She jumped back in surprise, then regained her composure. "Why doesn't anybody understand personal space?"

The bird shuffled its weight from foot to foot, staring at Nora expectantly. Nora stared back, unsure of what to make of this strange creature. Jessica seemed to be thinking the same thing.

"Okay, so we're stuck here," Nora said after a moment, more to herself than the parrot. "Charlie can't be in the car because Charlie will die in the car. Because Charlie is still going to die. Why the fuck is Charlie going to die?" Her voice caught. She steadied herself. "We need a plan. A proper one."

Jessica bobbed her head again.

"Any insights?"

Jessica hopped a step closer. "Forest house," she squawked, the nonsense words sharp against the still air of the room.

"Didn't think so. No. I've got to do this on my own. Shocker. What else is new?"

The bird gave a shake of her feathers, hopped off the bed, and went back into her cage across the room.

"Typical," said Nora. "You really are Charlie's pet."

Nora tossed over onto her back and closed her eyes to think. They couldn't get back on the road, that much was certain. But they had driven long enough and far enough that they were now somewhere roughly in the middle, or just to the left, of nowhere. Hopefully, nowhere enough that S.C.Y.T.H.E. wouldn't find them. That Death wouldn't find them. Maybe, somehow, by some fluke of fate, they were safe. That wasn't a word that came easily to Nora. Even at her desk or in the soft warmth of her bed, she was never confidently safe. Accidents could happen anywhere, and often did. But her anxiety-consumed mind needed safety right now, and in her exhaustion she allowed herself to have it, just for a moment. Just long enough for her muscles to loosen, her body to sink as much as possible into the stiff motel mattress, and finally, for Nora to drift into unbidden sleep.

NORA AWOKE NEARLY TWO HOURS LATER TO THE SMELL OF SOME-thing burning. She scrambled, trying to blink away the grogginess blurring her vision to a chorus of "shit, shit" from Charlie somewhere towards the other end of the room. When her eyes finally adjusted, she found him sucking his middle and index fingers, a still-smoking match in a freshly singed divot on the carpet at his feet.

"What the hell are you doing?" Nora swung herself out of bed and started towards him.

"No, no, close your eyes," Charlie said.

"Charlie." Nora crossed her arms in front of her chest, staring daggers.

"Well, it was supposed to be a surprise." He stepped away from the window, revealing a vending machine Moon Pie with a match sticking out of it perched on the sill.

Nora looked from the little cake to her brother and back.

"For our birthday," he said, waving his hands at the treat like a 1970s game show prize model.

"Oh," said Nora.

He dug into the waistband of his pajama pants and plucked out a photograph.

"Here," he said, offering it to her. "I've been saving it for you. For us, I guess."

"Oh," Nora said again. She took the photo, brows knitted. Her nap still clung to her enough to make the whole exchange surreal. The man in the middle of the photo stared back at her with eyes that pinched slightly at the corners the same way hers did, a dimple pocking his right cheek identical to the one on her own. He had one arm around another man, his other around a woman. Nora discreetly gave her thigh a small pinch with her free hand to make sure she was actually awake.

"He was exactly twenty-six there, just like us," Charlie said. "Look." He flipped the picture over in Nora's hand. On the back, in writing she knew nearly as well as her own, were the words "The Bird siblings, Virgo Bay, Nova Scotia, 1996."

Nora looked up at Charlie. "Virgo Bay? Why does that ring a bell?"

"It's where Dad grew up. I forgot about it too. He didn't talk about it much, but there were a bunch of other things from there in that old cigar box of his that Bubbie held on to. Coupla other photos and some seashells and stuff. That's where I found this." He poked at the photo, still flipped over in Nora's hands. She read the inscription again, her already-furrowed brow furrowing further.

"Dad didn't have siblings."

"Yeah, I figure that must've been his squad. My buddies and I all go by the West Side Horn Dogs, but to each their own. They seem like a fun bunch."

Nora flipped the photo back over and examined the three figures it held locked in time. The man beside her father was shorter, his hair straight and thinning where her father's curled around his brows in lush waves, but there was something famil- iar in the man's expression that Nora couldn't shake. The woman on the other side was a delicate thing with birdlike bones and fire in her eyes, standing a whole head shorter than Martin Bird. They were all soaked to the bone in their windbreakers, rain glistening on their faces, ocean waves lifted in a frantic dance behind them.

"This was two years before we were born," said Nora, trans- fixed. "Why don't we know about them?"

Charlie shrugged. "People get weird when they have kids. Friends drop like flies."

"I guess." Nora pried her gaze away and looked back to Char- lie. "Thanks for this."

"All good. Figured you'd have more use for it. Everything just gets lost or peed on at my place."

Nora nodded, slipping the photo into the pocket of her jacket, her mind still half in Virgo Bay.

"Anyhoo, shall we?" Charlie said. He struck the match from the Moon Pie against the motel-brand matchbook in his hand. The little makeshift candle took light, its reflection undulating in the window behind it. "Happy birthday!"

"Happy birthday," Nora said, allowing herself a small smile. She wouldn't let that carcinogenic chocolate time bomb of a snack cake anywhere near her internal organs, but it was an unexpectedly sweet gesture all the same. Maybe they could do this. Maybe they could actually do this. Together. The first thing they'd done together in eighteen years, and the most important of their lives.

"We blow it out on the count of three," said Charlie. "Ready?" The twins moved over the little flickering match.

"One," said Charlie. "Two. Thr—"

Someone knocked on the door to a neighboring room. Hard. Another knock sounded from down the hall. And another from the other side.

Nora froze. The knocking continued, getting closer, occasionally interrupted by the sound of a door opening, of words being exchanged, before more knocking resumed.

"Stay here," Nora said, her stomach suddenly somewhere below her knees. She slunk to the motel room door and pressed an eye to the peephole. A scattered herd of black-clad people lined the hallway, going door to door, a scythe and arrow emblem emblazoned on the backs of their jackets. Nora stepped back from the door, eyes wild. "No. No, no, no."

"Nor?"

"Shh!" She flicked off the lights and raced back to the window, blowing out the match with more spit than air. The room sank into a heavy darkness, the clouds beyond the window staving off any remaining whispers of setting sunlight. "It's them. They're coming."

Before Charlie could open his mouth to reply, a knock sent their door shivering on its hinges.

They were here.

5

We have to get out of here," Nora whispered.

"Okay," said Charlie. "How?"

Nora opened the window and looked down. They were two stories up, the tail of the leaf-filled, T-shaped pool stretching to just beneath them, concrete surrounding it. She looked up and to either side of the window, but the walls were flat and the fire escape was three rooms down. Charlie's gaze followed hers.

"Jump?" he offered.

"Absolutely not," said Nora. A twenty-foot drop wasn't likely to kill them, but the injuries could be immense. Compound fractures, wounds bad enough to require skin grafts, broken ribs that could pierce a lung. She once sorted a fatal fall that involved more impaling than she'd come across since her college medieval history class.

"You got a better idea?" Charlie said.

Another knock, this one even harder than the last. Nora suddenly couldn't move. It felt like the questionable beige carpet had reached up its fibers and countless years of grime and was holding fast to the soles of her shoes. She was trapped. By S.C.Y.T.H.E., by the drop beyond the window, by her own panic.

In a sudden whoosh of feathers, Jessica soared past Nora's head and out the window. Nora's heart lurched, her rooted feet suddenly free enough to carry her into a backward stumble. A floppy black item sailed after Jessica; Charlie's duffel bag, flying by in a blur of nylon before landing with a crunch somewhere below.

Nora's head whipped to the nearest bed, where Charlie hovered, his arms still outstretched from the throw. She couldn't process anything that was happening. The world seemed as blurry as the duffel bag that had just whizzed through the window. Charlie was looking straight ahead now, in the direction his things had flown. Time stopped and then sped up as Charlie took off at a run, barreling towards Nora. She tracked him in a trance as he raced around the bed and over the windowsill. Before she had time to protest, time to think, he was over the ledge and in the air, gravity ushering him swiftly down with greedy hands.

Nora fell against the wall, dizzy, acutely aware of Death's footsteps approaching as quickly as S.C.Y.T.H.E.'s enforcement agents. As quickly as Charlie was approaching the ground. The knocking grew louder, more urgent. Or was that Nora's heartbeat? In seconds that felt like years, Charlie landed in a heap on the accumulation of dry leaves that lined the bottom of the pool. The leaves enveloped him, swallowed him for long enough that Nora was sure they would be his grave. Then, like a whale cresting in the ocean, he emerged, swimming his way to the surface of the leaves and offering an enthusiastic thumbs-up back at Nora.

The knocking sound at the door morphed into something

angrier. Something blunter. As though someone was trying to kick it in. Nora forced her eyes away from the door and back towards her brother, who had made his way to the pool ladder and was climbing up, Jessica waiting patiently for him on the nearby diving board.

Nora was trapped. The only way out was in the clutches of the already-mysterious S.C.Y.T.H.E.'s most mysterious members and whatever mysterious horrors they had waiting for her. Or down, down, into a bed of leaves if she was very lucky, or a puddle of viscera on concrete if she wasn't. She had spent her whole life avoiding risk, and now she had to actively choose between two.

A door hinge creaked and gave way, and so did Nora. Without allowing her brain the time to think things through, she snatched Charlie's file from her bed and clambered shakily onto the windowsill. The ground seemed to retreat farther away with each fraction of a second she stared at it. The pool shrank to a fishbowl, the concrete suddenly all she could see. Charlie was a dot somewhere on that hard, bone-breaking ground.

She wouldn't jump. She couldn't jump. She knew this with everything that made her Nora June Bird.

As she shifted on the sill, bracing to climb down and face whatever would come next, her knee landed in the forgotten Moon Pie, its sugary frosting sliding beneath the fabric of her cargos. Her balance wavered, then gave way all together, and all at once and without any say in the matter, Nora was airborne. She thought she'd at least scream as she plummeted towards the earth, the ground rushing eagerly to meet her, but she didn't have time. Before she could rally her vocal cords for a shriek, she was engulfed in a bed of leaves. The smell of decay rushed up her nostrils as she scrambled to her feet. Charlie was at the top of the ladder with a hand extended as she emerged, still half in a daze. She let him haul her up the rest of the way and sank to her chocolaty knees on the concrete. Jessica hopped over to her and bit at the little finger of her right hand, the sensation forcing Nora back into her body.

Charlie grabbed his file from where it had landed poolside and helped Nora to her feet.

"Think we can get back in the car now?" he said.

Nora looked from Charlie to the file in his hand, head spinning.

"I'm not sure we have a choice."

6

Case # 90587
Arthur Phan
Age: 41
Cause of Death: Car Accident

Most days, Nora wished she didn't have to drive. She was
three minutes late to work that day after spending half an hour
stuck in the kind of unmoving traffic that made you wonder if
you would ever use the gas pedal again. It wasn't until she got
into her little office that she understood what had caused the
gridlock. A five-car pileup sat across her desk in the form of Arthur's file. She'd tapped her pen to her chin, eyeing the accident
through a narrowed gaze. These were always among her least
favorite cases. Delicate sacks of meat versus thousands of pounds
of metal. The battle wasn't even, and yet most people unwittingly
fought it on a daily basis. In Arthur's case, it ended in more pieces
than a body generally liked to be in. Nora moved his file to the
top of the pile. First of the day to die meant first of the day to sort.

Today was his lucky day, but only because it had been his un-
luckiest day possible first.

THE ROAD WAS FILLED WITH UNTOLD HORRORS. IT ALWAYS HAD
been. Why anybody thought cars were a reasonable option forever confused Nora, who had agreed to take a driving test only
when Bubbie became too frail to get herself to doctor appoint-
ments towards the end of her life. Charlie got his license almost
the moment he was eligible, their November birthday leaving
him the last in his friend group without that ticket to freedom.
As soon as he had it, Nora rarely saw him. It marked the beginning of the end of their childhood closeness in many ways, which,
though she would never admit it, was yet another reason Nora
didn't much care for the concept of driving. It had cost her her
brother once, and now there was a very real chance it would take
him from her again, only this time more permanently.

Nora kept her eyes on the road, her hands at ten and two, and
her foot primed to slam on the brake at any given moment. The
gray of the day had deepened into a velvety black that stood un-
interrupted by city lights as they traveled aimlessly down the rural highway.

The thought currently torturing her, the one that had fought
its way to the front of a very long line of thoughts waiting to do
the same, was, *How?* How had S.C.Y.T.H.E. found them? She'd
feared they were coming, but most of what she feared, which was
rather a lot, didn't actually happen. They must have tracked her
down somehow. But she couldn't imagine them accessing something as civilian as her phone location. That would require the

higher-ups to bring organizations from outside of the company into the fold, and that simply wasn't done.

Then it hit her.

"Charlie," she said, keeping her eyes sharp for any potential dangers around them. "Go into my purse for me."

Charlie reached down and pulled the little black bag from where it sat at his feet.

"I need you to get my name badge out."

One of the perks of being a S.C.Y.T.H.E. employee came in the form of a little metal rectangle engraved with your name and the emblem of the company. Beyond the aesthetic appeal, which was minimal, came the ability to blend seamlessly into the background the moment you pinned on the badge. They were mostly used by Collections Agents, who needed the near invisibility out in the field. The awkwardness of being found hovering over a body while making a collection in the days before the badges was still cringed about by some of the more senior staff. But every employee was issued a badge for emergency situations. Knowing exactly how the badges worked was definitely above Nora's pay grade, but some said it was Death's way of doing a favor for those doing a favor for Death. Regardless, it did things Nora couldn't explain, and she couldn't help but wonder if keeping track of her was one of them.

Charlie wrestled Nora's badge from the tentacles of a power cord and popped it on her lap. She let her eyes slip from the road just long enough to run across it. It looked like it always had, the silver tarnished at the edges and around the letters of Nora's name after nearly two and a half years of life in her purse. But the logo, the scythe and arrow that usually sat black and cold against the silver metal, was glowing red.

"Shit," Nora shouted. "Shit, shit, fucking shit!"

"Fucking shit," Jessica agreed from the back seat.

Nora rolled her window down and hurled the badge into the darkness. Wind whipped into the car, sending tendrils of her thin, ponytailed hair loose around her cheeks. She closed the window and forced her now-trembling hands back to ten and two.

"So, uh," said Charlie. "That was weird."

"They were tracking us," Nora said. "They know which direction we've gone."

"But they're not tracking us now?" said Charlie.

"No," said Nora. "I mean, I don't think so."

"Cool. So we can go anywhere then, and they can't find us, right?"

"I guess. But we have nowhere to go, Charlie." Nora's adrenaline was ramped up to "bear attack" mode. Which, to be fair, was only a few levels higher than where it usually sat, roughly between "pop quiz" and "we need to talk," but still. The thundering of her heart was deafening. "We can't go to either of our homes, they'll look for us there. And for all I know there's a S.C.Y.T.H.E.-wide alert with my info, telling agents across the country to keep an eye out for us."

"Okay, so we leave the country."

"Hilarious. Be reasonable, Charlie."

"You're telling me you don't keep your passport on you at all times these days?"

"You're telling me you actually packed yours?"

"Duh, you said we were going on a road trip. That usually means getting shit-faced in Tijuana at some point."

"Where would we even go?"

"Tiju—"

"Not Tijuana, Charlie."

Charlie shrugged and stuck a hand in the pocket of Nora's coat, pulling out the photo of their father and his friends.

"In that case, Virgo Bay, Nova Scotia sounds pretty peachy right now," he said. "Maybe these two wildcats are still there. Free room and board, plus a nice little change of scenery."

An eighteen-wheeler entered Nora's rearview mirror. It was the only other vehicle they'd shared the highway with so far that evening. Charlie was still talking, his voice animated, but Nora could no longer hear the words. In the panic over her name badge, she'd temporarily forgotten about the threat to Charlie, but last she'd checked he was still fated to die in a car accident on the highway. The truck drew up beside them on the right, and she allowed herself a peek inside the truck's cab, as if the driver would be twirling a moustache like a villain in an old cartoon. Instead he seemed like a perfectly average, three-dimensional man; white-haired, a round belly resting against the steering wheel. But his eyes drifted closed for longer than a blink before jolting open again.

Nora looked around, eager to change lanes, but there were only the two. The truck kept pace, though it drifted occasionally, ever so slightly, over the line separating it from Nora's car.

"Charlie," Nora said, swerving a little towards the concrete barrier between highways as the truck crept towards them again. Charlie followed his sister's head tilt to the truck on the passenger side. He looked back at Nora, eyebrows raised enough to crease his forehead with a look that said, "That guy?"

The swerving grew more aggressive with each passing mile, but Nora couldn't seem to pass the truck. Each time she sped up, the giant tires started to clip at her car's paint. After a few rounds of this, she noticed the swerving had developed a rhythm. Every eight to ten seconds, the truck weaved into Nora's lane, farther each time, before promptly righting itself again. She dared a look through the passenger window, and through her mind's eye the truck plowed through the lines and straight into the car, into the passenger side, into Charlie. The last time it had made its way into their lane, the truck's force had actually given Nora's car a small push. The next time could very well be the last. She counted to eight and slammed on the brakes just as the truck pummeled its way into their lane, straight through the barrier dividing the highway, and inexplicably emerged intact on the other side.

Nora ducked as the tail of the truck careened past them, narrowly missing the car's bumper. She dragged Charlie down into a huddle on his seat, and they remained crouched until the roar of the truck's wheels faded into the distance. Finally, Nora sat back upright, just in time to catch the truck weaving away in the opposite direction.

"Are you okay?" Nora rasped, mouth dry, eyes still fixated on the disappearing truck.

"Yeah, all good," said Charlie. "You?"

Nora could only give a weak nod.

"Jessica, you all right back there, baby?" Charlie asked the bird in the back seat.

"Fuck," Jessica squawked.

"That's what I like to hear," said Charlie. "So, Virgo Bay?"

Nora finally looked at him. "What?"

"Yeah, look. I can't find Virgo Bay on my GPS, but it looks like we can get to Nova Scotia from this ferry, right, which is only like an hour and a half from here. Then it's a few hours on the boat and we're there. I figure we can bug some locals for directions once we get there. I bet it's some little fishing village no one's ever heard of except the towns nearby. Bet the seafood is straight fire."

Charlie's voice and enthusiasm were unchanged by everything that had just occurred. It was as if nothing out of the ordinary had taken place, as if Nora hadn't just had to figure out how to save his life. His nonchalance was like ice water dumped onto Nora's head. "You realize we just almost died, right?" she said.
"You realize *you* just almost died, right? You saw how close we came. That truck nearly plowed into your side of the car like it did with the highway barrier. You were *this* close to being scattered into a bunch of different parts all over the road. Do you get that?"

"Yeah," said Charlie. "That would've blown. But hey, I'm not. So thanks for that."

Nora put the car back in drive and started forward again. "Jesus Christ. Does anything ever faze you?"

"Does anything ever not faze you?" Charlie countered.

Nora ignored him. "There's a ferry close by?"

"Yep."

"Does your cause of death still say 'car accident'?"

Charlie reached behind him to where his file sat just beside Jessica's cage. He gave it a quick scan.

"Yep."

Nora took a sharp inhale.

"Okay," she said resolutely. "We're going to Virgo Bay."

7

The next ferry was set to depart an hour after the twins pulled up to the docks. Nora examined the awaiting ocean through narrowed eyes, as though squaring off with a high school bully. The wind had picked up, its blustery fingers pulling the water into choppy waves. She didn't like any of it, and from the angry whitecaps foaming on the waves in the distance, it seemed the feeling was mutual.

Charlie trudged back to where Nora was leaning against her car by the dock, his hands full of to-go cups from the little café beside the ticket booth. He handed Nora her chamomile tea with honey and ripped a piece of doughnut from a paper bag held precariously between two fingers.

"You're sure your file didn't update again? Nothing about drowning or capsizing ferries or anything?" Nora said as Charlie plopped himself next to her on the bumper.

"Still just a plain old car accident," said Charlie. He took another bite of doughnut and stared out at the sea. "Sure is pretty out there, huh?"

"It's dark," Nora said. "Nothing looks pretty in the dark."

"Can't see the stars if it's not dark."

"It's too cloudy for stars."

"Doughnut?" Charlie waggled the little paper-bag-swaddled pastry nub in Nora's face.

Nora shook her head. The smell of salt and fish being dragged up from the sea by the growing winds turned her stomach. The prospect of a boat ride didn't help matters much either. She never trusted boats. Humans weren't meant to travel by water. They weren't meant to travel by air either, for that matter, and roads were also pretty sketchy. No, to Nora, humans weren't meant to travel at all, really. They were meant to stay safely tucked away in their beds eating soup. Maybe go for the odd walk through a familiar, well-lit park so their muscles wouldn't atrophy.

She took a sip of her tea and promptly burned her tongue, which felt like an omen.

"I'm going to wait in the car."

THE FERRY DOCKED NEAR A LITTLE COASTAL TOWN LINED WITH quaint Victorian storefronts, their quaint Victorian windows each framing a "closed" sign. It was only a little after nine p.m., but between the empty streets and the deep November darkness, it could have passed for midnight. This was almost definitely a bad idea. They had nowhere to stay and no idea where they were going. This was how you ended up being described in the past tense as "always lit up the room" in a crime documentary.

Nora drove around the commercial area of town twice before they finally noticed a single "open" sign, dimly glowing red and blue in the window of a twenty-four-hour diner called Mermaid's Landing. The mermaids that landed here were definitely not the

Disney kind, Nora decided. Three motorcycles sat parked out front of the run-down diner, its hand-painted sign so weather-worn that the blond mermaid logo looked more half-fish/half-constipated zombie than the sirens of myth. Nora parked.

"Want me to handle this?" Charlie asked, reading the concern on Nora's face. "I've gotta go drop some kids off at the pool anyway."

"Okay, gross. But no, it's fine. We'll go in together."

And so they did. The inside of Mermaid's Landing was both less ramshackle and more confusing than the outside. It seemed whoever ran the place couldn't decide between a traditional 1950s diner feel and an homage to the ocean theme, so they simply went with both. The scuffed black-and-white-checkerboard floor lay beneath a ceiling strung with fishing nets filled with plastic fish. The jukebox at the far end of the diner was wrapped in artfully placed artificial seaweed. Even the stools at the diner counter had little shark fins on the backs of the seats.

At one booth sat three men in leather vests and varying degrees of facial hair neglect, at another a teen girl in what appeared to be a life-ruining spell of quality time with her parents. Nora approached the counter, occupied only by an older man slowly making headway on an ice-cream sundae, the stool's shark fin peeking out from under suspendered corduroys.

The woman behind the counter, somewhere in the late stages of middle age and the early stages of complete apathy, greeted them with a blink. Her name tag read "Goldie" against the baby pink of her vintage-inspired, crab-patterned blouse.

"Hi," Nora tried when Goldie said nothing. "We—"

"What'll it be?" Goldie pulled a little notebook and even littler pencil from the apron on her waist.

"Oh, no, we just needed some directions."

Goldie snapped the notebook shut with an exasperated sigh. "Can't help you unless you order something."

"What? Really?"

"No grub no love, kid."

"That is definitely not how that goes," Charlie muttered.

"Fine, I'll take a tea," Nora tried.

"We don't do tea," said Goldie.

Nora sucked in a sharp breath. "Okay. Fine. A juice, then. Now, we're trying to get t—"

"That won't cut it," said Goldie.

"What?"

"Juice is two fifty. Directions cost more than that. Has to be food. No food? Just 'tude."

"This is ridiculous," Nora said, the frustration and fear that had plagued her all day raising her voice louder than she'd intended.

Goldie just shrugged as someone tapped Nora on the shoulder. She turned around to find the three bikers from the booth in a horseshoe around her and Charlie.

"These folks bothering you, Goldie?" said the one with the most ostentatious beard.

Goldie looked over the twins for a moment, considering. "Maybe."

"No, no, it's fine," said Charlie. "We were just ordering. The Hungry Man breakfast looks good."

"Hmm," said Goldie. The bikers didn't budge. "Where are you headed?"

"Virgo Bay," said Charlie.

Goldie's stony face eroded into something unrecognizable.

The bikers surrounding them took a step back. The air seemed to be vacuumed out of the diner for a moment. Even the teenaged girl with her parents looked up from her phone. After a silence that was too long for Nora's comfort, Goldie turned towards the kitchen. "I'll get that order going for you," she said, her voice suddenly small and without edge. The bikers slunk back to their booths.

"Uh, the directions?" Charlie called at Goldie's retreating back, but she didn't turn around. "The hell was that? All I said was 'Virgo Bay' and they scattered. What is this, a town of Capricorns or something?"

The old man at the counter chortled into his sundae.

"Let's go," Nora said, defeated. "We can find a place to stay for the night and try again elsewhere in the morning."

Charlie shrugged and started following his sister away from the counter when the old man turned around. "What do you want with Virgo Bay anyway?"

The twins stopped. "We're looking for some friends of our father," said Nora.

"In Virgo Bay?"

She nodded.

"You'd really be better off looking elsewhere. It's not an area for tourists. The locals . . . they're an odd bunch. Keep themselves to themselves. Don't welcome outsiders. That kind of behavior, well, it makes it feel like there's something to hide. Talk to your old man, maybe he can help."

"He's dead," Nora said matter-of-factly.

"I see." The old man patted his cheeks with a cloth napkin covered in embroidered jellyfish. "And he was from there?"

Nora nodded. "Yeah, he spent his whole life up here until he and our mom met." She didn't know why she was telling the man this. It was just wasting time. But there was something about his face, warm and well creased and worn red with a lifetime of exposure to the wind and sea, that made it feel worth a shot. "Martin Bird."

Something flashed behind the man's watery eyes before disappearing into the flecks of soft hazel. "Bird, you say? Hmm. Well, I grew up a few towns over from there. Never went to Virgo Bay myself, don't really remember exactly where it is. I haven't been back in a good long while and I don't remember much these days. But I can get you to the area if you like."

Nora looked at Charlie, her chest swelling with her longtime enemy: hope.

"That would be amazing."

"You got a pen and paper?"

"Notes app," said Charlie, holding up his phone.

"Fine, fine. But you really should know before you set off, Virgo Bay is not your average town."

"What do you mean?" Nora asked.

The man sucked his teeth, his eyes drifting to the middle distance as he seemed to consider his words. Finally, he looked back at the twins. "You start with a left at that stop sign by the convenience store. If you see the bakery, you've gone too far."

THE ROAD AHEAD SEEMED ENDLESS, CARVED INTO HILLSIDES AND nestled between evergreens along the wild coast. Nora kept her jaw clenched, Charlie's case file still etched in her head. Car accident. That's how he was slated to die. And though they'd left the highway, they would be in the car for another good few hours before they reached the approximate area of Virgo Bay. And with the file changing seemingly arbitrarily, any road seemed like a risk. This drive couldn't be over soon enough. But then what? Two strangers, who might not even still be there, would miraculously take them in? They'd stay off the roads forever so Charlie couldn't be killed? It all seemed like a long shot, but it was the best they had.

Charlie let out a gurgle from where he slept in the passenger seat. Nora took a quick look over at him. The way his brow hung close to his eyes like hers did. The way his nose curved up like hers didn't. The full lips that matched hers and the soft jawline that squished into his neck just slightly, while hers was taut. They were so different, and yet they were made of the same ingredients. She could see that, even when she didn't want to. Her old life was gone. Her job lost, her apartment a compost heap of rotting houseplants and groceries she never had the chance to eat, but as she listened to the rhythmic breathing from her brother's perpetually ever-so-slightly-plugged nose, she decided maybe that was okay right now. That maybe it was worth it.

The hours ticked by and the effects of the nap Nora had stolen at the motel began to dissipate. Her mind traveled back to the truck on the highway, the drowsy driver nearly bisecting her little car, and she gave her thigh a pinch.

"Do you know I spy?" Nora asked Jessica, eyeing the bird in the back seat through the rearview mirror.

"The first five digits of pi are three point one four one five," squawked Jessica.

"I'll take that as a no. Well, Charlie definitely wasn't your first owner, was he? The only pie he knows is served with ice cream. Where did you come from?"

"Shit, shit," squawked Jessica.

"Now that's more like Charlie. Can you give me something more than that?" Nora caught herself and sighed. "Am I actually having a conversation with a bird?" She decided she was. There wasn't much else to keep her awake. "Hmm. Are you from a pet store or something? Who left you with my brother? I mean, leaving Charlie in charge of anything is never a good idea. So it can't have been someone who knows him well, unless it was a prank. It's weird though, right? To just leave someone a bird? Do you remember their name or anything about them or when you last saw them or—"

Jessica suddenly let out a blood-curdling shriek, as if someone were hacking her to death right there in her cage. Charlie, suddenly awake, shrieked with her in alarm just as a rabbit hopped onto the road to the left of the car. In a flash, Nora knew she would swerve off the road. She could see the car sailing right and into the boulders bordering them. She could see it all so clearly, as if it were already happening. She would swerve right and Charlie would die.

She turned the steering wheel left.

The rabbit leapt to the right and hopped off towards the forest beyond the boulders as the car skidded off the road and onto the grass, crashing through a stake of wood, the street sign it held flying up onto the windshield and over the car as the impact forced them to a stop. Airbags tossed Nora's head back and threw her hands off the steering wheel. By the time the dust had settled, the front hood was smashed and steaming, the car unwilling to start. Nora quickly gave Charlie a once-over. His nose was bleeding from the airbag, but he seemed otherwise unharmed. For the second time that night, he didn't die. For her part, Nora's wrist was throbbing, but there was no time to think about that now.

"We need to get out of the car in case the engine catches fire."

Charlie held one hand over his nose, attempting to stop the bleeding with a pinch, and grabbed his duffel bag and Jessica's cage with the other. They exited the smoking car, and Nora promptly burst into tears.

8

The world had never been a safe place. Nora learned that on her first day of second grade, when Lizzie Tompkins snuck into her lunch box and ate her tuna sandwich ten minutes before lunch. Unfortunately for Lizzie Tompkins, what *she* learned that day was the reason her parents never packed her tuna sandwiches, which was only partially due to the smell and mostly due to a severe seafood allergy. The paramedics who showed up to deflate Lizzie Tompkins had to stab her with a needle, which Nora always felt was very much a salt-in-the-wound situation. It wasn't something she'd thought about again until a year later when her parents died, and then, for a week straight, it was all she could think about. Lizzie had an accident and lived; her parents had an accident and died. It didn't make any sense, and that was a painful revelation. Bad things were going to happen, and the universe or fate or whatever you wanted to call it didn't need a single reason for it.

Just now, Nora was sitting somewhere under a stack of roughly a dozen accumulated bad things, and she was nearly finished crying about it.

"I need water," she said as the sobbing finally ebbed into a light whimper. She hadn't had anything to drink in hours and knew all too well that dehydration was not a preferable way to die.

She was on the damp grass, cold seeping in through her cargos, a boulder at her back. Charlie's nose had stopped bleeding at some point, dried blood smeared across his lower face like lipstick applied by a toddler.

"I've got a 7 Up in my bag," said Charlie, pulling himself to his feet from beside her. He walked over to where he'd dropped the duffel and fished out a one-liter bottle.

"Why?" was all Nora could bring herself to say.

"I packed the essentials." He sat back down and handed Nora the bottle. She tried twisting off the cap, but her wrist sent pulses of pain screaming "absolutely not" down to her elbow. She winced and nudged Charlie with the cap until he took the hint and opened it for her. She glugged.

The car still steamed in front of them, the hood accordioned where it had struck the wooden post.

"How far are we?"

Charlie sheepishly dug into his pocket and pulled out his phone, the screen smashed, black, and streaked with multicolored lights. They would almost have been pretty if they didn't signify the demise of the twins' only means of directions. Nora's own phone had died some hours back, and neither she nor Charlie had a charger. Apparently that wasn't one of Charlie's essentials. She took another swig of the soda that had made the cut.

"For fuck's sake."

"I know, right?" Charlie leaned back against the boulder that could have killed him. "Hey, you still planning on crying some more, or should we figure out a plan? I'm freezing my balls off out here."

Nora looked over at Charlie in his blood-streaked T-shirt and threadbare flannel pajama pants. "You didn't pack a coat?"

Charlie seemed to consider the suggestion for a moment. "Huh."

"Christ." Nora hauled herself to her feet. "Okay, well, the road leads that way. I guess we follow it until we reach civilization. We should really get looked at by a doctor. I know neither of us lost consciousness, but that doesn't mean we didn't sustain concussions, and concussions can cause brain damage, which increases the risk of—"

"Doctor, got it." Charlie got back up and grabbed Jessica's cage from where it sat by his feet. The bird, for her part, gave an affronted squawk at the sudden movement. "I'll keep my eyes peeled for anyone with a stethoscope and college debt. Can we get this party started?"

Eventually the silver-speckled blanket of black above them began to crack with the first hints of morning light as they trudged down the endless winding road, taking turns with Nora's jacket to stave off hypothermia. Jessica, for her part, was back in Charlie's duffel and away from the bite of the air, and she'd yet to complain about this mode of transportation.

It felt as if someone had scooped out the bones and muscles and other fun goop in Nora's legs and replaced them with equal parts bricks and steel. "Fatigue" was too easygoing a word for the raw exhaustion that pressed down on her with each step, dragging her shoulders lower, stifling her stride. Beside her, Charlie marched along as easily as if they were on a late-night quest to the corner store for snacks. It was infuriating.

Eventually the paved road ended, gravel carrying on in one direction, paths carved into the grass by years of tire tracks splitting into two more. The twins silently agreed on the gravel road, following it along the coast until a little buttercream-yellow clapboard building appeared at the top of a hill, a wooden coffee cup jutting out beside a green-and-blue awning.

The sun was fully risen now, bathing the landscape in rays that promised heat and failed to deliver. The ocean sat in the near distance, waves lazily lapping in the light morning breeze. Long, browned grass curled over itself from harsher winds past, little houses scattered near the rugged beach below.

"Think they're open?" Charlie asked, jabbing a thumb at the café, his tone only half-serious.

Nora checked her watch. Even if the café was operating under regular hours—which she doubted, what with this definitely being the offseason for whatever picturesque little community they'd stumbled into—it was still too early for most of civilization. Still, it was worth a try. Above the little café sign was evidence of a residence. That meant the proprietors could be inside, which meant they could help.

Nora pulled back the screen door and gave a firm knock, which was promptly answered by silence. Another knock, this time met with a sharp gust of wind that crept down the neck of Nora's shirt, but still nothing from within. It had been a long shot. She shook her head at Charlie, who stood at the base of the three fat stairs leading up to the door, and began her descent. It was too cold to wait any longer.

Just as they got back onto the gravel road, the café door opened. A woman in a powder-pink bathrobe and matching slippers stood in the doorway, her already saucer-sized eyes widening as the twins turned around, revealing Charlie's bloodied face and the ash in Nora's cheeks.

"Goodness," the woman said. "You kids all right?"

"We were in an accident," Nora said, bristling at the word as it left her mouth.

"Well, come in, come in," said the woman as she stepped to one side of the doorway and ushered them inside with a wave of both hands. "It's right freezing out there, and it seems as if this young man here was the only one with the foresight to wear a coat."

Charlie smugly wrapped Nora's jacket tighter around his shoulders as he walked past the woman and into the café. "Yeah, I keep telling my sister to pack the essentials, but does she listen?"

Nora glared at her brother's back but quickly followed him inside, desperate to escape the morning chill.

The café was a bright little spot, painted in pastel blues and yellows, sunlight streaming in through bay windows that framed a table topped with a single white plastic flower in a vase. Four other tables dotted the room, a cashier counter at the far end separating the café proper from the kitchen. Charlie and Nora took the seat in the window as the woman instructed, then she disappeared behind the counter and reappeared just as quickly with two steaming mugs of strong black coffee.

Nora never drank coffee. She produced enough anxiety naturally that the assistance of caffeine didn't feel necessary. But that morning the warmth of the bitter liquid made it seem like a worthwhile trade-off. And besides, with all the adrenaline she still had coursing through her body from the past twenty-four hours, she could barely tell which jitters were her own and which weren't.

"I can wake my husband and get him to drive you to a hospital, if you'd like." The woman in the bathrobe hovered above the table. The sunlight left deep shadows in the lines on her forehead and around her eyes and lips, her gray hair in tight curls close to her head. "The closest one is about forty-five minutes back that way. Unfortunately we don't get ambulances coming out here unless it's tourist season, when all the houses are let. But Johnny'll drive you if I ask."

Nora opened her mouth to take the woman up on her offer, but Charlie got there first. "Actually, I'm starving. Don't suppose your kitchen's open for business, huh?"

The woman gave him a look reminiscent of one often worn by their bubbie, one that said she was inexplicably endeared by Charlie despite his complete lack of charm. "Oh, of course, you must be famished. Let me whip you up some eggs and toast, and we can figure out the rest once you've got full stomachs, eh? I'm Juliette, by the way. Juliette MacLean. Where are you headed?"

"Virgo Bay," said Charlie. "I'm Charlie Bird and this is my sister, Nora."

Juliette's saucer eyes expanded again. "You're Birds, are you?"

Charlie nodded. Nora was still busy calculating when in this conversation she could jump in and bring the subject back to the hospital trip.

"And you're looking for Virgo Bay?"

Charlie nodded again, a little slower this time. Even Nora let go of her preoccupation with a visit to the emergency room at the strange, hollow quality suddenly overtaking Juliette's tone.

"Well"—Juliette wrung her hands—"aren't you both in luck. You're only a few miles from your destination. Virgo Bay's just up the road a bit and down by the shore, if you follow that path in the grass just there." She un-wrung her hands just long enough to point at a path through the window before wringing them again.

"Oh, thank god," Nora said.

"Think old Johnny boy would take us there instead of the hospital?" asked Charlie.

"Oh." Juliette took a step backwards. "No." Then another. "But we sure can lend you an extra jacket. In fact, keep it. We've got a few old ones kicking around. It's a lovely journey, I'm sure. Very scenic. Couldn't be more than a couple hours' walk."

"Have you not been?" Nora watched, befuddled, as Juliette retreated another step.

"Me? No. No. It's not for me to go. But you? You're Birds."

"What do you mean?"

The woman gave an awkward laugh and tossed her hand at them as though she'd just made a joke that didn't land. "No, nothing, ignore me. I've been living here too long. Hey, why don't I start on those breakfasts for you, eh? I'll just be . . ." She took the remaining steps backwards and escaped into the kitchen.

"Okay, seriously," said Charlie. "Why do people keep doing that?"

"I don't know," said Nora. "But I don't like it."

Juliette's directions, which mostly consisted of vague gestures and the odd shout up the stairs to her husband, steered the twins down the hill and through a vast expanse of knee-high grass and nothingness. But their stomachs were full, their backs were warm with the thick, secondhand coats from the café, and even the pain in Nora's wrist was becoming such a staple part of her physiology she barely felt the need to acknowledge it. The thing was, through the exhaustion and the fear and the everything else Nora felt, the main thing she was feeling as they ventured farther into the grassy plains of the unknown was relief. Charlie was still alive. They no longer had a car for him to die horribly in. And they were so deep in the middle of nowhere that even the not-quite-explainable abilities of S.C.Y.T.H.E. would likely be stymied in tracking them down here.

By the end of the second hour of aimless wandering though, that relief began to waver, and Nora's patented anxiety started to creep back in. Charlie was still alive, but they hadn't checked his file in hours and his cause of death could have changed. They no longer had a car for him to die horribly in—or to get them anywhere, or as a means of escape in an emergency. S.C.Y.T.H.E. might have trouble tracking them down here, or they might not. There was so much about the company Nora still didn't understand. And if they couldn't track the twins down, neither could anyone else who might actually be able to help them.

Nora felt the hope drain out of her as the vast unfamiliarity surrounding them suddenly started crawling with danger. At the rate they were going, they could be lost out here forever, dead by starvation, dehydration, bitten to death by the cold. She was debating which she would prefer if given the option, when Charlie nudged her with his elbow. Nora looked up from her feet and followed his gaze. Roughly ten feet away sat a carved wooden signpost. It looked handcrafted and worn with age. Etched into the wood were the words "Welcome to Virgo Bay."

Nora looked at her brother. "Did we do it?"

"I think we did it."

They marched past the sign and down another hill. Nestled in the gulf beneath that hill sat a little cluster of houses in beige and various shades of blue. A farm with the stalks of long-ago-harvested crops and livestock grazing in far-stretching paddocks were just visible on the outskirts. A little stone church greeted them as they stepped into the tiny town's perimeter, its church-yard a garden rather than a cemetery, the flowers still alive despite the season. Huddled across the street was a squat old general store beneath a hand-painted sign. A stone fountain stood in the dirt road between them, directing whatever passed as traffic here to either side. This handful of structures appeared to be the commercial district. Beyond them, all Nora could see were the small collection of houses in the shadow of surrounding hills and the bay itself tossing waves at the other end of town. They walked slowly down the road, each taking a different side of the fountain, examining their surroundings. Nora took a deep inhale, absorbing the tiny town their father had grown up in. The sun seemed to hit it differently, casting shadows in strange places, illuminating each structure with a stage spotlight. The twins met back up on the other side of the fountain, where the dirt road reconnected. Charlie tipped a head to the top floor of the house they were passing. When Nora looked up, a curtain twitched in the upstairs window. Someone was watching them.

Nora took a step backwards and chanced a look behind her. The house there was only one story, and completely dark, but the blinds in the window nearest them shifted. Nora moved closer to Charlie, spinning around, eyes on the houses surrounding them. In each she found movement in the windows, the occasional silhouetted face appearing behind the glass.

"Charlie," she whispered, panic squeezing at her throat.

"I know."

They stood back-to-back now, eyes bearing down on them from every direction.

"We should go," Nora said.

Charlie nodded and they began their retreat just as a door opened from somewhere down the road. The figure of a man appeared, walking towards them. More doors opened now, more strangers filing out of their homes and moving slowly, zombie-like, in the direction of the twins.

"Run," Nora shouted. But before they had the chance, someone put a hand on Nora's shoulder.

9

Nora spun around and found herself face-to-face with a petite woman in her early fifties, with short salt-and-pepper hair, her delicate frame draped in peach pajamas.

"Can we help—" the woman began, but then she looked at Nora, really looked at her, and her face split into a warm smile. "I don't believe it." She turned her attention to Charlie and nodded, a surprised laugh escaping her lips. Then she pivoted to face the growing crowd in the street. "It's all right, everyone. Martin's kids have come home."

NORA BRAVED HER SECOND CUP OF COFFEE THAT MORNING WITH growing resignation. She and Charlie sat at a tall kitchen island in the house of the woman from the road, who had introduced herself as Patricia. Patty if you're a friend. Ricki if you wanted to be cute about it. Patsy if you absolutely never wanted her to speak to you again. Patricia/Patty/Ricki/Definitely-Not-Patsy had insisted the twins come to her home, and after she mentioned something about having a first aid kit with which to properly attend to them, Nora had agreed.

The house was compact and leaned heavily on its relative proximity to the beach when it came to decor. Crisp white walls and tasteful smatterings of driftwood and seashells with the odd pop of something blue. It was neither newly appointed nor obviously dated, and the muted, elegant, yet slightly rugged interior seemed to match the woman who resided there.

Nora was the first to speak, as much out of genuine interest as an excuse to procrastinate a second sip of coffee. "You knew our dad?"

Patty—because Nora decided she didn't want to be cute about it—gave a grin. "Of course I knew Marty."

Nora dug the photo Charlie had given her from the pocket of her coat and placed it on the island. She pointed to the small-statured young woman under her father's arm. "That's you, isn't it?"

Patty nodded. "Gosh, where'd you find that? I haven't seen that photo in years."

"Our bubbie held on to it for us."

"Your bub—oh, your mom's mom, I suppose. You wouldn't have met your other grandmother, would you?"

"No, Bubbie was our only family after . . ."

"We heard what happened, sweetie. I'm so sorry."

Nora's eyes turned back to the photo, and she forced herself to focus.

"But you knew him."

Another smile. "He really never mentioned us, eh?"

Charlie gulped down the remainder of the coffee in his cup and chimed in. "Did you date him or something?"

Another light laugh. "Well now, that's the first time I've been accused of *that*. No, dear, Marty was my brother."

This immediately sobered Charlie up and forced Nora's attention away from the photo. "What?" they spat in unison.

"Yup. The baby by five years. That's me there, and that"—she prodded a finger at the young man on the other side of their father—"is Charles. The monkey in the middle. You'll meet him at some point, I'm sure."

"That . . ." Nora stopped and tried again. "That doesn't make sense. Dad said he was an only child. Sorry," she added at the flash of hurt in Patty's eyes.

"Your father did what he felt was right, I'm sure," said Patty. "Families are complicated. Ours is certainly no different."

Something new flared up in Nora then. Something she hadn't felt about the injustices of life in a long while: anger. "He should have told us," she said. "We should have known." All those years when it was just Bubbie and the twins against the world. And then after Bubbie died and Charlie was even more Charlie than before, and Nora was alone . . . she could have had people. She could have had family.

"Well, I'm right glad you're here now. You have so many folks to meet. What brought you all the way out here, anyway?"

The twins exchanged a glance. Nora shook her head and gave her brother a look that said, "Bite your tongue." They had only just met this woman, they couldn't trust her with the truth, and more than that, there was no reason for her to believe them about something so outlandish.

"Charlie gave me that photo for my birthday," Nora said.

"*Our* birthday," Charlie interjected.

"Our birthday. We saw the location on the back and thought

maybe we could see where Dad grew up. He always told us he was from small-town Nova Scotia, but we couldn't remember exactly where, so when we found that information, it seemed like the right time to trace our roots." It wasn't a complete lie, Nora decided.

"Goodness, well, I'm glad you made the trek. But you must be exhausted. Unfortunately I don't have any extra rooms, it's just little old me here, but why don't you two shower and rest on the couches for a bit. When you're back up and running, we can make some introductions and find you somewhere to stay. Any idea how long you'll be with us?"

Nora looked out the window to the serene breeze playing with the branches of an evergreen. It was unimaginable that the quaintness surrounding them could ever be interrupted by the harsh practicality of S.C.Y.T.H.E. with its corporate gray and emotionless methods. It jarred her to find that the thing that once brought her comfort was now something to fear. Her reality had changed as rapidly as it had after her parents died.

"I think we might be here awhile."

THE STEAM FROM THE SHOWER FILLED THE BATHROOM, THE AIR wet and heavy as it enveloped Nora in its warmth. She let the previous night's chill slough off her, the perpetual goose bumps flattening across her body. She wanted to get into the shower, to scrub the past twenty-four hours off until they swirled down the drain, but there was something she had to do first. Charlie's case file sat on the counter beside the sink, the folder taunting her with its blandness. She hadn't looked at it since they'd left the car in a ruined heap on the roadside; there hadn't been a need. No car meant no car accident. But that could have changed, and the thought paralyzed Nora.

All she had to do was flip open the cover and skim the page. That was it. She'd done the same thing a million times at work. She'd done it several times with this very file. And yet, she couldn't convince herself to budge. She stared at the file. The file stared back at her. They were at a stalemate.

A knock thundered at the door. Nora jumped.

"Can you hurry it up in there? I've got dried blood in weird places and I'd like to wash it off. It's freaking me out a bit. That shit's not supposed to be on my outsides, you know?"

Nora glared at the door, then back at the file. Her face softened. Fucking Charlie. Can't be patient, can't stop almost dying. And Patty thought *her* family was complicated.

"Five minutes," Nora called back. She braced herself, set her shoulders back and her spine straight, and flipped the file open. Surely he was safe now. Really safe.

She ran a finger down the page until it landed on "cause of death." She leapt back.

This was much worse than a new cause of death. And much more confusing.

Nora threw her clothes back on and fled the bathroom, the shower still spurting hot water, steam escaping with her.

"Finally! Jessica wants a bath too. Her little feathers got all ruffled in my bag, poor princess."

The bird seemed to be shrinking back into herself from her perch on his shoulder, her face somehow conveying utter embarrassment at her current bedraggled state.

"Charlie, look." Nora shoved the file into his face, indicating exactly what was causing her current brand of panic. Charlie looked down, then back up, his face scrunched in confusion.

"I don't get it."

Beside "cause of death," everything was a blurry smudge of ink, only an occasional clear letter sneaking through before being swallowed back into the undulating black cloud.

"It's like. . . ." Nora bit her lip but forced herself through the rest of the thought. "It's like we have bad reception out here. Like we can't get a clear signal."

"Nor. You realize this is paper, right?"

"Yes. No. I mean it's paper, but it's special paper. It's S.C.Y.T.H.E. paper. Or maybe it's special ink or something, I don't know, I never asked questions. I have no idea how we find out when and where people die, or who that information comes from. It was never for me to know. But somehow this file, your file, keeps updating, and now it looks like it's trying to but can't."

"Huh." Charlie cocked his head, his position a perfect replica of the parrot on his shoulder. "So does this mean I'm safe, then? Like, if we can't read the cause of death, then I can't die?"

"I don't think so," said Nora, who had already run through that and every other possibility. "I think it means you're still supposed to die, but now we have no way of knowing how, or stopping it."

"That sucks," said Charlie.

"It really sucks."

CHARLIE LAY WRAPPED AROUND ONE OF THE PALE BLUE PILLOWS ON the living room sofa, Jessica curled into the crook of his neck, both sound asleep as Nora watched from the armchair across from them. She had allowed her brother a sponge bath in place of a shower—too many deaths happened in showers—and when he and Jessica had emerged, clean of dried blood and feathers unruffled, she had vowed not to let Charlie out of her sight.

The file lay open on her lap, the glitching ink still struggling against the page, the odd letter still sneaking through. Nora clicked the pen in her hand, sending the nib up and down, jotting each letter onto the file folder as they appeared. So far she'd managed an *S* and what was almost definitely a *T*.

Patty sat down on the love seat beside her, a steaming cup of tea in hand, and Nora promptly shut the file.

"What're you working on?" Patty asked, taking a sip.

"Just something for work," said Nora, forcing a smile.

"Work. God. My big brother has a baby old enough to work. What do you do?"

"Oh." Nora shrugged. "I'm an administrative coordinator. It's a lot of paperwork, mostly. Pretty routine. Usually."

"Sounds very grown-up. And what about him?" She bobbed her head at Charlie.

"Charlie? He . . . he floats around. Last I heard he was delivering for Domino's. Or working for the pot dispensary by his place, maybe. I can't remember which came first."

"You two aren't close then, I take it?"

Nora shook her head.

"Brothers are hard." Patty gave a smile, half lost in the past. "I get it. But they can be pretty special, too. I wish I'd realized that when I still had both of mine, you know. But then, it's always easier to appreciate someone when it's too late to let them know."

Nora looked over at her brother, snoring lightly on the couch.

"Yeah, well, I hope I've still got a long time before I have to start appreciating him." She shifted in her seat, then asked the question she'd wanted answered since she was a kid. "What was he like?"

"Marty?"

Nora nodded.

"He was different. Sweet to his bones. Water could've melted him for all the sugar he was made of. But god, he was stubborn. I think all us Birds are, in our way. And brave. He was the bravest of the lot of us, I'll tell you that much. I've always said it."

Nora picked at the file. She had only known her parents for such a short time, and Bubbie had only known her father for a little longer. She'd always wanted to believe she was like them, but given what Bubbie told her about her mother, vivacious and outgoing and carefree, Nora had hung all her hopes on her dad. But her dad had been brave. The bravest, even. And Nora, well, Nora would jump at her own shadow if she thought it could cause her harm.

"What made him brave?"

Patty leaned back into the love seat, drawing a long breath, eyes boring into Nora's. "Well, he left. He's the only one of us to ever move away from Virgo Bay. That's not easy, leaving your home, your family. And this town, well, it's a hard town to leave. But your father believed there was more to life than what this place has to offer. That there's a better way to live. And you know what? Maybe he was right. I hope he found what he was looking for in the end."

Nora tried for a smile. She hoped so too, but she doubted it. That end had come far too soon. Sure, he'd had Mom, who he'd loved in the way Nora always thought you were supposed to love someone: fully and vulnerably and even when it would have been easier not to. And he'd had Nora and Charlie, who, aside from the sort of bickering you'd expect from young kids who shared a birthday and little else, were pretty passable children if Nora was honest. And he'd had a job he seemed happy enough to leave for in the morning, and even happier to come home from each night. But it was all cut so short that Nora couldn't help but wonder if he'd even had time to look back on life and be happy with it. It had always made the pursuit of anything grander than adequate feel somewhat pointless to her. A life that was just fine seemed easier to sustain. Just fine didn't require risks.

"Sweet to see such a strapping young man all curled up with a little animal like that," Patty said, cutting through Nora's thoughts. "Has he had that bird for long?"

"Oh, no," said Nora, returning fully to the sunlit living room. "She just showed up a few days ago, apparently, and now they're best friends. It's all very Charlie."

"Funny how life works out. Well, why don't you try to get some rest? I'm sure your work can wait until you've napped a bit. I'll call round and see who's coming to lunch at Mom and Dad's. There's so many people who'll want to meet you."

"'Mom and Dad'? You mean your parents are still around?"

"Sure, and fit as fiddles. They'll be over the moon you've come."

Another pang. Nora's paternal grandparents were alive, despite her father's insistence they'd died years ago. She could understand wanting a fresh start, but he'd deprived her and Charlie of so many people who could have loved them when the world only gave them pain.

The thought weighed heavy against her, coupled with the

mounting weight of an exhaustion she'd been staving off since the previous night. She looked over at Charlie, still sleeping soundly on the couch.

"Okay," Nora said. She tucked Charlie's file behind her back for safekeeping and curled deeper into the chair. "I'll nap for a bit. But please . . ." Her eyes lingered on her brother. "Look after him."

Patty stood and walked over to her niece, giving her knee a quick squeeze. If she said anything after that, Nora had no idea, because within seconds she was lost in sleep.

10

When Nora opened her eyes again, the sun had moved out of the living room window and was streaming in through the adjoining kitchen. She found Patty there, tossing a salad in a big wooden bowl on the counter, but when she looked over at the couch across from her, Charlie was gone.

She bolted upright, immediately wide-awake.

"Charlie?" she called, panic rippling through her.

"Oh, you're up." Patty turned from the counter and let the tongs she was holding drop into the salad bowl. She leaned back against the sink and gave Nora a smile. "He's just popped out to the store for me. I'm all out of croutons, which is a cardinal sin in this town."

"Out?" Nora was on her feet. Out was a dangerous place to be. Any number of things could happen to someone in the outside world. Any number of things could happen to Charlie. "How long has he been gone for? Which direction did he go?"

"Goodness, you're a jumpy one. Charlie'll be just fine. He left about fifteen minutes ago, he should be back any moment. It's not exactly a big town. Besides, you don't have much to worry about in Virgo Bay."

"Oh?" Nora dug Charlie's file out from where it had slipped between the chair cushions and frantically searched for cause of death. The ink was still glitching. She slammed the file shut and looked back at her aunt. "Because everyone we asked for directions to this town seemed freaked out just by its name. If it's so safe, why did people get so weird every time we mentioned it?" She was already at the door pulling her coat from its hook and shrugging into it before she'd finished her sentence. Just as she reached for the handle, the door swung open and Charlie stepped through, a box of croutons under his arm, Jessica on his shoulder.

Nora stumbled back for long enough to absorb a wave of relief before charging forward and punching Charlie's shoulder.

"Ow, what the hell?"

"I told you to stay safe," Nora said. "What the hell do you call this?"

"Croutons," Charlie responded.

"No, I mean gallivanting around a strange town alone."

"'Gallivanting'? Sorry, my liege, I never meant to dishonor thee."

"Are you kids in some kind of trouble?" Patty chimed in, joining them in the little doorway.

"No," said Nora.

"Yeah," said Charlie, at the same time.

"I see," said Patty. "Well, whichever it is, I promise you couldn't be in a better place. A lot of people fear what they don't understand. We keep to ourselves here. We like our little community, our slow way of life. Those folks you asked directions from just don't quite get that. But if you are in trouble, you couldn't be safer than in Virgo Bay. And if you're not, well, the same still applies. We always say there's no better place for a Bird than this old forgotten town."

"That explains why Jessica likes it so much here," Charlie said. "She's a bird in every sense of the word, and I haven't heard a peep out of her since we got here."

Patty smiled, but Nora thought she caught something strangely cold in it, as though it didn't venture deeper than her lips. "I'd keep her caged while you're here all the same. Not everyone is quite so pet friendly around here." She took the crouton box from under Charlie's arm. "Let me just add these to the salad and we can get going for lunch. You came on the perfect day—Mom always makes her gourmet mac and cheese on Fridays, and I guarantee you won't taste anything better in all of the East Coast."

NORA AND CHARLIE'S GRANDPARENTS LIVED A TEN-MINUTE WALK from Patty's place. In truth, Nora was shocked to find that anything in the tiny town of Virgo Bay could be a ten-minute walk away from anything else. But the heads of the Bird family lived on the beach, separating them from the town proper by a stroll that was barely long enough to be considered leisurely.

The chill of the morning had subsided a bit, and the afternoon sun gave off just enough warmth to earn its keep. Despite the more palatable temperatures, Charlie had opted to wear the heavy coat gifted by Juliette from the café in order to hide the bloodstains on his white pajama top. Apparently packing a change of clothes was also not considered essential by Charlie Bird, but at least he'd had the good sense to leave gore out of the first lunch with his long-lost family. He also, inexplicably, carried his duffel bag over his shoulder, which Nora decided not to question for the sake of her own wavering mental stability.

They turned off the main road and down a narrow path that cut through the grass towards the coast, where a small, wooden house painted fire-engine red sat just in from the rocks and sand. The trim on the windows was freshly painted white, and smoke puffed like dragon's breath from the stone chimney. It looked at once like something out of a half-remembered folktale, and something as familiar as Nora's own reflection.

Patty led the way through the front door, the house alive with the sound of chatter and clanging cutlery.

"I told them you were coming, but patience is a bit too much to ask from these animals when it comes to feeding time, apparently," Patty said over her shoulder. "Make yourselves at home. I'll just drop the salad in the kitchen and then I'll be back to make all the introductions."

She slipped into the next room, leaving Nora and Charlie alone in a front hall of yellow panels that somehow felt both dated and modern, the fresh, buttery brightness of the paint combining with the retro warmth of the wood boards beneath. Just beyond this sat a living room with wooden ceiling beams and antique furniture, the fireplace glowing with a full belly of flame. But the most warmth Nora felt came from the voices and laughter that reached out like fingers searching for a hand to hold.

"This thing weighs a ton," Charlie whined, slinging the duffel bag off his shoulder.

"Then why did you bring it? Worried about a 7 Up shortage in Virgo Bay?"

"Nah, I leave the worrying to you," said Charlie. He unzipped the bag a crack and Jessica's head popped out. "I didn't want to leave her all alone."

"Charlie," Nora hissed. "Patty said not to. Not everyone is into bird mites and avian flu."

"Hey now, my pretty princess isn't carrying avian anything. She's perfectly healthy. I think once they get to know her and see how special she is, everyone will love her."

Nora opened her mouth, an extensive list of additional bird-carrying ailments primed on her tongue for rebuttal, when a shadow fell over them from the living room. Nora turned. A few feet away stood a man in his midfifties with a shortish, compact stature. He was thicker around the middle and had less hair than the last time she saw him, but Nora immediately recognized his smile from the photo Charlie had given her; it was a perfect replica of her own, with something of her father in there around his eyes.

"You're Charles!" she said.

"Not 'Uncle Charles,' eh? Guess I'll have to earn that." He took a step towards them, and the sudden movement sent Jessica fidgeting in the bag before her little gray head disappeared altogether. The motion caught Charles's attention. He looked from the bag to the twins. "What a fun little friend. You might not want to have her here, though. Mom and Dad aren't big animal people."

Charlie sighed but relented, zipping the bag back up and slinging it over his shoulder.

"You must be Marty's kids," Charles continued, adjusting the thick-rimmed glasses on his nose. "Of course you must. Who else would you be? You've really got the whole place buzzing. I guess we all figured we'd never get the chance to meet you."

"So did we," Nora said, trying to keep the pain from her voice.

"Oh, Charles. You're back." Patty reappeared in the hallway. "I thought you were gone another day or two." She turned to the twins. "Charles is usually the one in charge of the town's supply runs. We get most of our produce, meat, and dairy from Uncle Vic's farm down the road, but this time of year there's not much growing, and we like the odd treat once in a while."

"So I get the monthly road trip assignment," said Charles.

"Usually it's just to one of the bigger towns nearby," said Patty. "But there've been some supply chain issues, and they don't send much out this far into the middle of nowhere anyway, so sometimes he needs to make the trek to a city. Then he'll usually stay the night, sometimes two if there's anything interesting going on in town. I figured he might miss you kids altogether."

"Thank goodness I came back early," said Charles.

He and his sister exchanged smiles. Then Patty put a hand on each of the twins' shoulders and started ushering them in the direction of the voices.

"Well, you've met two of us birdbrains. Come on, I'll introduce you to the rest and we'll get some food in those bellies of yours. You both must be starving."

They followed Patty through the living room and into a dining room bustling with more people than Nora knew what to do with. And most of them had her eyes. Or dimple. Or Charlie's crooked smile.

As soon as they entered, the room stilled. Every eye in the house fell on them, forks lowering, heads shaking in disbelief. A woman at the far end of the table dropped the serving spoon into the dish she was holding and shoved it into the lap of the person she was serving as soon as she spotted the twins. She rushed over, wiping her palms on an apple-patterned apron, and immediately pulled Nora into her arms. She smelled like homemade pastries and fresh mint. And then she stopped smelling of anything at all, because she was squeezing so tight Nora couldn't manage another breath. On average, a human can survive up to six minutes without oxygen, only four before brain damage sets in. Nora counted down from ten and gave the woman's back a quick pat, signaling the end of the hug. She decided that would be a sufficient length for both displaying affection and retaining vital cognitive function.

When Nora pulled away, she finally got her first good look at the woman. She only came up to Nora's nose and, at only five foot four herself, Nora saw that as something of a biological feat. The woman was older than she'd appeared from far away, her skin falling like melted wax down her neck, but her dark eyes were sharp and her physical health was evident from the remaining gentle throb where she'd just been pried off of Nora's ribs.

"Apologies, I'm not usually so forward. Only, you really do look just like him." The woman's voice was less emotive than her words, but a shallow pool of tears formed a rim under her eyes. Then she turned to Charlie. "You, not so much."

Patty slung an arm around the woman's shoulders. "Kids, meet your grandmother Ruby."

"Holy shit," said Charlie.

"You sure sound like him, though." A tear escaped Ruby's watery eyes and skidded down her cheek. She quickly swatted it away and regained her composure. "Please, come in, let's get you something to eat. Everyone?" She turned back to the overflowing table. "Meet my grandchildren."

NORA HAD TRIED AND FAILED TWICE TO GET SOME SALT. SHE WAS seated between Charles and Charlie—a Chuck sandwich, as Charlie had unfortunately decided to call it—and they were both too engrossed in other conversations to pass her one of the little shakers that sat at either end of the table. Charlie's side had a set of kissing pigs, Charles's a pair of cardinals with chipped ceramic wings. Nora didn't have a preference between them but felt a little bad for the damaged cardinals and had hoped out of pity to give them something to do.

Ruby sat at the far head of the table, a tiny matriarch on her wooden throne, while her husband, a tall man with broad shoulders and thick gray hair, helmed the other end. This, Nora learned after her asphyxiating first encounter with Ruby, was Richard. The twins' grandfather, if you wanted to get technical about it, which Nora always did. He was what she imagined her father would have looked like if he'd been allowed to grow old: strong featured, clear-eyed, and still physically imposing despite a personality that was anything but. Nora immediately decided she liked him. Of all the unexpected family she met that day, he was the most familiar, the most like home.

Then there were the others. So many others. Ruby had two brothers, Vic and Vince, who were her equals in small stature, while Richard had a sister, Dorothy, who also happened to be Vic's wife. They had five kids, whose names Nora could barely remember. One of them—Hannah? Anna? Alana? Or maybe it was Christine—was married to a man they all called Pickles for reasons Nora had yet to suss out, and their son was the closest to the twins in age, his face offering an estimate of late thirties. None of the others had partners or children, but the high median age at the table didn't stop the lunch from being a rambunctious one. Everyone talked over everyone else, but in a way that showed enthusiasm rather than disinterest. Dishes floated around the table, passed from hand to hand, like this was a dance they'd rehearsed for years. Nora had never been a part of anything like it. But she *was* a part of it, albeit quietly and without salt, and that warmed her along with Ruby's gourmet mac and cheese.

"And what do you do?" The question came from one of Dorothy and Vic's children, and it was aimed directly at her.

"I'm an administrative coordinator," Nora said without hesitation. A job title like hers was bland enough that it rarely led to follow-up questions, and on two separate occasions led to a hearty yawn.

"Ah," came the reply. "Well, we're farm folk, us lot. Except for Pickles. He manages the shop. Not much for manual labor, Pickles."

"You're all farmers?"

"Oh, just my family," said Vic. "Though we recruit the others for extra hands from time to time."

Nora couldn't fathom a life that revolved around unpredictable livestock, rusty tools, and heavy machinery. One of Nora's early cases involving one of those riding lawn mowers farmers use to traverse their acres of land had quickly dispelled any romantic notions she'd had about a quiet pastoral life.

"Most of us are retired," Patty chimed in. "No one really

needs much money out here; the only things we pay for are what we buy from town. The rest we provide for ourselves. Plus there isn't much that needs doing in a place so self-contained."

"Sounds like a dream," said Charlie.

"It can get a little monotonous at times. I think that's one of the reasons your dad wanted to move away. To find some new opportunities."

"Well, we don't have to talk about that now." Ruby patted at her lips with her napkin. "Besides, what opportunity could be better than being with family? I'm just so overjoyed you're both here."

"We're happy to be here too," Nora said, and meant it. For once she felt a sense of calm, of ease. S.C.Y.T.H.E. and even Charlie's potential death shifted to the back of her mind for the first time since she came across his file at the office the previous morning. In that moment it was like those worries were somewhere far away from this house, somewhere beyond the border of Virgo Bay.

WHEN MOST OF THE FAMILY HAD DEPARTED AND ONLY THE TWINS' newfound grandparents, aunt, and uncle remained, Ruby gave them a tour of the little red house. She walked them up the three carpeted stairs to the upper level, where a cozy master bedroom sat at one end and a desk tucked into the alcove sat at the other, sandwiching a small powder room between them. Back down the carpeted steps and down a narrow wooden staircase into the basement, Nora found herself in what felt like a wood cabin. Crisscrossed snowshoes hung on the wall above an old TV, in a large open space ringed by doors.

"That's Patty's old room over there." Ruby pointed at one of the three closed doors. "And that one was shared by the boys."

Nora turned to face Ruby. "This is where Dad grew up?"

Ruby nodded. "Spent every day of his life in this house until he left us for good. You can go have a look if you'd like. It's been a few decades now. I'm sure the smell's mellowed out."

It was Charlie who opened the door, pushing it inward to reveal their father's life before the twins, preserved like a time capsule. The walls were blue, and two twin beds in hand-carved wooden frames sat at either side of the room. There were no posters on the walls, no rock stars or bikini models staring back at them, but Nora immediately recognized the art that hung above the far bed as her father's: sketches of animals, landscapes, portraits of his siblings, all in various states of completion.

She moved towards them. They were just as awful as his drawings in adulthood. He never could get proportions right. She cocked her head at a deer with the stubby limbs of a tortoise.

"You can stay here if you'd like," said Ruby. "For however long you're staying."

"Are you sure?" said Nora. "We wouldn't want to impose."

"Impose? We have over two decades to catch up on; you're welcome to stay until we've managed that."

Nora looked at her brother. "Charlie?"

Charlie lowered himself onto the bed opposite her, his body sinking into the mattress. "Yeah, I mean I'm not exactly *dying* to leave in a hurry, if you catch my drift."

Nora tried to imagine S.C.Y.T.H.E. tracking them down here. Which, of course, she could, because it was a negative thought and those were her specialty. But even if the organization and all of its unknowable resources were on their trail, surely the twins had enough of a head start to allow them to stay put for a day or two. Besides, they still had no car and had barely slept since leaving home, and Nora knew the risks that came with going so long without a proper night's sleep.

"Okay," said Nora. "Yes. We'll stay."

11

Nora couldn't rest. Or at least, her mind couldn't, its TV static buzz creeping down her limbs until the list of ills that came from lacking sleep were drowned out by a restlessness she couldn't shake. While Charlie napped effortlessly—again—Nora shrugged her coat on and slipped to the shore. She found a rock near enough to the ocean that she could feel its mist on her face but far enough that nothing else from it could touch her. She sat down and took stock.

Charlie's file sat open on her lap. The ink still twitched and blurred where Charlie's cause of death should have been. She added another letter to the few she'd been able to make sense of so far. S-T-A. It wasn't much, but maybe it was a start. Stalked? Not that she could imagine anyone stalking Charlie, especially not all the way out here. Starved? After the meal they'd just had, she seriously doubted it. She clicked her pen. Come on. This was her specialty. Her area of expertise. If anyone could come up with ways for someone to die, it was Nora Bird. Starch . . . allergy?

She closed the file and looked out at the sea, regarding it with distrust. It regarded her with the apathy of an ancient life source that didn't really need to feel any particular way about the opinion of a being with a fraction of its size or lifespan. The sun was still high in a sky spattered with only a few light clouds, its touch warm on Nora's cheeks. She lifted her hood to shield herself from the UV rays and brought her knees to her chest, wrapping her arms around them. She felt a strange sense of peace here on this little rock in this little town at the edge of the world, and that terrified her. There were too many dangers lurking—the usual ones and the new ones aimed at her brother—for her to feel any ease. But there was something about this place—the quiet, the slowness, the warmth—that made staying on edge hard, even for her.

Someone was walking towards her. She could hear the sand and pebbles squelching under rubber soles. When Nora pulled her hood back, she gasped in spite of herself, but the veil of brightness from the sun's reflection off the water quickly receded from her vision and instead of the tall, broad form of her father, she found Richard standing there.

"Mind if I have a seat?"

Nora slid her bum over. "Pull up a rock."

"Thanks." He sat down and stared out at the ocean for a long moment, letting the gently lapping waves fill the silence. Finally, he turned his focus to Nora. "You know, it never gets old. I've lived in this town almost my whole life. In that house for much of it. And I still come out here every day and find myself amazed all over again by the beauty of the place."

"It's special here," Nora agreed.

"Special. Yes." He crossed one leg over the other. "I'm glad you finally get the chance to see it. Always broke my heart a little to know that there were Birds out there who'd never get to experience Virgo Bay. But Patricia tells us you had quite the adventure getting here."

Nora's mind flashed back to discovering Charlie's file and all that came after it. "It's a hard place to find," was what she settled on.

"So I've heard. But you were in some sort of accident? Patricia said you injured your wrist."

"Oh." Nora cupped the wrist in question with her other hand. In truth, she'd somewhat forgotten about it. The pain felt much more manageable now that she had a full stomach and a few hours' rest. "It's nothing."

"I can look at it, if you'd like," said Richard. "My father was a doctor. I've done a bit of training myself. In fact, I was something of a town physician back in the day. Mostly retired now, of course, but usually I'm the one who tends to the bumps and bruises around here. Anything that doesn't require a hospital, I look after it."

Nora pushed up her sleeve and held her arm out for inspection. "It won't kill me," she said matter-of-factly.

Richard gave a bright laugh. "No, I can promise you that much." He rotated Nora's arm gently, had her move and twist in different directions and gauged her pain. "Well, my dear, I can offer you a clean bill of health. Not a sprain nor a break on you. It's a hefty bruise, and will likely be tender for a while, but you'll be right as rain soon enough. We can get you an ice pack when we're back in the house if you're in pain, though."

Nora slid her sleeve back down, the slight chill in the air biting at her exposed skin. "Thanks."

"It's what I'm here for."

"I always thought my dad would have been a good doctor," Nora said.

"Oh no, not Martin." Richard laughed again. "He was a sweet boy with many talents, but the sight of blood turned his stomach. There aren't many patients whose ailments would be improved by watching their doctor be sick all over his own shoes."

"Oh," said Nora. She never knew that about her father. There was so much about him she didn't know. It was something that always sat there at the back of her mind but had never really felt the need to come forward until now. "Well then, I guess it was good he went into architecture instead. Buildings don't really mind what comes out of you. You can even add extra bathrooms if it's a big enough concern."

"That you can. So he was happy, then? Your father? He found a job that made him happy?"

"I think so. Yes. It made me want to get into architecture too, actually, though for different reasons."

"And what are those reasons?"

"Well." Nora lowered her legs and swung her feet. She felt like a child talking about what she wanted to be when she grew up. "Architects can design buildings to be safe. People live in buildings, and work in them, and shop in them, and spend their whole lives surrounded by walls. And those walls should feel like . . . like a sanctuary, I guess. No matter what you're doing within them."

"I understand exactly where you're coming from. Did you know my father founded this town? He landed here some eighty years ago, on this little forgotten patch of land with nothing and no one in it. He had been looking for a place to lay down roots and raise his young family away from all the stress and the chaos of the world after Mother died. A sanctuary, as you call it. Over time, the odd outsider would find us and stick around, but for the most part it's just been us. But tell me, why didn't you end up pursuing architecture in the end?"

The answer to that question was the same as the answers to most questions in Nora's life. Because it would have been a risk. She had watched her father try and fail to land a job in the field for over a year, forcing her mother to work longer hours and bringing a tension into the house that hadn't been there before. Nora needed to provide for herself, and that required stability. When S.C.Y.T.H.E. had reached out to her less than six months after her graduation, promising her a decent salary, benefits, and the ability to learn more about death (and, by extension, how to avoid it), she'd jumped at the opportunity. Of course, now, miles from home and with an entire brother's life to babysit, Nora couldn't help but wonder if her risk assessment skills had been off. But it was too late to change things now.

"What did Ruby do before she came here?" Nora asked in place of giving her answer.

"Ruby?" Richard ran a finger under his nose and looked out at the sea again. "She worked in . . . transportation."

"Like, truck driving?" Nora asked, trying to picture the tiny woman in the cab of an eighteen-wheeler.

"Mm. Now, what say you and I go back inside for some hot cocoa? Then we can talk sleeping arrangements and figure out what you kids will be needing for your stay."

Nora gave one final look at the foreboding ocean, the deep blue concealing a myriad of things with too many legs or teeth or, somewhere very far below, likely too many eyes as well. She gave it a nod of recognition, and in response a small wave broke into foam on the shore. Nora turned and scurried after Richard and the little red house just beyond.

12

Dinner was a stark contrast to the meal that preceded it. Instead of every Bird in town reaching over one another in the packed dining room, only the immediate family and the twins sat around the table. Patty insisted that despite appearances, they didn't spend every meal together—even a close family had its limits—but this was a special occasion. Ruby and Charles whipped up some salmon with roasted potatoes and the rest of Patty's mostly untouched salad from lunch, and the six familial strangers sat down to eat in the last winks of sunlight.

After dinner, they stayed around the table and talked about nothing in particular, which Nora found both infuriating and a relief. She could feel the million and one questions she had about her father, about this place, about the family she never knew existed pressing hard against her throat, fighting to get out. But at the same time, the ease with which this meaningless, carefree conversation rolled reminded her of coming home from some after-school program or other to a table full of hearty foods that were mindlessly devoured while Dad cracked a joke or Mom told a story about something especially nonsensical that happened at work that day. There was something comforting about conversations without an agenda, which seemed to be the only genre of conversation she ever had at work, where each person involved had an end goal. This was just talk for the sake of lingering a little longer in each other's company. The only agenda here was simply to be.

After a while, Charles got up and started to clear the table.

"Let me help." Nora rose from her seat and grabbed Charlie's plate, making sure to keep the knife pointing outward and as far away from her as possible as she stacked the dishes on top of her own. She'd once had a case involving a steak knife, a post-meal cleanup, and a man's unsuspecting abdomen that she'd never forgotten.

Charles, unlike his namesake nephew, was only too happy to take on the role of dishwasher, tossing a blue gingham towel to Nora for drying. They found a rhythm and carried on in silence for a while before Nora decided to take a stab at small talk.

"It seems nice out here," she tried. And while it was true, it was also all she could think of to say. This man who shared her smile and knew her father's deepest secrets was a stranger to her. For all she knew, the most they had in common was genetics.

"I'm partial to it," Charles said, flashing Nora's smile back at her. "Might be a bit too slow-paced for you kids though."

"I like slow-paced," said Nora. "It's safer that way."

"Oh, if safe is what you're after, you can't get much safer than Virgo Bay."

The words slipped through Nora like a warm sip of tea, and for that moment she gave herself permission to agree with them. It seemed true enough in a way. S.C.Y.T.H.E. would certainly struggle to find the twins all the way out here, which made for one less thing to worry about. Now most of Nora's boundless worry could be comfortably concentrated on keeping her brother alive. In its own strange way, that came as something of a relief.

"Safe is good," she said.

"Your dad would argue with that," Charles replied on a chuckle. "That kid was always a little daredevil. Fearless."

"Just like Charlie," said Nora, trying to keep the hint of resentment from her voice. She'd always longed to see her parents reflected back in her, but from what little she'd known of them, they simply weren't—not in the way they lived on in her brother. Sure, she'd once dreamed of being an architect like Martin Bird, but her reasons for it couldn't have been more different, her character less similar, even her stature and the way she carried herself so far removed from the people who'd created her.

"Ironic that he should carry my name," said Charles. "When you seem to be the one carrying my nature."

This caught Nora off guard, and for a brief, wild moment she wondered if Charles had somehow read her thoughts. "Really?"

Charles nodded. "I see a lot of myself in you, Nora. You seem to see the world the way I do, which is quite something to find in someone I never thought I'd get the chance to meet. I'm very glad you're here."

Nora forced her eyes to the counter to hide the tears forming at their base. After her parents and Bubbie died and she and Charlie grew apart, she had never expected to feel anything close to "family" again. But as she and Charles stood there in the kitchen of her grandparents' house, their synchronized washing and drying an effortless dance, a lost but familiar warmth fell over her that brought a smile to her lips.

"I am too," she said, and then, almost in spite of herself: "How come Dad never told us about you guys?"

Charles stopped washing for a moment, adjusting his glasses with a sudsy, rubber-gloved hand. "That's a tricky question to answer. Hard to say. Martin was different than the rest of us, in a way. He always wanted more, though *why* is still beyond me. I guess we weren't enough for him, so maybe he figured we wouldn't be enough for you kids either. Or maybe he just wanted a clean slate. We didn't even know about him and your mom until after the wedding."

"That doesn't sound like Dad," said Nora. "I can't imagine him wanting to shut anyone out."

"Well, people change. Not that any of that matters now. I'm sure he had his reasons, and none of us held it against him. We knew he was off to live a very different life and that he would find his way to what he wanted, whatever it took. And here you both are. I'd say he did a very good job of it."

Nora allowed another small grin. "I just wish I'd known about you all."

"Likewise, my dear."

"You mean you didn't know about Charlie and me?"

"Well, we only ever got the barest hints of information up here. Martin wrote us letters, mostly. We did receive word when the two of you were born. I still remember learning I had a nephew named after me. And we heard a bit here and there about your milestones. But I know he had to move you kids around a bit for work, and then after he . . . well, I had no way of knowing where you'd ended up. So many times on my supply runs, I'd thought how pleasant it would be to drop in for a visit, to watch the only little ones in the family growing up, but you could have been anywhere in the world by then as far as I knew. To think you were only a ferry ride away all this time."

Nora smeared the last water droplets out of a glass and placed it gently in the drying rack. Not for the first time since they'd arrived in Virgo Bay, she felt a flare of anger at her father. All this time she'd seen him as this infallible man who'd been stolen from her, but he stole from her too.

"That would have been nice," was all she could think to say.

"Ah well, the past belongs in the past," said Charles. "There's no changing it now. The only thing we can do from here is decide what the future looks like. And I hope mine looks like a proper chance to get to know my niece and nephew."

"I'd like that," said Nora. She'd never had an uncle before. Her mom had been an only child, and for her whole life she thought her father was too. But her school friends had uncles and aunts, and though a few were not the best examples of the role, they had, for the most part, always seemed like a second, more lenient set of parents. In high school her friend Sarah Levinson's aunt had bought them cocktails in a can to celebrate the end of the school year. Nora hadn't drunk hers, of course, because even at that young age she knew that far too many bad things could happen when alcohol was involved. But the gesture had always stuck out to her as something that would technically qualify as "cool," in a dictionary definition sense, and that was something few adults could be, according to her teenage sensibilities. Teachers and parents were old and boring, but aunts and uncles got to be cool, and Nora was being offered the chance to experience that dynamic for the first time. Granted, she could now legally purchase her own booze, and the uncle in question was wearing a stuffy argyle sweater-vest, but who was she to turn her nose up at the opportunity to have this new species of relative in her life?

They exchanged another identical smile, and for the first time Nora couldn't help but see her father in Charles's expression. Despite the lack of shared features, the warmth and the way one eye crinkled more than the other when he smiled were exact duplicates. Even if she was currently mad at her dead dad, Nora couldn't help but breathe in the similarities.

As the day slipped away and night glided into its place, the varied age demographics came fully into play. Charles was the first to leave. Apparently, he had the farthest to walk, his house an exhausting fifteen-minute journey away, which he emphasized twice. Nora suffocated the urge to make a joke about the Jewish people wandering the desert for forty years without this much kvetching. These were her non-Jewish relatives, she reminded herself; they might not be as used to comedy.

Ruby and Richard were next to depart, preceded by a duet of yawning in C minor. Patty seemed bent on lingering awhile after her parents went off to bed, determined to continue braving her role as host against any tiredness that may have crept in. But eventually she too succumbed to the epidemic, her eyes already heavy with sleep as she shuffled out the door at Nora's insistence. That left only the twins, who made their way down to the basement to get settled.

"Think I can finally let poor Jessica out now? Gran and Pops are on a whole other floor, so they definitely won't hear her now," Charlie said as soon as the door to their father's old room was closed.

"I still don't understand why you brought that thing," Nora said instead of answering his question. Charlie was already unzipping the duffel bag as she spoke, Jessica's head appearing and disappearing like a Whac-A-Mole as the opening around her grew.

"You've been such a good girl," Charlie cooed. "So quiet. Not a peep all through dinner. Such a good girl."

"She has been weirdly quiet since we got here. You think she's had enough oxygen in that bag?"

"Oh sure, I've kept all kinds of things in there before."

"And they all lived?"

Charlie wasn't listening. Jessica was on his forearm now, hopping up to his shoulder and back down, her head bopping. He bopped his head along with her. "How's my pretty, pretty girl?"

Jessica said nothing.

"Huh. You think she's giving me the silent treatment?" he asked Nora before turning his attention back to the parrot. "You can be just like my ex sometimes, you know."

"Amanda or Roberto?"

"Dude, catch up. They were both years ago."

"Sorry, I canceled my subscription to Charlie's Love Life Updates after it raised the price."

"Inflation's a bitch." Charlie dug back into his bag and pulled out a glass pipe and a colorful packet of weed. "Watch my sweet girl for me, will you? I'm heading out back for a little evening refreshment."

"Oh sure, you didn't bring a jacket but you packed your weed," Nora snapped as Charlie sauntered to the door.

"I told you, only the essentials."

He disappeared just as Nora threw her dirty sock at the closing door. Infuriating. If there's one thing she could count on, it's that she couldn't count on Charlie for anything practical. She looked over at the bird on the bed opposite her.

"How do you put up with him?"

Jessica once again said nothing.

"Not feeling chatty, huh? Well, fine. Turn around. I'm getting changed and I don't need any commentary."

Nora picked up the nightgown Ruby had left on Martin's old bed for her. It was thick flannel, with a ruffled bib and a high collar. Not Nora's usual style, but it was clean and didn't smell like sweat and two days' worth of BO, so it was already a great improvement over her own clothes.

Once fully flanneled, Nora peeled back the blue-and-red bedsheets and crawled under the covers. The mattress was harder than she'd expected, the sheets scratchy, but on them lingered the slightest hint of a scent she recognized. Or maybe she was imagining it. Either way, she sank deeper into the bed and let herself imagine, for a very brief moment, that the blanket was her father's arms holding her in a hug. She could still remember what that felt like, just a little. Warm and comforting, like none of the dangers in the world could touch her. And like the sudden drop of something weighing roughly a pound or so onto her big toe. Wait, no, not that part. She opened her eyes. Jessica stood perched on her foot, watching her intently with pale yellow eyes.

"I thought I told you to turn around," said Nora. Still Jessica said nothing. Instead she hopped down and made the steady climb up Nora's bent legs, coming to rest on one knee. "All right, fine," Nora said. "Moment over. I'm mad at Dad anyway. But fuck, it's hard to be mad at someone dead. Have you ever tried it? They can't explain themselves. They can't apologize. There's nothing remotely satisfying about it. I guess it would be easier if he was freshly dead, like the souls my colleagues have to deal with. At least they can talk back. But then I think you'd just end up feeling too sorry for them for being dead that you couldn't even stay mad at them. How unfair is that?"

Jessica bobbed up and down.

"Maybe someone pretending to be dead is the next best thing," she said, still speculating. She'd experienced more than enough of that growing up. The deeper she fell into her fear of death, the more a teenaged Charlie had tried to scare it out of her. It started when they were fourteen. She'd just returned home from a grueling day at school (dodgeball followed by an oral presentation in which she'd mispronounced "pianist" rather profoundly) and walked into Bubbie's living room to find Charlie dead on the couch, a pool of blood surrounding him. After a shriek so high-pitched it upset the neighborhood dogs more than a block away, Charlie came clean and was forced to spend the rest of the evening apologizing to Nora and scrubbing strawberry Kool-Aid off the couch cushions. Nora hated him for it, naturally, and hated him just as much when he faked his death in four more ways over the course of the next two years, mastering the art of shallow breathing and rolling his eyeballs in ways eyeballs were not meant to roll. But secretly she was a little grateful to him too, because each time he turned out to be alive, she got to be angry and swear at him and cry in his arms—something she never got the chance to do with her parents no matter how badly she'd needed to.

Nora shook her head. "Whatever. I have more important things to worry about." She cracked open Charlie's file from where she'd left it on the bed before going up to dinner. She tapped her pen on the letters she'd written along the inside of the file. "S-T-A . . ."

Jessica cocked her head, enthralled.

"S-T-A." Nora repeated. "S-T-A."

"Stare," Jessica said.

Nora looked up in surprise, a second voice in the room unexpected after hers had dominated for so long. Then she shook it off and turned back to the file. "Yes, you are staring at me. Quite intensely. It's very off-putting."

Jessica hopped to Nora's other knee.

"S-T-A," she said again. Then leapt up. Jessica went sailing in a flurry of feathers, catching herself midair and landing on the other bed with an affronted squawk, but Nora barely noticed. "Stairs!"

She raced out the door and careened into the open space between bedrooms, reaching the bottom of the rickety wooden staircase just as Charlie's silhouette appeared at the top.

"Charlie," she called out in warning, but all that did was confuse Charlie, who was too mellow to understand warnings in his current state, causing him to miss the top step and begin a painful tumble down the rest. Nora had seen this before. Not in person, but in case file after case file that had once stood stacked on her desk at S.C.Y.T.H.E.: broken necks and cracked skulls resulting from a heavy fall down the stairs. In her mind's eye she watched as Charlie thudded to the wooden floor by her feet, another staircase death to add to the roster. But before her mind had time to move on from this thought and connect to her feet, Nora was already bolting up the stairs, throwing herself in Charlie's way like a stuntman's crash mat with bones. Any thought of her own welfare was uncharacteristically gone from her mind for just long enough to propel her upward before the twins collided and tumbled down, down, landing in a heap of limbs and groans at the bottom.

Nora smacked at her brother's meaty form, which was lying like an anvil across her rib cage. "Off. Off," she wheezed. Charlie rolled off and lay there, dazed, head-to-head with Nora, their legs stretched out in opposite directions. Neither had what it took to move.

"Did you die?" Nora asked, still scrambling for breath.

"I don't think so," Charlie said back.

"Good. Good."

"Was I going to? Was that the thing?"

"I think it might've been."

"So we stopped it?"

"I stopped it. You nearly marijuana-ed yourself right into it."

"People don't die from weed, dude."

"They do when it impairs their judgment, or depth perception, or—"

"That was pretty sick though."

"What?"

"You, like, used yourself as a human shield or whatever. Highly out of character, but pretty sick."

Nora lifted her head and turned back to look at him. "You were going to die, Charlie. Maybe. I told you I wouldn't let that happen."

"Well, thanks."

"Just try not to maybe almost die again. Are you hurt?"

Charlie patted himself from his head down to as close to his toes as he could reach. "My elbow got a nice whack. Otherwise I think I'm good. You?"

Nora's wrist was throbbing all over again, and her knee would be too bruised for Jessica to perch on for a while, but otherwise she was fine. No broken neck. No cracked skull. Somehow she'd taken a risk and come out of it alive. "I'm okay. What the hell were you doing up there anyway? You were barely gone long enough for one of your famous Charlie solo parties."

"There was somebody out there," he replied.

Nora sat up. "What?"

"Yeah, I saw someone standing there in the dark. They had something in their hand. I dunno. I'm sure it was nothing. I'm high as fuck, dude, I got spooked."

"Why would there be somebody out there at—" Nora checked her watch. "Twelve oh seven a.m.?"

"Search me. Maybe old Granddaddy Boulder Shoulders felt like a late-night walk. Or he and Gram-Gram wanted to get freaky without us hearing. Maybe they swing? Did you notice any pineapples as part of the decor?"

"Pineapples? Jesus, Charlie." Nora shook her head. "We can't really apply city logic to a town like this. It's such a different way of life here. I guess it could have been someone foraging or something. Night foraging. Maybe that's a thing? I don't know. But I don't like it."

"You don't like anything."

"Okay, come on, that is not true."

"Name one thing you like."

"Chamomile tea."

Charlie faked a yawn as his review of that answer. Nora took off her other sock and threw it at him. This time it easily hit its mark. Charlie jumped up, dusting himself off as if he'd just been doused with tarantulas. "Nor, gross, I don't want your foot fungus."

Nora, who had never had any fungus in her life, not even shiitake mushrooms, and did everything in her power to keep it that way, blanched. "How dare you!"

"I'm going to bed. You going to bed?"

Nora let her shoulders drop. They, like the rest of her, were heavy with exhaustion. "Yes. Of course. It's after midnight. Have we discussed the health risks of getting too little sleep for a sustained period of time?"

"Not for about six minutes."

Nora glared at him.

"Aw, and you've run out of socks. Sucks to suck. Cute nightie, by the way. Is it from the Mrs. Claus collection?"

Nora retrieved the offending—but fungus-free—sock from where it had landed by the stairs and charged at Charlie, who knew this was coming before she did and was already halfway to the bedroom.

After a truce brought about by Charlie's threat to start using his own socks as ammunition, the twins took to their beds. Jessica curled herself into Charlie's neck and they were both snoring before Nora had finished tucking herself in to her satisfaction. She rolled her eyes. The lights in the room weren't even off yet. Charlie always could sleep without effort, as if he didn't have a million worries suddenly cued to the stage by his head hitting the pillow.

Nora pulled out Charlie's file one last time. With any luck, this was it. The last way he would be fated to die. She ran her eyes down the page, but the answer revealed itself with the same clarity as before, which is to say none. The cloud of ink remained, the letters lost somewhere within. Nora looked at her own writing.

S-T-A. They were the only letters she'd been able to make out so far, and they might not even be in the correct order. She turned back to the gyrating ink. In a space that had never shown the hint of a letter before, a shape appeared. Half a shape, anyway. It looked like a *U* with the two stems shaved low. Nora threw the file to the ground with a grunt of frustration and curled under the covers that smelled like her dad.

WHEN NORA WOKE UP AGAIN, IT WASN'T YET MORNING. THE HOUSE was still, the darkness in the room heavy with the final hours of night. And yet, something had woken her. She didn't have to pee; a little jostle confirmed that. She looked across the room to her brother's bed, but he remained fast asleep. At least from what she could tell. Something was blocking the upper half of the bed. Nora tried to focus her eyes, but they were still too filled with the weight of sleep, the darkness too thick to make sense of what she was seeing. She tapped her watch, the little light setting her wrist aglow and efficiently blinding her in the process. The only thing she could make out through the spots of light now dancing across her eyeballs was the glint of something raised just above Charlie's bed. A glint of something polished, and sharp.

"Knife," Jessica squawked, echoing Nora's own fuzzy thoughts. The word set both parrot and woman into motion, Jessica flapping wildly, Nora attempting to untangle herself from the covers that presently bound her legs.

By the time she'd freed herself, the holder of the weapon was out the door and thundering up the stairs. Nora flopped to the floor, and Jessica hitched a ride on her shoulder as she bolted after the intruder, but it was too late. She reached the top of the danger stairs to find the back door gaping open, the night sheltering the knife wielder in its boundless black.

"Did you see who it was?" Nora asked the parrot, struggling to steady her breath from both the panic and the exertion.

Jessica didn't reply.

"Holy shit, holy shit," said Nora.

"Holy shit, holy shit," Jessica agreed.

They trudged back down the stairs, Nora defeated, Jessica bobbing her head. The lights were on when they got back into the bedroom, Charlie hunched over a mess of bedding.

"There you are!" he said.

"Yeah, I—"

He scooped Jessica off Nora's shoulder. "I was looking all over for you, beautiful." He gave the bird's head a smooch and turned back to Nora. "What the hell do you think you're doing, sneaking off with my little sweet pea in the middle of the night?"

Nora just stared at him for a moment, words lost to her in the wake of everything that had just occurred. She'd barely had time to realize how close she'd come to death in an effort to protect him from a similar fate. That thought alone sent the ability to speak far from her tongue. Instead she kicked his shin.

"Ouch, what the fuck?"

"Charlie," Nora said, words returning to her. "Someone just tried to kill you."

"What? What are you talking about?"

"You didn't hear anything just now?"

He shook his head.

"Unbelievable." Nora took a sharp inhale. "Charlie. Someone was just in here with a knife. I tried to chase them down, but—"

"You what?"

"I'm trying not to think about it. The point is, someone wanted you dead. Not just your file this time. An actual human being. With a knife. And I—wait. Your file."

Nora dove for the manila folder on the floor beside her bed. The ink cloud beside "cause of death" had not changed shape.

"S-T-A. It wasn't the stairs that were going to kill you, Charlie. I was wrong. You were supposed to be stabbed."

"Why the hell would someone stab me?" Charlie asked. "I haven't been here long enough to piss anyone off yet."

"I don't know, but we need to find out quick. Because according to your file, they're not done with you."

13

Case # 10452
Toni Jackson
Age: 48
Cause of Death: Stabbing

Murder had always felt far removed from Nora's world. Sure, death happened—and in Nora's case it seemed to happen more often than most—but it wasn't until she began working at S.C.Y.T.H.E. that she fully realized how Death itself wasn't always the one to take a life. That thought still struck her as so very strange. Life was already such a vulnerable thing, a piece of cracked china in clumsy hands. The fact that anyone had it in them to deliberately smash it baffled her no matter how many times she came across it. The shooting she'd sorted last week felt just as incomprehensible as her first murder case, a stabbing after a drug deal gone wrong. And yet, like every other hand of Death, murder had finally reached out to her, its fingers stretching hungrily towards her brother.

* * *

NORA COULDN'T GET BACK TO SLEEP THAT NIGHT. SHE SAT LIKE A sentry, stiff-backed in her bed, guarding Charlie with Jessica by her side. The lights stayed on. Her pulse stayed raised. Her mind hummed with everything the night had presented her. Charlie wasn't just destined to die; he was destined to be murdered. But why? And by whom? It didn't make any sense, which fit nicely with the theme of the past forty-eight hours of her life.

If someone here wanted Charlie dead, then the twins needed to leave Virgo Bay. But they couldn't. Nora's car was still a smoking heap somewhere miles away. They were stuck here for the foreseeable future, which meant she needed to figure out who was after Charlie, and quickly. But that wasn't exactly Nora's area of expertise. If listing all the ways a person could die were an Olympic sport, Nora would easily bring home gold for the US, and then be accused of doping given such a faultless performance. It was one of the skills that made her such an efficient administrative coordinator at S.C.Y.T.H.E. and, she was certain, was the main reason she'd made it to twenty-six without so much as an urgent care visit to her name. But when it came to people and why they made the choices they made, she was out of her depth. She'd never solved a murder before, much less one that had yet to take place. But she didn't have any choice. She couldn't go to anyone in town for help, not when they'd all just become her suspects.

BY THE TIME THE REST OF THE HOUSE WAS AWAKE, NORA HAD CY-cled through every possible way her brother could be murdered two and a half times. Each incarnation became gorier and more upsetting than the last. The box of cereal waiting for the twins on the dining room table was embedded with razors. The milk was poisoned. The note from Richard and Ruby saying they'd gone on their daily morning beach walk and would be home by nine thirty would somehow leap up and sever Charlie's carotid artery with a jarringly potent paper cut. Nothing was safe. As usual, but even more so.

They needed to discuss this. They needed a plan—again. But they didn't get far before the twins' newfound and potentially murderous grandparents came through the back door, their cheeks flushed from the brisk morning breeze that tapped lightly against the dining room windows.

"You kids aren't just getting up, are you?" Ruby said, hanging her hand-knit scarf on a hook by the door. She slipped off her shoes and flitted to the kitchen, clearly in the midst of a mindless daily ritual. "You're missing a beautiful morning out there. Not many more days of sunshine left this season."

Nora looked from one grandparent to the other. Richard was still hanging his coat, his morning rhythm more leisurely than his wife's. In the kitchen a kettle began to hum. Richard wiped his boots on the little rug by the door, stomping to get the sand off. Charlie spooned another heaping mound of cereal into his mouth and crunched. The kettle's whistling began to emerge. All the sounds stacked on top of one another like a seven-layer dip of auditory overstimulation. Nora could barely think, much less plan.

She leapt up, grabbing Charlie by the wrist and yanking him away from his breakfast.

"You know, you're right," said Nora, her voice tight. "It does look beautiful out. We were actually just talking about going on a walk, right, Charlie?" She didn't wait for him to reply. "It'll be a great opportunity for us to explore Virgo Bay a little. See the sights."

"There are sights?" Charlie asked through a mouthful, still trying to shake Nora off him as she dragged him towards the door.

"You're not going out like that, surely." Ruby appeared in the dining room, cradling a steaming mug in her hands.

Charlie was still in the pajamas he'd been wearing since Nora had picked him up two days ago.

"I've got some old clothes you can borrow, Charlie," said Richard. "As for Nora, well, my Ruby's always been barely a hair higher than a field mouse, but I'm sure Patty will have things that will fit you just fine. You look about her size. Nice to see the Bird genes still kicking around in both of you."

"That's very kind," said Nora, his seemingly earnest generosity propelling her out the door even faster. The confusion over whether or not she could trust either of them made her head spin. "We'll get changed when we get back, but we'll be fine like this until then, right, Charlie?"

"I mean, are you even fine right now?"

Nora gave a nervous laugh. She grabbed both of their coats, shoving Charlie's into his chest harder than was absolutely necessary. "We'll be back in a bit."

Charlie offered a bewildered shrug to Richard and Ruby as Nora ushered him out the door. As soon as the sun hit her and the oppressive air of that little red house melted away, Nora could breathe again. She let the breeze press against her cheeks for a moment, revitalized by the refreshing bite it carried, then pulled her coat in tighter to stave off any threatening chill.

"So that was weird," said Charlie.

"Shh." Nora guided him away from the house and onto a nearby path. She needed them to be as far away from earshot as possible, not only from their grandparents but from anyone else in town.

"I was still eati—"

"Shh."

The path ended at a line of evergreens on the cusp of a dense wood. Nora hesitated. She didn't trust nature; too many unknowable things lived in it: poisonous things and biting things and stinging things and bacteria that could eat your brain. People died getting lost in nature, or trying to pet nature when it didn't want to be petted. But it also offered the currently elusive promise of privacy, because who else would possibly choose to venture in there? She could feel the warmth of eyes on her back. This town was too small, too insular. They needed to be alone. Nora nodded to a gap in the trees and they slipped through.

"Can I talk now, or are you going to shush me again?" said Charlie.

The trees that enclosed them were tall and thin, their spindly trunks stretching to somewhere just out of sight. The sun's rays couldn't quite navigate their way through the dense foliage of the many conifers still plump with their spiky attempt at leaves, casting the forest in a green-tinted haze. Nora felt like she was wearing sunglasses all of a sudden, the world just slightly dimmed. Branches squeaked and cracked in the wind, dead leaves rustling on the ground under the feet of invisible creatures gathering winter supplies. The twins weaved around trunks and over roots until a dirt path opened before them, guiding them deeper into the wilderness.

"You can talk now," Nora decided at last.

"Cool. Okay, so first of all, what the fuck?"

"Can you be more specific?"

"Yeah okay, let's start with why you didn't let me finish breakfast."

"I needed to talk to you," said Nora.

"You haven't said words in like ten minutes."

"Eight," Nora clarified, confirming on her watch. "And that was because I didn't want to be overheard. You remember what happened last night, right?"

"The stair thing or the knife thing?"

"Knife."

"Yeah, I remember the knife thing."

Nora shook her head. His tone was too blasé. How was she more freaked out by his almost murder than he was?

"Charlie, someone wants to kill you."

"Right, we established that."

"Do you have any idea why someone might want to kill you, Charlie? Anybody you could've pissed off back home that might have followed us here? Any newfound family members you've hit on?"

"Got nothing for you, sis. Anyone who wanted me dead back home would've just killed me there to save the gas money. And I'll have you know I've been on my best behavior up here."

"Okay." Nora clenched her jaw. "What do we do about this? I mean, we're trapped here, in a town where someone we haven't identified wants you dead for reasons we don't know. That's not good, Charlie, you get that, right?"

"I'm not dumb," said Charlie. "I know it's bad. But what are our options here?"

"Exactly," said Nora.

"You've lost me again."

"I brought you out here so we can figure out our next steps. We need to strategize. To be one step ahead of whoever had that knife. To figure out who it was so we know who to trust. Or better yet, to get the fuck out of here. So, let's plan."

"Right. Great. Good thinking," said Charlie. "So . . . any ideas?"

Nora just glared at that. This was the way things had always been. Well, almost always. Back when they were kids, Nora and Charlie had been inseparable. On the first day of kindergarten, when she found out she'd been placed in a different class than her brother, Nora cried for so long that the school relented and allowed them to be together, even though it made the class numbers uneven. Charlie was her best friend. He looked after her. If anyone so much as looked at her funny, they would have to answer to Charlie Bird. Which usually involved language officially deemed "not schoolyard appropriate" in parent-teacher meetings. Then their parents died, and everything changed. They changed. When Nora needed her brother most, he just kind of stopped. Stopped sticking up for her, stopped trying hard in school, stopped taking anything seriously, stopped being Charlie. Instead all he wanted to do was have fun. High school was a nightmare. There wasn't a single party that Charlie Bird didn't attend, assuming he wasn't throwing it himself. While Nora, still swallowed by a boundless well of fear, retreated deeper into herself, only emerging to save Charlie from Charlie. Now she had to save him from Death too, and she'd already done that like five times now.

"We need a car," Nora said, falling back into her usual role without further resistance. "If not mine, someone else's. Maybe we can borrow one. Or maybe we find out when Charles is heading out on his next supply run and go with him. But we need to get out of here. Failing that, we need a phone charger. My phone's dead, but if I can get it charged, then we can call for help. If we're dealing with a murderer, then we need the police. The FBI. Whatever they have up here. Mounties? Or is that just in cartoons? Anyway, whatever, that's the best I've got."

"Well, I guess we don't need my plan, then," said Charlie. "Too bad, it was a real good one too. Oh well. Hey, what's that?"

He pointed off the path and into the thick web of trees beyond.

"Can you seriously not focus on one thing for more than two seconds?" Nora said, but followed his gesture into the thicket with her eyes, to what looked like some kind of man-made structure in a clearing forty or so feet away. "Oh, for fuck's sake. What now?"

"Only one way to find out," said Charlie. Before he even had time to take a step towards the structure, Nora had her fingers wrapped tight around his jacket collar.

"No," she said. "Absolutely not. Are you serious? You're literally on the verge of being killed at any moment and you want to go explore the creepy abandoned building in the middle of the woods? Charlie, can you please use your brain for a sec?"

"It isn't abandoned," Charlie said, as if that were the main issue. "Look, there's smoke coming out of the chimney."

Nora found the stone chimney through the trees, slender coils of gray smoke escaping its mouth and disappearing into the treetops high, high above. Any saliva in Nora's mouth vanished.

"Fuck," she said. "We have to get out of here."

She took Charlie by the wrist again and started dragging. It felt like walking an unruly puppy. The wind had picked up now, tree branches creaking like breaking bones high above. Then another sound snuck into Nora's brain from just above them, buzzing there, familiar but impossible to pin down. It was rhythmic, back and forth, back and forth. Then the buzzing stopped, and the creaking, and the wind rushing, and any other sound, and suddenly she knew exactly what she was hearing. She could see how this would end. It was all right there in her mind's eye. But it was too late. The saw had stopped cutting, the heavy branch plummeting towards Charlie's oblivious head. There was no time to warn him.

Nora felt the warmth from where her hand wrapped around his wrist. Her own wrist still pulsed from its growing collection of injuries; her strength, already questionable under normal circumstances, was dulled by the pain. And yet, without fully thinking about it, without time to inhale and collect herself, Nora yanked. Hard. Hard enough to throw off their collective balance and send them both to the leafy ground just as the fat branch hit the earth, bouncing once and then coming to rest at their feet with a thunderous thud.

The sound of retreating footfalls followed, echoing through the forest, louder and more assured than the little critters who had been rummaging in the leaves. Someone, almost certainly the same someone who had just sent a tree branch down on them, was fleeing the scene.

Nora dragged herself to her feet, her tailbone throbbing. She looked down at Charlie, who sat propped on his elbows, staring at the branch with wide eyes.

"Are you okay?" she asked.

"Did you just save my life again?" Charlie said, his voice flat, his mind clearly still catching up with what had just occurred.

"Yeah," Nora said. She carefully dusted off the back of her cargo pants, trying to shed the damp leaves that clung there.

"You're good at that," said Charlie.

"I wish you were better at it," she said. "We really need to go. Now. Whoever that was could still be around here somewhere, and who knows what they have planned next."

Charlie stood up without protest. His face was as close to mirthless as Nora had seen it in years. This seemed to have finally driven the severity of the matter home to Charlie. He led the way out of the woods, saying nothing.

When they got back to the little red house, they were greeted by a cacophony of voices emanating from the living room. Nora threw a look over her shoulder at Charlie that said, "Oh fuck," as they took their shoes off. Great. More people they couldn't trust.

ONCE INSIDE THEY FOUND A HEALTHY FIRE UNDULATING IN THE hearth, surrounded by Richard and Ruby on the couch, Patty perched on a footstool, Charles on the matching chair, and a man Nora couldn't remember the name of on a seat across from them. The man was the relative closest in age to the twins, the only child of Pickles and his wife—Nora knew that much. He wore khaki pants smeared with mud, his stubbly cheeks still rosy from the crisp November air. Based on his position and elevated breathing, he must have arrived only minutes before the twins.

"Uh, hi," Nora said to no one in particular.

"Oh good, you're back," said Richard. "There's a fresh pot of coffee in the kitchen to warm you both up. A good walk always deserves a little brew, I say."

Nora blanched at the suggestion, her anxiety already threatening diarrhea without the help.

"How'd you kids sleep?" Patty asked from her perch.

Nora gave her a sharp appraisal. Could she have been in their room with a knife last night?

"Great," Nora said through a tight jaw.

"Glad to hear it," said Patty. "Hopefully the boys' room was up to snuff. God only knows what those scoundrels got up to in there." She tossed a look at Charles, who volleyed it back the way only a brother could. "Anyway, Mom said you were in need of some clean clothes. Guess Marty never taught you kids how to pack, eh? Typical Marty. Nora, I left some things on your bed for you. Not sure they'll be your style, but hopefully they'll keep you warm at least."

"That's very kind of you," said Nora.

"And, Charlie," said Richard. "You're welcome to take a look in my closet, but it occurred to me that your father left some of his old things downstairs. I thought they might be more to your taste."

"Thanks," was all Charlie said.

"If nothing works, I have a few old things," said the man Nora couldn't name. "You could come over if you want, Charlie."

"As you can see, Phil's fashion sense is impeccable," said Patty, indicating the man's muddy pants.

Phil. Nora made a mental note of that. Phil with the muddy pants and the rosy cheeks and the glint of something suspicious in his eye. Could he have been the one out there in the woods today? He looked agile enough to climb a tree, his sinewy muscles visible even under his thin moss-green Henley. Under normal circumstances, ones where they weren't related and he wasn't possibly trying to kill her brother, Nora would say he was a good-looking guy. A little old for her, maybe, gray flecks hidden among his brown stubble and creases beside his eyes, but his jaw was strong and his expression sharp and alert. He seemed to be watching the twins more intensely than the rest, his gaze torn between them. His sharp eyes tore through Nora like an X-ray. She wondered if he could see through her ribs to where her heartbeat was quickening with her growing discomfort.

"We'll go get changed," said Nora, more as an excuse to get away from that stare than an actual desire to get out of her clothes.

"Is there anywhere to get a car fixed around here?" Charlie asked from beside her. "Or a phone charger we could borrow?" His voice was flat. He scratched at his mat of bleached hair. Nora blinked at him, glad that one of them remembered the plan but shocked it was Charlie.

"No phones to charge, I'm afraid," said Richard. "Not much need for them when everyone you know is just around the corner."

"I can fix a car," said Phil, almost too quickly.

"Phil's very handy," Charles confirmed. "He also happens to have the only proper tool kit in Virgo Bay, which helps."

Which meant he might have been the only person in town with a saw, Nora thought. And now he wanted access to the twins' only possible means of escape.

"That's okay," said Nora. Charlie gave her a confused brow raise but she continued. "We just need to figure out a way home, but we don't want to put anyone out. It's an old car. I've been meaning to get a new one anyway. Charles, maybe we could come with you on your next supply run?"

"I don't see why not," said Charles. "I'd love the company."

"But he just got back from his last run," Patty said. "He won't have another until next month. That's not to say you're not welcome to stay that long of course, but—"

"No," Nora said, more forcefully than she'd intended. She willed her voice to soften. "That's okay. I've got . . . work."

"I'm happy to have a look," said Phil. "Really. Charlie, why don't you come along and show me where you crashed? I can get on it later today."

"No," Nora said again. "I mean, I'll go. Charlie had some things around here he wanted to do. Right, Charlie?"

Charlie finally caught on with the help of a subtle pinch to the side from Nora.

"Uh, yeah."

"Well, that settles that," said Ruby. "Now shake a leg and get changed. I could use some help putting lunch together."

Nora found the pile of clothes waiting for her when she got downstairs. She sifted through the neutral fabrics, holding each item up to her front. Just about everything looked handmade, the simple cuts sewn with relative skill. She selected a pair of gray pants and a pale salmon top and made for the door to find somewhere private to change, but was promptly interrupted by a groan from Charlie, who was almost entirely submerged in the bedroom closet.

Nora froze. Was that a groan of pain? Had Nora missed something somehow and, in doing so, allowed Death to finally claim her brother?

"Charlie?" Nora called.

Charlie poked his head, still in its proper place on his neck, out of the closet. "I don't see any of Dad's stuff. It all looks like Charles's. I'll hulk out of these sweater-vests."

"Jesus Christ," Nora muttered to herself. "Maybe Dad's stuff is somewhere else? I don't know, Charlie. If you can't find them, then borrow Richard's clothes. Just stay away from that Phil guy. He's my top suspect right now."

"Wait, seriously? He's kinda hot though, right?"

"*Cousin* Phil clearly got here just before we did, and he knows those woods. He could easily have known a shortcut. Plus his clothes are covered in mud. From climbing trees? And he has all the tools in town, apparently. Not to mention how keen he was to spend some one-on-one time with you."

"I mean, I also wouldn't mind—"

"*Cousin* Phil," Nora repeated. "Stay away from him. Please, for the love of god."

"Okay, okay," said Charlie, his more serious tone returning. "You're right. That's all sus as fuck. No hot cousin Phil time. Noted."

"Thank you. Now, I'm going to change into something that doesn't smell like sweat and mental anguish. Please try not to get killed while I'm gone."

Charlie gave her a salute, and Nora finally made it out the door. Back in the common area, she decided to change in Patty's old room. It seemed appropriate since she was getting into her clothes. Why not embrace the transformation fully? But as she reached for the handle, the third basement door caught her eye. It was narrower than the bedroom doors, clearly a closet of some kind. The kind of closet where folks might keep a bunch of old clothes belonging to their son, maybe. Nora knew her father's things would be Charlie's preference over the stodgy wardrobe of their grandfather. Though nothing could quite compete with Charlie's novelty T-shirt collection, family photos suggested Martin Bird had a decent sense of style in his day, always in something acceptably well cut and rich or darkly colored to accent his eyes, although Nora couldn't account for how much of that was her mother's influence.

Nora opened the closet and was promptly greeted by a wall of dust. She coughed and sputtered as the motes clambered up her nose. Clearly this thing hadn't been opened in a while. When she'd finished frantically waving away the settling cloud, Nora inspected the shelves within, stacked with dinosaur-print linens and a few well-loved plush toys. Beneath the shelves, a garbage bag sat slumped on the floor. She slid it out and opened it to find a mass of tangled old clothes staring back at her. Vindicated, she went to close the door when something else caught her eye. Something familiar.

In a cardboard box on the floor next to where the bag had sat was a stack of file folders. Nora looked at them with narrowed eyes. Those files . . . she shook her head. S.C.Y.T.H.E. intentionally used the most generic brand of generic file folders for their cases. These could hold anything, and likely did: tax records, old receipts, more of her dad's impressively bad artwork. And yet, the familiarity of their innocuous beige niggled at her.

She glanced behind her, twice over each shoulder just in case, then plunged in, plucking the first file her eager fingertips touched. She pried it open, a puff of dust wafting out, then promptly slammed it closed. Then opened it again. Then closed it.

No. This wasn't possible. She grabbed another file and

opened that one. Then another. With bated breath she grabbed one more, but as soon as she read the first words, she immediately regretted it. And even more than that: she regretted coming here, and everything that led up to it.

ONCE SHE WAS CHANGED, NORA WENT BACK INTO HER DAD'S OLD bedroom and threw the bag of clothes at her brother. He was sitting on the bed, Jessica cradled in his arms like a baby.

"You found them," Charlie said, sifting through the bag.

"Yeah," said Nora, still numb from shock.

"Jeez, Dad really had a thing for paisley, huh?"

"Charlie," said Nora, "I found something else."

"His underwear? Because honestly I'm good going commando."

Nora just shook her head. "You need to see it."

Charlie followed her back to the closet in the wood-paneled basement common room. Nora tossed another look over each shoulder and opened the door again. She handed Charlie the file that had sent her reeling. He looked it up and down, then handed it back to Nora, face scrunched.

"So . . . Grandma Ruby's a zombie?"

"No," said Nora as though she could confidently state *anything* at that point. "I think . . ." She patted her tongue against the roof of her mouth, trying to find any hint of moisture left. "I think she was a S.C.Y.T.H.E. agent."

"Then why does that file say her name?"

"I don't know," said Nora. "But we need to find out."

14

The afternoon snuck up quickly while Nora wasn't looking. She'd been too busy trying to untangle the knots in her head, each new element of this mystery tied up tight and suffocating, that she'd barely noticed time slipping away. The mindless tasks Ruby had assigned her in preparation for lunch only served to send her further into her thoughts, the constant busywork preventing her from properly addressing her small but enigmatic grandmother about what she'd discovered.

Nora barely ate a thing. There was no room in her for anything other than questions right now. Phil had left in the late morning, leaving only Ruby, Richard, Charles, Patty, and the twins for lunch. After everyone had their fill, Nora tried to offer Ruby help with the dishes in the hopes of a moment alone, but it was Richard she found herself in the kitchen with instead.

By the time they'd finished tidying, Phil was back and looking for her.

"You good to go?" he asked Nora. He'd changed his pants. She eyed the mudless jeans suspiciously.

"Go?" she said, still catching up with the passage of time.

"Your car," said Phil. "You still okay to show me where you crashed it? My tools are in the truck."

"Right, no, I'm ready," she said. But was she? She might not be Phil's target, but if it *had* been him in the woods that morning, she wasn't convinced she was safe with him. And "safe" was always her first priority. But if she didn't go, Charlie would have to, and she knew that outcome would likely be worse. She'd have to do this. And, if she made it out alive, she'd confront Ruby when she got back.

Phil's pickup sat waiting for them on the grass just outside the little red house, its paint scuffed, mud caked onto the wheels, years of overuse written across its exterior. It looked ready to slough off its doors like a shedding snake and retreat into the wild. If Phil didn't kill her, Nora figured a ride in the rust-mobile might do the trick. But at least it was running, which was more than she could say for her own car. She swung herself into the passenger seat, trying hard to ignore the torn leather on the seats or the unknowable stains inexplicably spattered across the roof.

Phil slid in behind the wheel. "You remember the way?"

"I think so," said Nora.

Phil nodded and turned his focus to the road, driving them to the outskirts of Virgo Bay and making a left at Nora's cue. They drove in silence for a while, Nora slipping back into the knots of her mind, when a sudden slam on the breaks jostled her forward and out of her thoughts. Her seat belt locked, digging into her collarbone.

"What is it? What's going on?" She looked around, eyes wild. They were on the paved road she'd driven down on her way to town, nothing around but the mass of trees and rocks that made up the landscape. She turned to face Phil, suddenly hyperaware of their proximity, of their isolation, of just how vulnerable she was, alone in the middle of nowhere with a stranger.

"You need to tell me which way to turn," Phil said.

Nora barely heard him over the pulse in her ears. "Oh. Down there," she said, trying to keep her voice steady.

Phil gave another nod and drove on. Nora watched his hands on the wheel, suddenly attuned to every detail around her. His hands were cut and calloused, the profile of his face more weatherworn than it had seemed in the house. There was something almost robotic about him; something in his stillness, his quiet, the calm in his manner. All things that scared Nora, if only because she couldn't manage any of them herself.

They slowed again, and Nora saw her poor wounded Civic come into view, a shiny black heap of abandoned metal on the grass. In an act of cosmic mockery, two perfectly unflattened rabbits sat nearby, nibbling at the greenery around one of the car's sedentary tires, basking in their driving hazard-y life choices.

"Gonna go out on a limb and say this is it," Phil said as he pulled up behind the car. Nora hopped out as soon as the truck stopped, relief flooding her the moment she felt fresh air on her cheeks. There was something about being caged with someone who could maybe be an attempted murderer that did unhappy things to Nora's already-delicate bowels.

The driver's side door slammed shut and Phil rounded the truck with a red tin toolbox in hand.

"You have a saw in there?" Nora asked stiffly.

Phil looked at her blankly before turning to the car. "This is going to be a big job," he said. "Can't guarantee anything. I'm not a mechanic. But I'll do what I can."

He gave the car a thorough once-over before hunkering down under the crumpled hood. Nora felt her anxiety simmer into uneasiness and then, as more time passed, turn into restlessness. If Phil was going to hurt her, he didn't seem in much of a hurry about it, and she couldn't get any closer to answering her questions about Ruby from way out here. But there was something else she'd wanted answers about, another knot in her mind that she'd double tied and left at the back.

"Do you get out into the woods around Virgo Bay much?" she asked, then immediately realized that if it had been Phil out there this morning, she had walked right into a confrontation with a killer without meaning to. Thankfully Phil just kept on poking around under the hood.

"Not too much these days, but I played in there a bit as a boy," he said.

Nora exhaled. If it was him, he didn't seem about to own up to it, and she was definitely not going to press. She quickly got to her point. "There's an old building of some kind in there. A house, I think. It seemed . . . I think it was inhabited. I just wondered who lives out there."

This time Phil's head peered over the hood of the car. He didn't look at Nora, really; if anything he seemed to be looking through her. "Like I said, I haven't been out there much in a long time."

"But it's such a small town," Nora said, perplexed. "And you've lived here your whole life, right? Surely you'd know who's living in the woods."

"Well, I don't," Phil said, his tone the most animated Nora had heard it. "Now, you want me to fix your car or what?"

Nora took a step back in spite of herself, the uneasiness his tone triggered in her tingling down her knees. Then it hit her. Phil himself could be the resident of that strange house in the woods. It would explain how he'd found the twins so easily that morning, it would explain why his truck was so beaten up and painted with mud. And surely, even in a town like this, a man of Phil's age didn't still live with his parents, but if he didn't live with Pickles or at the farm with Vic and his family, or in one of the little clapboard houses around Patty, he had to be somewhere. Nora studied the top of his head, as though it would tell her what parts of his story were true and which were lies. Then he looked at her for another moment.

"You're not from around here," he said. "You have no idea what the wilderness holds in these parts. What harm could come to you out there. If you know what's good for you, you'll stay out of the woods."

THEY RETURNED HOME AN HOUR LATER, NORA NOT DEAD. PHIL HAD decided he'd work on the car the next day when he'd have more hours of sunlight. The weather had begun to turn sometime before they began their journey back into town, fat clouds rolling in. By the time they pulled up at the little red house, speckles of rain were dotting the truck's grubby windshield. Nora waved a tight goodbye and hurried into the house as Phil drove off.

Inside, the fire was warm, Charlie curled on the couch in front of it like a cat, belly up, leg twitching slightly. Somehow he'd managed to nap while Nora was receiving threats from their hot but sinister cousin.

Ruby came down the stairs a moment later and tipped her

head in greeting. "He's been like that for over an hour," she whispered, indicating Charlie with her chin. "Should I be concerned?"

Nora shook her head. Of all the things in the world she had to be concerned about, and there were always many, Charlie napping wasn't one of them. Charlie Bird was not a man of many talents, less due to inadequacy than a total lack of effort, but he'd always excelled at naps. One time in senior year he left school at lunch, planning to grab a few quick winks and be back for fifth-period biology. He didn't wake up again until after breakfast the following morning.

Just to be absolutely certain, Nora approached her brother and shoved a hand under his nose. A steady rhythm of air hit her knuckles. He wasn't dead, he was just Charlie.

"He's fine," Nora said. "And there's really no need to whisper. Charlie's slept through . . ." She thought back to the figure with the knife in their room last night and shook it away. "One time when we were little, I fell out of bed and broke my arm. Mom and Dad called an ambulance. The whole street woke up from the sirens and the flashing lights, but Charlie didn't realize anything had happened until he saw me in a cast the next morning."

"Lucky boy," said Ruby. "I can hardly remember the last time I slept through the night."

Nora nodded. Neither could she. It was one of the few things she had in common with the agents of S.C.Y.T.H.E. Death and all the terrifying unknowns that surrounded it had kept her up all night for years, long before she started her job in the field. But for her agent colleagues, modern-day grim reapers in many ways, who saw the effects of death firsthand on a daily basis, it was even harder to shake it off at the end of the day. Nora searched Ruby's eyes. Was that why she couldn't sleep too?

"Where's Richard?" Nora asked.

"Your brother inspired him," said Ruby. "He's napping up-stairs. I was just about to make some tea. Would you like a cup?" She moved towards the kitchen.

"I'll help," Nora said. She grabbed a pair of mugs and pulled the milk from the fridge while Ruby filled the kettle. As soon as the water was boiled and the room felt quiet enough for the question, she dove in. "Richard said you used to be in transportation before you moved here. What did you transport?"

Ruby plucked a couple of tea bags from a little jar beside the sink and plopped them into the waiting mugs. "Oh, a bit of this, a bit of that," she said.

"Souls?"

Ruby froze in the middle of pouring the kettle. The water rose to the top of the mug and spilled over the side, steam swirl-ing. She quickly put the kettle down and mopped up the water with a dishcloth before it had the chance to scald her foot below the counter.

"What did you just say?"

"Working in transportation" had long ago become a common euphemism among Collections Agents, who couldn't directly state the nature of their jobs. Nora was only disappointed in her-self for not picking it up right away.

"I saw the files," she explained. She tried to meet Ruby's eyes, but neither seemed quite ready for that.

"How on earth . . . how do you even know what those are?"

"So it's true," said Nora. "You did work for S.C.Y.T.H.E."

Ruby shook her head. "I worked for the R.C.M.P."

"Like . . . Mounties?" said Nora. "So they're *not* just in car-toons?"

This drew a small smile from her grandmother. "Not the Mounties, dear, the R.C.M.P. Removal and Collection of Mobile Phantasms. We're a Canadian organization. We follow the same basic business model of international companies like S.C.Y.T.H.E., though we're not directly affiliated. But how . . . ?"

"I'm a S.C.Y.T.H.E. administrative coordinator," said Nora. "Was an administrative coordinator," she corrected, mostly to herself.

"I see," said Ruby. She fidgeted uneasily with her dishcloth, going over the spot where the water had spilled again as if there was any moisture left.

"You took all those files. Files from the late sixties."

"Yes," said Ruby.

"And *your* file's in there."

Ruby stopped fidgeting but still didn't look up. "And I suppose you intend to turn me in?"

"What? No," said Nora. "I just need to understand it. I need to know why you have those files here."

The front door opened then, Patty's voice reverberating from the next room.

"Anybody home? My oven's doing that thing again, and I've got a chicken so frozen it might as well be a penguin at this point."

Ruby held up a finger to Nora. "Later, all right?" she whispered.

Nora nodded as Patty appeared in the kitchen doorway, a chicken on the tray in her hands.

PATTY ENDED UP STAYING FOR DINNER, JOINED BY VINCE FROM THE farm and Charles a short while later. This seemed to be something of a routine. Despite the little red house's position at the far end of town, it appeared to be a hub for both the Birds and the few neighbors who weren't related. Nora kept one eye trained on Ruby over forkfuls of Patty's chicken. The flash of fear, or possibly anger, in her grandmother's eyes when she confronted her in the kitchen set Nora on edge. Not that that was particularly hard to do.

Could Ruby have felt threatened somehow by the twins' arrival in Virgo Bay? Would the otherworldly consequences of violating death-industry protocol—the same consequences she herself was running from—be enough to make her want to kill Charlie? It was about as likely as any motive she could think of for Phil, which was about a three out of ten on the motive-plausibility scale, but she couldn't shake the sense that there was more to Ruby's story. The question now was how much of that story Ruby was willing to share.

This time, as dinner finished, neither Nora nor Ruby moved to do the dishes. Instead, Charlie and Patty were saddled with the job. Ruby, meanwhile, insisted on a nice stroll down the beach, just the two of them, which meant Nora was either going to get some answers or get knocked off. Which, she supposed, was still getting answers in a way, though it was definitely not her preferred method. She would have to be vigilant.

The sun was already a distant memory when their boots hit the sand, a silver-speckled sky winking down at them. The waves tumbled gently on the shore. Nora sent them a warning glare. When she and Ruby had made it far enough from the house for their voices to be swallowed by the wind, Ruby chanced a look at her granddaughter. It was the first one since their conversation before dinner. Nora, for her part, had barely taken her eyes off her grandmother. Ruby was in her mideighties, if Nora had to guess. Not exactly who you'd expect to see in a mug shot. But people in desperate situations were capable of a lot more than they would be otherwise. Nora knew that fact firsthand. It was the same fact that had left her stranded here at the end of the world with her brother, a bird, and a murderer.

"I never expected to have to talk about it again," Ruby said. "It was all so long ago."

"But you knew that, even all these years later . . . if it came to light . . . you could face some serious consequences," said Nora tentatively. She understood the threat all too well. It had made her reckless in her own way. Had it done similar, or worse, to Ruby?

"I love this place," said Ruby, as if they were having a completely different conversation. "I knew from the first day I came here it was special. And just how lucky I was to have it."

"Ruby, why do you have those files?"

"It was your grandfather's idea for me to come," said Ruby, still lost in a separate exchange. "He was the only one in his family to go away to university, you know. His father did not like that, not one bit. We met the year he graduated. I was two years into my job with the organization. It all happened so fast."

"What did?"

They rounded a bend, and the thick woods down the path came into view. Nora could swear she could see movement among the trees, even from all the way down on the beach. When she looked back, Ruby had a hefty piece of driftwood in her hands. Nora swallowed a growing wave of panic. Why did she agree to come out here alone in the dark with someone who could be a killer? If Ruby had wanted Charlie dead due to some abstract threat about her past life, surely a more direct one meant Nora had a target on her back by now. One made of neon lights and fun little sound effects set to go off for hitting a bull's-eye.

"Everything," Ruby replied, though Nora could barely remember what she was replying to. The old woman's grip on the driftwood tightened. "I was going to die."

"What?"

"I don't know what the system's like now, but back in my day, all the daily cases were left on one desk in the middle of the room. Every morning, we'd go in and grab a bunch from the pile and get to work. Which was all well and good until I found my own file. Nora, I was only twenty-two. I had barely lived yet. I couldn't accept that I had to die. But I didn't have a choice. I was going to have a heart attack from some sort of genetic abnormality I didn't even know about until that morning. I didn't know what to do. So I called Richard. We'd only just started going together, but I knew somehow I could trust him. Just a few hours later he'd brought me and my brothers—all the family I had left—to Virgo Bay. I wasn't thinking clearly and I took my files with me. They were already in my car, and it was all such a scramble."

"But I don't understand," Nora said, wondering for a very brief and potentially certifiable moment if circumventing the afterlife could be a hereditary ailment. "Why would Richard bring you here? How could that prevent your death?"

But Ruby wasn't looking at her now. The old woman's eyes were fixed on the house down the beach.

"Ruby?" Nora tried again.

In reply, Ruby flung the driftwood behind her. It nearly knocked directly into Nora's head, walloping her in the shoulder instead before thudding into the sand. Nora shook her nearly in-jured head and looked back to where Ruby had been standing, but she was gone. Nora blinked into the darkness. Was that just a murder attempt?

When she finally spotted the tiny woman amid the blue-black shadows of night, Ruby was barreling towards the house as fast as an eighty-year-old can barrel. Nora grabbed the discarded driftwood for defense and took off after her, realizing only as she neared the house what had sent Ruby running. Smoke billowed out a side window, where the fireplace decidedly wasn't. A thick, black cloud pierced the navy sky, swallowing a cluster of stars.

15

Nora whipped the wood behind her with the same force Ruby had used and quickened her steps. The smoke was billowing out of the kitchen, the same kitchen where Charlie had just been doing the dishes, vulnerable to anyone who might want to harm him. Which, as of now, could be anyone in this nightmare town. Ruby was through the door only a few strides ahead of Nora, who stumbled into the house in a flurry of panic and breathless wheezing. Richard and Vince were rushing around with buckets of water and the kind of inexplicable sense of purpose that comes with having the better part of a century under your belt. Patty, meanwhile, pushed past Nora and into the open air to catch her breath. But Charlie . . . where was Charlie?

Nora dodged her grandfather as they passed in the living room, and rushed into the kitchen. The smoke in there was so thick it split the room almost in half horizontally, leaving only the lower portion with any degree of visibility.

"Charlie?" Nora screamed into the near-invisible kitchen before the heavy air sent her sputtering. "Charlie!"

A warm palm landed on her shoulder. She whipped around, half expecting to see her brother there, but instead she found his namesake. The expression on Charles's face sent a wave of dread up her spine. It seemed to be a look of pity. What did he know? Where the fuck was Charlie?

Charles guided Nora out the side door in the dining room. Her lungs stung as the sea air hit them, pulling an ashy cough out of her, but she barely noticed. The majority of fire-related deaths were due to smoke inhalation. If Charlie was still in there . . .

She moved to run back inside, but Charles grabbed her shoulder again. Patty had rounded the house and come to join them now, her arms crossed over her chest. The rest of the household was slowly filing out, but there was no sign of her brother.

"Where the hell is Charlie?"

"Hey, it's okay," said Patty, her voice hushed. "When the fire started, Charlie went downstairs for that parrot of his. I told him to take it to my place for safekeeping until we get things under control. Mom and Dad . . . they wouldn't want her here. Plus I didn't think they'd want to see him doing mouth-to-mouth on a bird."

"Charlie's okay?"

Patty nodded. "You can go see him if you'd like."

Nora started a deep inhale but stopped halfway. "Why would he have to do mouth-to-mouth on Jessica if he got her out of there just after the fire started?"

"Jessica," Charles said with a wry smile. "That's cute."

Patty threw him a look. "She was unconscious when he found her. Um. You know. Birds have such little lungs. It must have made her extra sensitive to the smoke."

Nora furrowed her brow at this but quickly dismissed the whole scenario. Instead she fumbled her way onto the grass and took off towards Patty's house.

Sure enough, Charlie was safe and sound inside, curled on the couch with Jessica in his arms. Nora leaned against the doorframe for support. At this rate she was regularly producing enough adrenaline to fight off three full-grown grizzly bears a day.

"She okay?" was all Nora could muster. She indicated Jessica with a lazy head loll.

Charlie looked up from the bird in question. "Oh hey. Yeah, I think she will be. It was touch and go there for a sec, though."

"I'm sorry," said Nora.

"Thanks. Nice walk with Grandma?"

"Kind of. She's a fugitive from Death."

"Huh."

"So that's something to bond over." Nora pulled herself upright and dragged her heavy limbs to the couch, dropping herself beside Charlie. She gave the bird's head a little pat with one finger and quickly thought better of it as she remembered she hadn't brought any hand sanitizer to Virgo Bay. "Do you think it's a bit weird that Jessica was unconscious when the smoke was mostly contained in the kitchen? Or that there was even a fire at all?"

"You think this was another way to get me dead?" asked Charlie.

"I mean, I don't know what Jessica would have to do with that, but it seems likely."

"Two in one day feels excessive."

"Three," Nora corrected. "The knife thing was after midnight. Someone's clearly determined. But who? And why?"

"Think it's your grim reaper pals?"

"No," said Nora. "If S.C.Y.T.H.E. had found us out here, we'd know. Besides, they don't kill people—that's strictly against company policy. It has to be somebody from here."

"Then your guess is as good as mine," said Charlie. "Everyone here seems so chill between murder attempts."

Nora leaned her head back against the cushion with an exhausted sigh. "Patty was the last one to use the oven, right? And then she told you to come here, alone."

"Wait, I thought you thought it was Phil."

"I did. Or maybe Ruby. But it could be Patty, couldn't it?"

"She does have too many dried starfish to be completely stable. Wait, you think it could be Granny? She's like a hundred, isn't she?"

Before Nora could reply, the front door opened and Patty wafted in. Her pale blue shirt was smudged with ash. Charlie and Nora exchanged a quick look that said something to the effect of "oh shit" as Charlie swung his feet off the table. Nora decided that was a wise choice. If Patty already had some kind of motivation for killing Charlie, she didn't need further validation.

"You kids okay?" Patty asked as she slumped down into the armchair near the couch. "How's the parrot?"

Charlie pulled Jessica in closer to his chest protectively. "She'll be all right."

"And so are we," Nora added quickly, standing up to leave. "But you must be exhausted. If things are under control back at Ruby and Richard's, we can leave you to rest."

Nora studied her aunt, waiting for a protest at their leaving, or a sign of disappointment at their well-being, but instead she got a "Thanks, I'm pretty tuckered out."

On the walk home, neither twin seemed fully capable of tying their thoughts to their tongues. Nora tried twice, only managing a few odd sounds that contained too many vowels. She was exhausted, too little sleep and too much attempted murder pressing down on her, turning her limbs to lead and her mind to the consistency of pudding. The whole thing seemed to be taking a similar toll on Charlie, though he eventually remembered how to form words.

"We okay to sleep under the same roof as Ruby tonight?" he said at last.

Nora shrugged. Maybe. Maybe not. Either way, they didn't have anywhere else to go. There wasn't a single person in town they could trust. At least (Nora was pretty sure) she could take on Ruby if it came down to that, though she really, really didn't want it to come down to that. The thought of a physical altercation with anyone, even an octogenarian, gave her heartburn. All it took was a hit at the right angle to send a bone from your nose straight into your brain and then boom, dead. Though given the current pudding-like texture of her brain, she half wondered if that move would still be fatal. Clearly exhaustion-fueled delirium had taken full effect. She found her tongue.

"We'll lock the bedroom door tonight."

"That won't do a whole lot of good if they actually manage to burn the house down this time," Charlie replied.

"I really hate this town," said Nora.

16

They returned to the little red house to find it empty of all
but its primary residents. Ruby had gone to bed while Richard finished cleaning up the mess in the kitchen. The walls
directly around the oven were singed, and the coat of ash on the
floor was currently being herded into neat piles by Richard's
broom, but otherwise the room seemed as it had been. Nora
walked in, grabbed the dustpan from the counter, and held it for
Richard, in part to be helpful and in part to distract him while
Charlie scrambled downstairs with the contraband Jessica, hoping not to be seen.

"Thanks," Richard said, smiling over the ash at his granddaughter.

"I'm glad you're okay," said Nora. "You and Vince seemed to
have everything under control. It was impressive. Not something
I could've done. Fires are terrifying. I don't even like birthday
candles."

Richard gave a hearty chuckle at that. "I'm sure you'd do just
fine in an emergency. You are a Bird, after all. We're built of tough
stuff. Even Charles."

Nora emptied the dustpan into the garbage under the sink, swallowing her disagreement with a polite smile. She might be a Bird, but she was built mostly of multivitamins and anxiety.

Charlie materialized in the doorway and gave Nora a discreet thumbs-up. Jessica had been safely smuggled back into the bedroom. Nora gave a small nod back, then looked at Richard as he struggled to his feet.

"Any idea how the fire started?" she asked as casually as possible. Charlie sidled up beside her, his own interest less subtly worn on his face.

"It's the strangest thing," said Richard. "Some of the oven's wire covers were cut, leaving the wires exposed."

"Cut?" Nora echoed. Charlie gave her a look that said, "Yup, that tracks for a murderer."

"Well, damaged," Richard quickly corrected. "It seemed to be working just fine yesterday, but I suppose that's what happens when you use the same appliances for too long. I'll have to get Phil down here tomorrow to see what he can do with the old thing."

"Phil," Nora echoed again, temporarily forgetting how to form words of her own. Phil had been there that morning, then again that afternoon. He had the tools and the knowledge to do something like this. Nora still couldn't quite fathom why he'd want to, but right now the *why* didn't matter as much as the *who* and the *how*, so it would remain an *if* rather than a *when*.

"Oh that's right, he'll be working on your car tomorrow, won't he?"

"Car," Nora repeated.

"We do keep that boy busy."

Nora wasn't listening. Instead she was imagining all the ways

Phil could sabotage her car. If he could expose some wires in the oven and set the kitchen on fire, cutting the brakes on a Honda Civic would be a breeze. Or maybe he'd do something to start a fire there too. Maybe that was his thing. Not that that would explain the knife situation, but a man could have range.

"Nora?"

Nora blinked at the sound of her name.

"Sorry," she said. "What was that?"

"I said he seems keen to have you both here. Phil's not usually quite so lively," said Richard. "Must be nice for him to finally have some folks in town closer to his age. He always used to joke about how much he'd hate having newcomers around, but I guess he's changed his tune."

NORA HELD CHARLIE'S CASE FILE OPEN AND PROPPED AGAINST HER raised knees. Across the bedroom, Charlie was already asleep, Jessica perched on the pillow beside his head. Nora furrowed her brows at the dancing smudge of smoky black that held Charlie's cause of death somewhere inside, trying to decipher the indecipherable once again. Jessica abandoned her post on Charlie's pillow and made her way to Nora, seeking attention wherever she could get it. She climbed the wooden bedpost and hopped onto Nora's knee, peering down at her expectantly.

"What do you want?" Nora said without looking up from the file.

Jessica just stared at her intently.

Nora sighed. "We really need to have a chat about boundaries," she said as the parrot bopped her little head up and down. "Unless you think you can make sense of this?"

The bird made no attempt to make sense of anything. In fact, her rapt attention only made the whole thing seem harder to unravel. Nora closed the file and lowered her knees, letting Jessica hop her way over her torso so they were face-to-face.

"Phil," she said, thinking out loud. "Richard says he doesn't like outsiders for some reason. If he's the one who lives in the woods, maybe he's hiding something there. Something so terrible he doesn't want anyone finding out about it. The townspeople might know not to go into the forest, but outsiders wouldn't, right? So maybe he . . . maybe he wants to kill Charlie so we don't discover whatever's out there in the forest. And maybe he's not trying to kill me because . . . because. . . ."

"Forest," Jessica squawked. "Let's go play in forest house."

"Well, that was creepy," said Nora. "Do you ever say anything that isn't swearing or weird?"

"Let's go play in forest house," Jessica repeated.

"Okay. Tomorrow I'm teaching you boundaries *and* decent conversational skills." Nora chanced a look down the foot of her bed to the locked bedroom door. The knob had remained still, no sound of footsteps on the other side for as long as they'd been in bed. There were no windows down there by which someone could break in, and nothing appeared to be booby-trapped. Nora's eyelids each weighed roughly as much as a full-grown Great Dane. She gave Jessica a groggy glance.

"I need to sleep," she announced. "Sleep deprivation increases the risk of heart attacks and stroke. I need to sleep. Jessica, this shift is on you. If anything dangerous happens, scream. Blink twice if you understand me."

Jessica stared at her a beat, then blinked once, more from the right eye than the left.

"That's going to have to do," said Nora. She left the lights on just in case, rolled onto her side, and drifted into a restless sleep.

THE NEXT MORNING, NORA AWOKE TO FIND THE ROOM UNCHANGED from the night before. Charlie was still asleep, the steady rise and fall of his chest confirming his status as not dead. Jessica was back on his pillow, and the bedroom door was as firmly closed and locked as it was possible for a door to be. Nora checked her watch. It was just after seven thirty a.m. If yesterday was anything to go by, her grandparents would likely not yet have left for their morning walk. Good. She needed to talk to Richard. He was on a rapidly shrinking list of people who hadn't actively done something to make Nora suspect them of wanting to kill Charlie, which was the best she had to work with right now.

She went upstairs to find Richard tidying the stack of magazines on the living room coffee table, his broad form hunched over the low surface.

"Morning," Nora greeted as cheerily as she could manage.

Richard turned around. "Oh, good morning, Nora. I figured you kids would still be asleep at this hour."

"Well, Charlie is," said Nora. "And will be for a good while. He's really good at sleeping." She rubbed her eye with the heel of her hand, still drowsy. Sleep was just one of the many ways the twins were different. "Actually, I had a question for you."

"Go for it," said Richard.

Nora glanced around. "Where's Ruby?"

"Oh, she's just in the shower. She should be down in a sec."

Nora nodded as casually as possible. The old woman had secrets, big ones, and until Nora knew them she couldn't trust her.

"Charlie and I took a little walk into the woods yesterday," she began. Richard seemed to subtly, almost imperceptibly stiffen at this. Or did Nora imagine that? She continued, "We came across an old house out there. I was just wondering about it. Seems like a weird place for a house when there's so much cleared land around."

"Oh that," said Richard, straightening, his expression unreadable. "That was my father's house, the first house built in Virgo Bay, as it happens. There used to be a path through town to his front door, but it's become overgrown over time."

"Who lives there now?"

Richard paused. "Now? No one. It's been vacant for years. I wouldn't go venturing out there, if that's what you're angling at. It was already fairly ramshackle when I was a boy; I would bet it's deteriorated into a real death trap by now."

Death trap. That was certainly one way to put it. "But there was smoke coming from the chimney," Nora said, almost in spite of herself. She needed answers; she had no way of saving Charlie without them. That meant she had to ask questions, no matter the risk. She hated all of this.

"Nora, your grandmother says you've been asking about her life before Virgo Bay. I understand you're curious—you've just discovered this whole facet of your past you never even knew existed. And I'd like to answer as many questions as I can. But we'll take things one day at a time, okay? Life out here . . . it's complicated. Now, what has your grandmother told you?"

"What we tell everyone, dear." Ruby appeared at the top of the stairs, looking down at her husband. "That Virgo Bay is a special place."

Nora looked between them. Her tiny, fleece-clad grandmother had just silenced Richard with a single sentence. Richard offered Nora a tight smile and went to the hallway to put on his boots.

"You have a lot of questions," Ruby said as she walked down the stairs and joined Nora in the living room.

"And you have answers," Nora said. "Why don't you want to tell them to me?"

Ruby's face softened into what almost looked like a sad smile. "Some things require patience, Nora. Stay here long enough and you'll understand."

BY THE TIME CHARLIE WOKE UP, THEIR GRANDPARENTS WERE AL-ready well into their daily walk. Nora had Charlie's file open next to Ruby's on the kitchen table. She was bouncing back and forth between the two when Charlie stumbled in, scratching the scruff on his face.

"Any idea what's killing me today?" he asked.

"Look at this," Nora said in place of a response. She jabbed a finger at the "cause of death" section in Ruby's file. The space was blank. "And then yours." She pointed to the inky blob on Charlie's file. "Ruby said she was supposed to die by heart attack, but her cause of death is empty. That means something happened to erase her cause of death, right? Possibly the same something that's happening to yours. She's still alive and it's been decades. I think that means you can live too. I just need to figure out how. She's keeping secrets, Charlie. And so is Richard. Hell, this whole town seems to be. And a lot of them are about that house in the woods."

Charlie took this all in quietly from the chair beside her.

Finally he said, as though it were obvious, "So we go to the house, then."

"What?"

"Yeah. Seems simple enough. If there's something about that house that nobody here wants us to know, then we gotta go know about it."

"Charlie. Jesus. You have the self-preservation skills of a lemming. We can't just go to the house of secrets in the middle of the woods that everybody wants to keep us from."

"Why not?"

"Because, Charlie. That's how you die. We go there and the killer is waiting and then you're dead. You know, that thing we're trying to avoid?"

"If nobody's talking, then how else are we gonna get answers?" Charlie asked.

Nora deflated. He was right. He was dumb, but he was right. If their family had anything to say about it, whatever was hiding in that house would remain hidden. The only way to learn what it was, and what it had to do with saving Charlie's life, was to go there and find out for themselves. No, not themselves.

"I'll go," said Nora, fighting every risk-averse cell she was made of. "If there's a killer there, you need to stay away."

"Because you're killer-proof?"

"No, but as of right now I don't seem to be a target."

"Breaking into a killer's house might change that."

Nora knew that. Of course she knew that. She'd already run through three different scenarios ending in her murder before Charlie had finished his sentence. But what other choice did she have?

"I'll be fine," Nora lied.

Charlie gave her a look that said, "I know you're lying, but I appreciate it all the same."

"All right," Nora said, already regretting it, "I'm going now, before I realize what I'm doing. Stay put, and stay away from . . . I guess everybody, if you can." She grabbed a small, serrated knife from the block on the kitchen counter and stuffed it into her coat pocket, just in case. Charlie stood and looked as if he might try to stop her from leaving, but the resolution on Nora's face forced him back into his seat. Nora didn't know if it was the sleep deprivation or sheer desperation allowing such wanton recklessness, but she vowed not to examine it too closely until she was safely back in the little red house with answers, and a way to save Charlie. If she was ever back in the little red house again.

17

The sunny sky of the previous day was tucked somewhere behind a blanket of ashy clouds, rain spitting down in tiny, sparse droplets. Nora shrugged her hood on and marched onto the dirt path towards the woods, one hand wrapped firmly around the hilt of the knife in her pocket, her breathing ragged. *Don't think about it, don't think about it, don't think about it.* Don't think about all the ways this could end, all the cases she'd sorted for the S.C.Y.T.H.E.'s Murder Department that started off with one stupid person doing one stupid thing, usually alone, often in the woods. Don't think about shotguns or blunt force trauma or that one case with the poison ivy and the bear trap. Don't think about anything at all if she could swing it, which of course she couldn't. Nora Bird was built to think and think too much. But then she thought about Charlie, and how all those ways a person could die would very likely be used against him. And that thought, and that thought alone, propelled her forward.

The trees looked more ominous than she'd remembered them, their bark darkened by the rain. They towered high above her, their branches taunting her with the threat of falling swiftly towards her head. She pulled the hood down lower, as if that were enough to protect her from a heavy tree limb. Even the sounds of the forest, the rustling of furry feet on dead leaves, the rushing wind, the morning birdsong, seemed to have stilled into an eerie calm. Rain spattered her half-exposed nose. She was walking into the eye of the storm, and she hadn't even brought an umbrella.

The question now was how to get back to that strange house. She and Charlie had merely stumbled across it by chance, and stumbled away from it in such a hurry that she'd barely noticed how they got back, pure adrenaline fueling her. Now, alone in a knot of unapologetically indistinguishable nature, Nora was dizzy with the directional chaos before her. The path split in a fork just down from the entrance. She hadn't noticed this the previous morning. Her talk with Charlie had stolen too much of her focus. Which was impressive for any talk with Charlie. One path seemed to keep towards the thinner line of trees by the entrance of the woods. Nora reckoned she would still be able to see little glimpses of the beach just beyond from that route, a trunk-curtained window to whatever passed for civilization in Virgo Bay, a tether to the world beyond the forest. The other path led deep into the heart of the woods, foliage thickening and grasping along either side so that the dirt trail was rendered nearly invisible as little as ten feet away. Nora knew exactly which path she wanted to take. And, just as certainly, which path she needed to take.

This trail turned to slick mud beneath her shoes the farther she traveled into the forest. She shuffled her feet like a penguin with a full bladder, desperate not to slip and break her neck. It was a delicate balance, keeping half her focus on the muck below her to avoid tripping over obstacles and half on her surroundings and any threats they held. After waddling around for substantially longer than the human form was meant to waddle, Nora looked up from an especially untrustworthy-looking patch of mud to find the hint of a roughly carved stone wall peeking through the soggy trees. She stifled a gasp and poked her head around the nearest trunk, examining the structure. It was a squat thing, as colorless and rugged as the day, with only a few small windows and a heavy-looking wooden door visible from this vantage point. It reminded her of a quaint Victorian cottage, only less expertly constructed and almost definitely cursed. She'd go so far as to call it haunted, but ghosts were rare and frightened her far less than the thought of whatever, or whoever, might actually be lurking in there.

Before Nora could take in anything else, the door creaked open. Nora pulled herself back against the tree, heart thundering in her ears. She carefully rested her head against the bark so that it angled towards the house, enough to catch a glimpse of the blur of human hurrying out the front door. He was moving quickly, hands in his pockets and head bowed, but Nora knew exactly who it was. For a man who hadn't been in the woods since childhood, he sure seemed to be making up for lost time now. Nora scrambled around to the other side of the tree as Phil hurried past. As soon as his footfalls faded and the stillness returned, Nora sank down into a squat, releasing the breath she'd been holding since she first heard the door open.

So this *was* Phil's place. And everyone had lied to her about it. But why? What didn't they want her to know? What was he hiding? And why would it motivate him to want Charlie dead? Nora waited until a light bout of hyperventilation had passed, and then forced herself back upright. She cut through the trees and closed the distance between herself and the stone house. Up close, it was better constructed than she'd given it credit for. Good bones, she would say if she were an architect, but she wasn't, so she only thought it. She ran a hand over one of the cream-gray stones that made up the structure. It appeared to have been hand carved. The artisan craftsmanship of the house was something Nora had always complained was lost to time. These days buildings were tossed together with more regard for speed and cost than art and safety. Even the quaint wood and clapboard houses of Virgo Bay, sturdy and charming though they were, would likely have failed the Big Bad Wolf test. But this was a house built to last, crafted by someone with long-dead sensibilities. Richard's father, her great-grandfather, must have been an impressive man, she thought, remembering the house's origin as the first in town.

She abandoned the wall and looked down at the doorknob with a frown. Its metal was weatherworn but delicately shaped. Nora contemplated it. No one in this town seemed to lock their doors, and even with Phil's suspicious activities, she doubted he would bother to lock his either, especially all the way out here. That meant all she had to do was turn the handle and she'd be inside, looking at whatever awful thing it was that the town didn't want her to see. All that separated her from those secrets now was the wooden door in front of her. She shuddered. It would be so easy to turn around. To go back the way she'd come and leave whatever horrors the stone house contained to remain unknown.

She turned the handle.

A cough of dust tumbled out the door as it opened. Apparently, Phil wasn't into housekeeping. Nora braced herself and chanced a look through the open door. What she saw shocked her, if only because it was so remarkably un-shocking. The floors were polished wood, coated with a thin layer of dust. An old-fashioned stove sat near the door to her right, heavyset and cast iron. A few cupboards hung above it, one open just enough to reveal a stack of mismatched dishware. There was a counter in a light wood by the oven, and a matching table under a narrow window. The kitchen area opened into a space with a fireplace in its belly, the smoke in the hearth indicating it had just recently been extinguished. Nora's mind raced back to the kitchen in the little red house, oozing with black smoke. *Oh sure, Phil puts out fires when they concern him, but he seems to have no trouble starting them when they don't.* Nora shook the thought away.

The house had the heavy stillness of a recent departure. By the fire sat an armchair upholstered in muted florals, and a rocking chair made of the same wood as the furniture in the kitchen. It didn't feel like the house of a youngish man, though Nora supposed growing up away from any peers might have that effect. She crossed through the kitchen and spotted a narrow staircase tucked behind a jutting pillar of stone between the two rooms. So far there had been nothing out of the ordinary about the house aside from a questionable swan-shaped lamp on the end table beside the armchair. Nora looked up the stairs. There were only ten or so steps, but from where she stood safely at the bottom, in the soft embrace of the remaining warmth from the dead fire, it may as well have been the stairs to the top of the Empire State Building.

Nora looked back over her shoulder to the front door. It was still open, an easy escape route. She gave herself a nod of encouragement and hauled her wobbling legs up the steps.

The upper floor felt nearly as narrow as the staircase, as a sudden wave of newfound claustrophobia—which was frankly long overdue for Nora—crept its way up her spine. She opened the first closed door she could reach and stepped inside. The walls were bare, but powder-blue wallpaper still winked out from under years of discoloration. Against one formerly blue wall at the back of the room sat an old-fashioned metal crib and a small bed, a large dusty birdcage between them. Nora took a step inside, her utter bafflement clouding her logical inclination to avoid creepy old nurseries. Was this where Phil grew up? The origin of whatever evil he currently harbored? Or did he have children? But why would he need to keep that a secret? Well, Nora considered, there weren't any women of childbearing age in town, at least not that he wasn't directly related to. Could he have kidnapped someone? That wasn't much of a leap from murder. Maybe it was someone Charlie knew somehow. Nora's head was spinning. Even with her renowned worst-case-scenario-concocting habits, she was starting to sound crazy to herself. She was in over her head here.

She turned to leave the room, when the floor creaked from somewhere down the hall. Nora froze. It was the house settling. That's what Bubbie would always say when Nora would go diving into her bed in the middle of the night, crying about monsters or intruders or really big raccoons. Houses settled, especially old ones. Though why their settling had to be so unsettling never quite made sense to Nora, even when she eventually grew up and learned how house foundations worked.

Another creak. Either this house was really making itself

comfortable or there was someone else in it with her. Nora had seen Phil pass her outside. He was heading back the way she'd come, out of the forest and into town. No, this was someone else. Someone walking straight towards her. Beads of sweat burst onto Nora's brow, her cheeks flushing red as blood surged into her head, presumably to pick up the slack from her brain, which had just hung a little "out of order" sign outside her prefrontal cortex. Her eyes darted around the room. Next to the crib was a small closet, as narrow and foreboding as everything else in this house. Without time for a second thought, she dove for the closet door and slipped inside.

The footsteps grew louder, closer. Nora begged her lungs to inhale more quietly, but they were too busy panting in fear to notice. The door to the nursery groaned as it opened even wider than Nora had originally pried it. The creaking approached her, slowly, rhythmically. The footsteps sounded heavy, and as they neared, Nora heard a small dragging sound accompanying them. She clapped a hand over her mouth and nose. Asphyxiation statistics buzzed around her, but she swatted them away with the assurance that whatever was on the other side of that closet door would be worse.

With a squeak of protest, the closet door inched back, slowly, achingly slowly, until the room reappeared in front of Nora, only this time she wasn't alone. The person attached to the footsteps, the one who'd opened the closet door, stood there towering beside the crib, spine twisting into a hunch, a shock of stiff white hair above sunken eyes so dark they were nearly black, reflecting no light.

Nora screamed. No, Nora tried to scream, but she quickly

realized the sound wouldn't come, so she did the next most reasonable thing. Nora ran. Back down the stairs, back through the kitchen, back out the door that was still mercifully open, and back into the woods, which were now being pelted by heavy drops that hit hard with the force of a howling wind. Nora didn't care. She didn't care about the rain or the wind or how badly her lungs stung from running and from the scream that never came. All she cared about was getting as far away from the white phantom in that secret stone house in the woods as her slippery feet would take her.

NORA TUMBLED THROUGH THE FRONT DOOR OF THE LITTLE RED house with as much force and as little intention as a candy wrapper on the wind, the gust behind her made of sheer panic. She ran her wild eyes over the living room, half expecting to find Phil there again, another deadly trick up his sleeve. Instead she saw only Ruby and Richard sipping coffee on the couch, their serene little vignette promptly shattered by Nora's impressively dramatic entrance. Mud caked the hem of her pants; her brown hair sprang from the hair elastic at her nape; her eyes were wide and feral.

"There's someone in the woods," she said, her voice foreign to her own ears, the strain making it high and tight. Ruby placed her mug on the coffee table and looked to Richard, but Nora was having none of it. "No. No. No more lies. There's someone in that house in the woods. Who is it? Is it someone evil? Someone violent? Someone who eats faces as a hobby? What the hell is going on?"

Ruby somehow shrank despite her already-tiny stature, her proud shoulders rounding. "I suppose we'd best tell her," she said to Richard.

"About time," he responded. "Why don't you have a seat, Nora?"

She shook her head. Her nerves were so shot she already half felt like she was sitting, and her feet were too rooted to the floor for her to attempt the real thing.

"Very well," Richard said. "There is someone out in the woods, yes. The same someone who's always been there."

Nora squeezed her temples. "I don't get it. You said your *dad* built that place, right? But he must be, like . . ." She squinted at her grandfather and placed his age somewhere towards the second half of his eighties. "Over a century old."

Richard nodded. "One hundred and twenty-seven."

"I don't . . ."

Richard smiled at her, though whether in pity or apology she couldn't tell.

"Papa will know you're here by now, no doubt. I'm sure he was thrilled to see you, though I'm sorry he gave you a fright."

"You're trying to tell me that your dad is over a hundred and twenty and lives in the woods alone?"

"Things work differently here in Virgo Bay, dear," Ruby said. "I told you this is a special town."

Nora crossed her arms over her chest, as much in impatience as it was a means to steady herself. Her grandfather took a heavy inhale.

"We lost my mother when I was very young," said Richard. "Too young. You, of course, understand that pain. My papa, he never really healed from that loss. He was all alone in the world with three broken children to raise in a heartless city. But there are dangers in the city, and Papa couldn't bear the thought of losing us too, so he decided to move us somewhere safe. Though when he went out in search of some land to settle on, he didn't expect to find this place."

"You know a thing or two about Death given your line of work," said Ruby. "Which means you know how little any of us really knows about it."

"Your grandma tells me you followed in her footsteps," Richard added.

"What Oliver, Richard's father, found when he came here," Ruby continued, "was one of Death's Blind Spots."

At this Nora finally sat down, her legs unable to hold her up with the added weight of all she was hearing. She'd heard of Blind Spots before, as rumors and conspiracy theories passed around the office, but neither she nor anyone else really gave them any credence. The idea that there were places on earth that Death couldn't reach seemed like wishful nonsense. But if that man in the woods really was the father of an octogenarian, it definitely forced Nora to reconsider everything she thought she knew about life, and death, and anything in between.

"You mean," she tried, then choked on a wave of emotion, then tried again. "You mean no one can die here?"

For someone who had spent all her life running, fearing, learning about, and running farther from Death, the very premise flooded her with more emotion than she knew what to do with. She felt like she needed a whole second body just to process the influx of tears and tension and relief and anger.

"It's not quite that simple," said Ruby. "Death can't see us to claim us, so we'll never get sick or die of old age as long as we remain within the borders of Virgo Bay. Only our own doing, or the actions of another human, can take a life here. But once we leave town, we're on the same clock as anyone else. It may even be accelerated due to our time on the outskirts of the normal life cycle, though there's no real way to be sure. Your father was the only person to leave this place for an extended period of time."

Nora sat in the silence that followed her grandparents' words, trying to absorb it all. As long as she was here, she wouldn't die. All the ailments and illnesses she'd spent her whole life fearing suddenly couldn't touch her. The sensation that washed over her as that reality sank in was unlike anything she had ever felt. She felt light. All the weight of the anxiety she had carried for so many years lifted. Her head and limbs filled with helium. She felt like she could float up and up and up forever and would never fear the fall. She was free.

But Charlie wasn't. Charlie was still in as much danger as ever. If murder took a life in Virgo Bay the way it would anywhere else, nothing had changed for him, and that thought brought Nora back to earth.

Charlie. Wait. Where the hell was Charlie?

"Where the hell is Charlie?" Nora said as she thought it.

Ruby cocked a brow. "I assumed you'd have more questions."

"I do," said Nora. "Lots. But my main one right now is, Where is Charlie?"

"Phil and a few of the boys stopped by on their way to work on your car and asked Charlie along," said Richard.

"Charlie's out there with Phil?" Nora leapt up from her seat. "I need to borrow your car."

"We don't have one," said Richard. "But I'm sure Charles wouldn't mind if you borrowed his. He's out there with the boys, but his keys should be on the table by his front door if you want to grab them."

Normally, breaking into somebody's house and stealing their car wouldn't be Nora's ideal rainy-day activity, but Charlie was off in the middle of nowhere with someone who might be trying to kill him, so there wasn't much time for good manners.

"Which house is his?"

18

Charles's house, it turned out, was a clean white clapboard just down from the little general store and directly across from the church with no graveyard at the entrance of town. The front door, like every other front door in Virgo Bay, was unlocked. Nora climbed the steps and crept inside. The quiet bounced off a neutral interior that was somehow pristine and cozy at the same time. The floors and countertops were a creamy marble, their sheen clear and bright, putting the sky just beyond the windows to shame. A gilded birdcage sat beside an austere cream sofa, which Nora regarded as very brave. Pale-colored furniture always seemed too big a risk to her. Charles also seemed to have the only TV in town, which she supposed was a perk of being the one to do supply runs. She found the little table by the front door, simple and white, a glass bowl perched on top with only a single set of keys inside. Nora slipped the keys from the bowl, whispered an apology to Charles, and went around the house to where a gray-blue van was parked in the driveway.

Nora had never driven recklessly in all the years she'd been driving. Cars were enough of a hazard without adding your own.

But that afternoon, head flooded with too many thoughts and gut twisting with too many fears, Nora found herself speeding around the bends of the road that she'd already crashed on once. When she finally came upon the wreckage of her car, Charlie wasn't there. And neither was anyone else, for that matter. Phil's pickup truck sat just behind her car, a toolbox on the grass between the two, but there were no people in sight.

She quickly parked Charles's van behind the other two cars and hopped out, scanning the surroundings, the woods to one side and the boulders to the other. They could have taken Charlie into the forest. If they'd ventured deep enough, she'd never find them. Fucking Charlie. Nora had told him in no uncertain terms to avoid Phil. To avoid everyone. But instead he'd decided to throw himself at the others. Did he have a death wish? Anger and concern fought for emotional supremacy within her, each evenly armed.

Nora started to cross the street towards the woods, when the wind picked up the echo of voices. They were coming from the opposite direction, from somewhere behind the rocks. Nora followed the sound until she found a break in the boulders and slipped through. Beyond the rock wall sat layers of cliff side looking out over the turbulent sea. Both sky and ocean were so gray she could barely see the horizon between them. On a lower cliff up ahead, she spotted the backs of four men, roughly mousesized from her vantage point. She scrambled after them, uncertain of what the hell they were up to but convinced it was no good. She caught sight of the brassy mass of Charlie's hair bopping along with the others. He was still alive. For now.

The unmarked path down the cliff was a bumpy mess of wet grass tufts and half-hidden stones. Nora did her best to avoid both as she hurried down, her eyes locked on the men. By the time she'd nearly closed the gap between them, they'd reached the cliff's edge. What the hell were they doing? They seemed to be talking, joking maybe, playfully slapping one another's backs in that way men seemed to do when they couldn't figure out how to show actual affection. They all stood in what could have passed for a friendly half circle under different circumstances. Someone pointed over the edge, and they all stepped closer to look down into the sea. Nora immediately pictured Phil giving Charlie a shove just forceful enough to send him tumbling to the jagged rocks below. Her feet had already picked things up to top speed before she could tell them to, which brought her inches from the small crowd when it happened. She barely recognized the sound of her brother's yelp, Charlie's silhouette suddenly jerking forward, arms flailing in a desperate attempt to regain balance before his head slipped out of view to the sound of loose rocks breaking free on the cliff side and a chorus of gasps. It was impossible to tell from Nora's vantage point whether her brother had tripped or if he'd been pushed by one of the men around him; all she knew was that he was toppling forward and she needed to keep him from completing the fall. No one else seemed quick to do the job, though whether that was from shock or something more malicious she couldn't be sure. Before she could catch up with herself, she was holding on to Charlie's legs as the rest of him dangled helplessly over the cliff's edge.

Charlie had never been a delicate boy. Even when they were kids, despite being twins, he had always dwarfed Nora. She was narrow while he was broad, short while he was tall, thin while he was stocky. None of this worked in her favor as she tried to hold on to his lower half, the rest of him swinging like a rag doll over the sheer drop.

A second pair of hands gripped Charlie's ankles, just above Nora's. Nora looked over to find Charles holding firm. He wasn't a huge upgrade as far as strength or size, but at least she was no longer attempting this alone. Vince, the fourth member of this death excursion, grabbed on next. Eventually, and with what Nora was certain was reluctance, Phil hooked a fist around Charlie's waistband and they all pulled in tandem until he was upright again. Nora continued pulling until they were a solid fifteen feet away from the cliff's edge, and then tentatively let go. She looked at each of the men individually, her eyes aflame. They each made a sheepish expression in turn, like kids being scolded by a strict teacher.

"What the hell?" Nora demanded. She let her focus linger on Phil longer than the rest, trying hard to show him that she knew exactly what the hell.

"I had to take a leak and Charles spotted a pod of whales," Vince said quickly.

"Charlie said he'd never seen whales," said Charles.

"Sorry," said Phil. "We just got distracted. I promise I'll get to your car."

"And you?" Nora turned on Charlie.

"I wanted to see whales," said Charlie with a shrug.

Unbelievable.

"How did you get all the way out here anyway?" asked Phil, eyes narrowed.

"I borrowed Charles's car. I hope that's okay, Charles," said Nora.

"Oh," said Charles. Then: "Of course."

"Thanks. Okay." Nora choked back the kind of tears that usually crept up her throat when she was overwhelmed. "Well, I'm sure Charlie has been enough of a distraction. We'll leave you guys to it, right, Charlie?"

Charlie gave a salute.

"I might head back with you, if that's all right," said Charles. "I'm not much of a car man myself, and that was more than enough excitement for one day."

CHARLES DROVE THEM BACK TO TOWN, WHICH WAS JUST AS WELL because Nora was still shaking too hard to even think about operating heavy machinery. Charlie rode shotgun, his face cast out over the sea, reflecting back at Nora from the side-view mirror. She never could make sense of him. What kind of maniac willingly goes to the edge of a cliff with near strangers when he knows someone wants him dead? In his shoes, Nora would be hard-pressed to leave the house. A house that was outfitted with fresh locks. And an alarm system. And a really big dog. But that would never be Charlie. Even a middle ground between a safe house and the cliff's edge would never be Charlie. Nora leaned her head against the car window and felt the cool of the outside world pressed against it. It steadied her nerves just a bit, just enough to make it back to the little red house.

Charles dropped them near the door and headed home. The rain was still falling, and while Nora was mostly spared its touch under her coat and hood, Charlie was soaked to the bone. Still, Nora wasn't ready to let him go inside just yet. She had too much to say, and most of it was for his ears only.

"Charlie," she said as he moved to the door.

The way he stopped, like a dog whose leash had just been yanked, said he knew that tone. His shoulders went up defensively. "What? Hey, look, I figured there'd be a bunch of us going and Phil probably wasn't dumb enough to try anything with witnesses around. A little guys' outing sounded fun. And this place is really lacking in the fun department, Nor. I figured I'd take what I could get."

"What you could 'get' might be dead, Charlie. Phil isn't our only suspect, remember? The whole town is a question mark. And I was right, they *have* all been hiding something."

"You found something at the house in the woods? I figured that would be a dead end. Like, no offense, but sometimes your imagination gets the better of you."

Nora's jaw tightened, her cheek muscle twitching. She'd been given that lecture enough as a child. The last person she needed it from was Charlie.

"Yeah, well, turns out I was right. Kind of. It's not Phil living in there, it's Richard's dad, Oliver."

"Wanna run that by me again?"

So Nora did, along with everything else she'd learned from Ruby and Richard about the town.

"Death's Blind Spot," Charlie said on a whistle once Nora had stopped talking. "That would make a sick band name. Can I have that?"

"You don't even play an instrument, Charlie," Nora said, letting herself get sidetracked by her brother's usual nonsense before her own sense returned to her. "That's not the point. The point is, this place . . . it's safe."

"Aside from the person trying to murder me."

"Aside from that," Nora agreed. "But think about it, Charlie, a place where you can live forever without life harming you."

"Without life," Charlie interjected.

"If we could just figure out who's after you and stop them, properly stop them, we could stay here, with our family, where it's safe. You wouldn't have to worry about making rent or paying back whoever you owe money to this month. And I wouldn't have to worry about . . . I wouldn't have to worry."

Charlie shoved his hands into the pockets of his jeans. "Weren't you just complaining about how we can't trust anyone in this hellhole?"

"Sure, but in the end there's only one person we actually can't trust. We just need to weed them out, and then this could be our home. Right?"

Charlie just shrugged. "Dude, I'm wetter than a soccer mom at a Magic Mike show out here. Can I go get into something that isn't actively growing moss?"

"Okay," said Nora, deflating. "Yeah, of course. Go dry off, and just think about it, okay?"

Charlie gave a salute and disappeared inside.

19

Case # 64889
Gus Richards
Age: 111
Cause of Death: Flu

By the time lunch rolled around on the day Nora sorted Gus's case, he was the talk of the office. Until that point, the oldest soul collected at Nora's branch had been a one-hundred-and-three-year-old woman named Doris who had to be reassigned to a new agent after relentlessly flirting with her initial collector. Gus's case was fascinating, and until his agent returned with firsthand intel, everyone spent the day speculating on how he'd managed to evade Death for so long. Nora, having finished her shift and gone home, had to wait until the next morning to find out this crucial information. She spent the night trying to decide who among her colleagues to approach; unfortunately, her social anxiety got the better of her and she never got to learn Gus's answer. Not that it mattered, she reasoned. There was nothing he could say that she didn't already know. There simply weren't any secret tricks for keeping Death at bay, no matter how much she wished there were.

NORA WAS BECOMING UNCOMFORTABLY ACCUSTOMED TO NOT SLEEP-ing. Back home she was in bed by ten, asleep in give or take an hour depending on her current level of anxiety, and waking up well rested by six a.m. as a result. But now, with the newfound thoughts and worries and uncovered secrets a constant cacophony of concern in her head—which only grew louder as soon as that head hit the pillow—Nora was lucky to drift off at all before the first hazy hints of sunrise.

That night, the thoughts keeping her awake were different than usual. Since arriving in Virgo Bay, they'd been consumed by Charlie's situation: trying to decipher his cause of death, trying to determine his would-be killer, trying to keep him alive. But tonight, her grandparents' revelation drowned anything else out. It was too big, took up too much room between the walls of her skull for any other thoughts to squeeze through.

Nora first learned about Death's Blind Spots a week into her time at S.C.Y.T.H.E. She had finished her daily file deliveries late, which in turn led to Nora finding the last agent on her roster already at his desk. She handed him his cases for the day and had every intention of hurrying back to the sanctuary of her office when the agent—a man named Michael somewhere firmly between the age of fifty and whenever it was that people stopped bothering to manage their nose hair—did the unthinkable. He roped Nora into small talk. It was a grueling ten minutes filled mostly by polite nods at golf-related anecdotes and the occasional mention of grandchildren, but somewhere towards the end of the exchange, Michael mentioned something about an upcoming trip to Florida, and how it "must be one of Death's Blind Spots. Why else would old coots hanging on by a thread flock there in droves?"

Nora had given him a confused look, which prompted even more words out of his mouth, but these she found herself rapt by. The prospect of a place that Death couldn't reach sounded like an impossible fantasy. And her coworkers quickly confirmed that to be the case. Like poltergeists and possession, Blind Spots were widely rumored, but only crackpots in the industry actually believed in them. It seemed that even those who worked in the Death field felt as mystified by the concept as civilians, and so had filled in the blanks their own way. That's what her supervisor had explained when Nora approached her with questions. And she'd believed it, because when something sounded too good to be true, it very likely was.

But somehow, a century ago, her own family had proven that crackpot theory true, and now Nora was there, in a Blind Spot where Death couldn't find her unless a human did her harm.

She flipped onto her side, restless with the energy of hope coursing through her. Just that morning Virgo Bay had seemed like an absolute nightmare town, but one conversation with Richard and Ruby later, and it was suddenly a haven she would never admit to dreaming about. Sure, it had its quirks. Remote, no real amenities, at least one murderer. But aside from that, she'd landed in her own personal utopia, and any desire she had to return to her old life seemed to melt away like cotton candy in the rain. Who could ever want to leave a place like this?

Charlie. He'd want to leave. The man could get bored at a rave (and had, on more than one occasion). Virgo Bay wasn't exactly his pace. Nora would just have to find a way to convince him otherwise. He wasn't always receptive to sense, but she had to try.

She tossed back over to her other side. Jessica greeted her from the edge of her pillow with a tilt of her head. Nora looked up at the bird.

"You'll help me talk to Charlie about staying here, right?" she whispered. "Once the whole murder thing is done. You must feel it too, what makes this place special. Maybe that's why you've been so quiet. You don't want to leave either, do you? Who would?"

Then Nora finally allowed herself to answer that question in a way she wasn't ready to before.

"Dad," she said. "Dad left."

The thought made her stomach ball up into something hard and uncomfortable. Martin Bird had been the only one to leave, and he'd paid the ultimate price for it. If he'd just stayed there, like the rest of his family, he'd be alive right now. He'd have raised his family in Virgo Bay, and Nora would have grown up without knowing fear or loss or death. The thoughts kept flooding her. All that wasn't and could have been. Her anger flared again, the one pointing directly in her dead dad's direction. It lit a flame behind her eyes, but there was too little kindling, and a rush of tears quickly came to wash it away. She choked on a sob, desperate to avoid waking Charlie and letting him see her like this again. She had to keep her shit together for once.

"Why?" she barely mouthed at Jessica. "Why would he leave? Why couldn't things have been different?"

Her cheeks were slick and streaked now, her nose helpfully contributing to the general sheen on her face. Jessica hopped towards Nora and tucked her little gray head under Nora's chin, which only served to make the tears stream harder. Nora untucked her arms from the blanket and wrapped them around the parrot, pulling the creature close to her chest.

"Thank you," she whispered into Jessica's feathery head.

"Mars bar," Jessica squawked back, but Nora was too busy stifling sobs to notice.

NORA WAS HALFWAY UP THE STAIRS THE NEXT MORNING WHEN SHE heard the sound of hushed voices in the kitchen. She stopped and crouched on the step she'd landed on, careful not to shift the wood and elicit a creak. It didn't take her long to place two of the voices: Ruby and Richard weren't quite at a whisper, and their tones—Ruby's cool but gentle, Richard's warm and robust—were easy enough to detect. The third voice was kept so soft that Nora had to strain even to hear it, much less determine who it belonged to.

"We told her not to go, but she's so stubborn," hissed Ruby.

"She's her father's child," Richard agreed.

"So then she knows," said the voice Nora couldn't place.

Nora's heart picked up its pace until it was at a full-blown gallop. They were clearly talking about her. But why? She crawled up a step, carefully, desperate to keep the wood beneath her knees quiet.

"She only knows what we've told her," Ruby said.

"We need to keep it that way," the mystery voice replied.

Nora pulled herself up another step. She needed to see who the voice belonged to.

"Why are you doing this?" said Richard.

"Richard, please," whispered Ruby. Then: "Tell us what you need."

"I need Charlie taken care of," said the third voice.

Nora's palms were suddenly Slip 'N Slides as they reached for another stair to slink up. She'd hauled one shaking leg to the next step, when it happened. The stair groaned beneath her weight, the sound catapulting into the kitchen, where the clandestine meeting was taking place. The voices all hushed in unison. Nora slid down to her bum as the back door opened and shut above her, nonchalant kitchen sounds—dishes clanging and water running—taking the place of conversation. Nora shook off the defeat and forced herself the rest of the way up the stairs. They'd heard her coming; not finishing the climb would only raise suspicions.

In the kitchen she found Ruby filling the kettle at the sink, Richard rummaging through the fridge. They both stopped their busywork as she entered, feigned looks of surprise on their faces.

"Morning, dear," Ruby greeted. "You're up early. Can I get you a tea? Coffee?"

"I'm thinking eggs for breakfast," Richard chimed in from the fridge. "How do you like yours?"

Nora chanced a look out of the window over the sink, just above Ruby's bent head. She could see the shape of someone retreating from the house, moving swiftly to the dirt path beyond. Short, salt-and-pepper hair over a neutral outfit.

"Actually," said Nora, "I don't have much of an appetite. I, uh, forgot to do something downstairs," she added by way of excusing herself before thundering back down the same wooden staircase that had betrayed her.

She practically leapt on Charlie's sleeping form as soon as she was back in their room, but all her prodding and jostling wasn't potent enough to rouse her brother. Nora looked over at Jessica, who was currently perched on the bed frame.

"Little help?" Nora said.

The bird fluttered down and nudged Charlie's head with her own. When that didn't work, Jessica opted instead to bite his nose. Charlie swatted her beak away and rolled over.

"Infuriating," muttered Nora. She shook her head and leaned in close to her sleeping brother. "I'm about to go through your Internet search history," she threatened in his ear.

Charlie bolted up. "I'm awake. I'm awake!" He blinked the last of his sleep away and focused his eyes on Nora. "Okay, that was low. This'd better be good, Nor."

"It definitely isn't good, that's just it," said Nora. "Shove over, will you?"

Charlie shuffled towards the wall, and Nora perched beside him.

"I just overheard Ruby and Richard talking to someone about us. It was all very hush-hush and they did not sound happy."

"You woke me up because someone's not happy with me? Nor, if you keep that up, I'll never sleep again."

"Charlie . . . it was Patty."

"What?"

"I saw her walking away from the house. She said . . . she said she wanted you taken care of."

"That would be really nice in a different context," said Charlie. "But she's probably not talking about a spa day, huh?"

Nora shook her head.

"And Gran and Gramps are in on it?"

"I don't know," said Nora. "Richard seemed reluctant about the whole situation."

"That's nice of him."

"But Ruby basically shut him down."

"Bummer. What were they mad about anyway?"

"They didn't say exactly, but it sounded like Patty didn't want us knowing about the Blind Spot."

"So she wants to keep all that sweet, sweet immortality for herself, huh? Is that why she wants me dead?"

Nora shrugged. "I doubt it. If that was the case, she'd want me dead too. And she really, really seemed focused on you."

"Her and Ruby," Charlie said. "So it's not just women I've dated who want to kill me."

"Charlie, please," Nora said. "Can you just try to be serious? Fake it if you have to."

Charlie wiped his hand down his face and seemed to sober up. "All right. So the plan is still to get out of here, then? Do we still think Phil's on the no-no list, or can we trust him with the car?"

This stopped Nora in her tracks. *Get out of here.* That thought had been so appealing just twenty-four hours ago, but now . . . Even with more arrows pointing to more suspects, she couldn't help but want to stay here now that she knew what staying here would truly mean.

"Maybe we can find out Patty's motives," Nora said, pulling at the wrinkles in her pants. "There must be a reason she's after you. And then maybe we can resolve all of this."

"What, just have a cute little chitchat about her trying to murder me?" said Charlie. "And what about Phil? He was probably the one who cut that tree branch to fall on me, right? And who started the fire? And who pushed me over the cliff yesterday? If they're both in on it, and the grandparents are in on it, we probably shouldn't stick around. That's four against two, Nor, and they've got creepy homeschooler vibes on their side."

"Hear me out," Nora tried. "What if all of that was Patty? We never saw who was in the woods that day, and she had been using the oven to cook when the fire started. Plus, it was hard to tell if you were even pushed at all or if you just slipped yesterday."

"So we're not leaving?"

"Let's just . . . let's just see if we can sort this out."

Charlie scratched at what was quickly becoming a full-blown beard. "You do what you want, I guess. But as soon as we have a way out of here, I'm bouncing."

"You can't," said Nora, practically pleading. "Once you leave, Death will find you. At least here you stand a chance. We just need to do something about Patty, or whoever's trying to kill you, and then you're safe. Then you'll live."

"Here?" He stood up. "Nora, I don't think anybody lives here, really. They just kinda exist."

"What's the difference?"

Charlie gave Nora the first look of his she couldn't read, then left the room.

Nora remained sitting stiffly on his bed, staring at the closed door in his wake. Jessica hopped over to her and plopped herself on one of Nora's crisscrossed ankles, staring at her expectantly.

"They think *I'm* the stubborn one?" Nora shook her head. "All right, I need to figure out what the hell is going on before Charlie actually gets himself killed. It must have something to do with the house in the woods, right? Why would Richard's dad live way out in the woods, tucked away from everyone? It doesn't make sense. And why would it be bad for us to know about this town being a Blind Spot? Patty was so angry that Richard and Ruby had told me. Though they didn't tell me everything, apparently. They made sure to let Patty know that. So what are they still hiding?"

The parrot just continued to stare.

"Okay. Guess you're not the right person to be asking, huh? I mean, you're not a person at all. You probably don't even know you're a bird, much less anything I'm talking about. But who the hell can I talk to about this stuff? Who would know why Charlie's being targeted?"

Jessica cocked her head. "Charles," she squawked.

Nora blinked at the bird. "Huh," she said. "That's actually not a bad idea." She picked Jessica up off her ankle and set her onto the bunched-up bedspread, then made her way to the door. She stopped for a moment and turned to look back at the bird, who was still looking at her with blank, expressionless eyes. "How did you . . . ?" She shook her head. "Never mind."

And with that, Nora set off to find Charles.

20

Charlie was sitting down to breakfast when Nora emerged from the basement for the second time that morning. She gave him a curt nod of the head as she shoved her feet into the boots by the side door.

"Where are you off to?" Charlie asked through a mouthful of generously sugared bran cereal.

"I'm visiting Charles," said Nora. "He might know what's going on."

"And we can trust him?"

"No. But so far we can distrust him less than a lot of the others. Richard and Ruby out for their walk?"

"I guess."

Nora nodded. "I'll be as fast as I can. Please, please, for the love of god, *please* stay away from them as much as possible. And if Patty or Phil stop by, come find me. Okay?"

Charlie gave one of his infuriating salutes and Nora was out the door.

It was another gloomy day, the sky as thick and milky as the kind of upscale tea latte you'd never find in a place like Virgo Bay.

Nora breathed it all in, the salty scent of the sea gently tickling the back of her throat, the long grass brushing her boots, the quiet so complete it almost felt rude when birdsong or lapping waves occasionally interrupted it. This was not the kind of place Nora had ever pictured herself, but now she could see herself learning to love it. The slow pace, the ease . . . it was growing more and more appealing. She might not even miss her vitamin subscription service in a place like this—she'd have no reason to take them anyway.

Nora crunched across the grass and down the dirt path to what passed as Main Street in this little town. Just as she reached the general store, a familiar figure stepped out. Patty had her coat wrapped around her small frame, a length of freshly purchased rope held tight to her chest. Spotting Nora she immediately dropped her hands, letting the coil fall to her side in a firm grip. Her smile seemed forced, her teeth glinting despite the dimness of the day.

"Good morning," she greeted, tone pinched. "Where are you going?"

"I'm popping into Charles's for a quick chat," said Nora, who saw no reason to lie.

"Oh," said Patty. "And Charlie's back in the cottage on his own?"

"No," said Nora, who suddenly saw many reasons to lie. "He's out for a walk. Not sure which direction he went."

Patty nodded. She fidgeted with the rope for a second, then seemed to realize she was drawing attention to it and lowered it again.

Nora swallowed down the nervousness marching up her

throat and forced herself to say, "New rope?" Which she realized was an odd question, if she was being honest with herself, but she was in an odd situation, so she supposed further oddness was to be expected.

"Yeah," said Patty. The word hung in the air alone for longer than it should have. Then she added, "It's for Uncle Vic. He needed it for something at the farm."

"Nice of you to run errands for him," Nora said.

Patty shrugged. "He's busier than I am."

Nora opened her mouth to press her aunt further, but before she could, Patty jumped back in. "Well, I should really get this to Vic. Do me a favor and tell Charles I say . . . hi." And with that, she hustled away.

Nora shoved her hands in her pockets and hurried to Charles's place. Her encounter with Patty nearly made her change her mind and head back to the little red house instead. If Patty figured out Nora had lied, she could easily catch Charlie alone. Hell, even if Ruby and Richard were back by now, who was to say they wouldn't help their daughter in whatever awful thing she had planned with that rope? But Patty had rushed off in the opposite direction, and Nora needed answers like she needed Valium on plane rides, so she prayed her lie had done the trick, and knocked on Charles's door.

The door pulled back a moment later and Charles emerged, his sweater-vest of the day a Nordic-patterned navy-and-white work of—if not art, then craft at least. He adjusted his glasses as he took in his guest.

"Oh, morning, Nora. What brings you to my doorstep?"

"Could I come in?"

Charles looked over his shoulder into his immaculately appointed little house. "My place is a bit of a mess right now, I'm afraid."

Nora's face fell, which seemed to elicit an almost fight-or-flight response in Charles, who didn't strike Nora as the type to be particularly comfortable with other people's emotions. "Oh, no, I, um, yes, sure, why not?" he stammered, stepping aside to let Nora in. She found the space almost as she'd remembered it, though the kitchen was, she had to admit, a bit of a mess. A stack of dishes sat unattended in the sink, a wood cutting board strewn with vegetables in various stages of chopping.

"I'm sorry to interrupt," Nora said, taking in the room.

"That's all right. You're family, family doesn't interrupt. I was just making myself an omelet for breakfast. Would you like one?"

Nora could feel the hollow spot in her stomach where a breakfast should be. The smell of recently minced garlic and onion drew a small gurgle of agreement from her gut.

"Let me help," said Nora. "I just came to ask a few questions. There's no reason we can't cook and talk."

In response to her offer, Charles gave a smile that was almost shy. He found another cutting board in one of his well-organized cupboards, and together they sliced up some more vegetables and one very generous slab of ham. A few cuts into a red pepper, Nora worked up the courage to start. "I was just wondering if I could ask you a few questions about the town."

"Of course," said Charles. "This town is as much your home as any of ours, as far as we're concerned. You deserve to know whatever you'd like to know about it. You are a Bird, after all."

Nora nodded her thanks. "The house in the woods," she began, tentatively easing into the topic. "It's Richard's dad who lives there, right?"

Charles stopped chopping for a beat. "It looks like you already know a decent amount about this place," he said.

"Not as much as I'd like," said Nora.

Charles went back to cutting. "Yes, that's Grandad out there."

"All alone?"

"Yes."

"But why?" Nora asked, unable to keep the intensity from her voice. "Why does he live away from the rest of the family?"

"He prefers it," said Charles. "Though I couldn't tell you why. Years ago, the woods weren't so dense and he was much more connected to the rest of us, but I suppose when you've lived as long as he has, the company of others might begin to bore you. He's lived mostly in solitude for decades now."

Nora wiped her hands on a towel and contemplated this. She understood being a bit of a loner, but not a complete hermit. Something must have happened to make him a recluse.

"Did you ever ask him why?" said Nora.

Charles shook his head. "I haven't really seen him in years, if I'm honest. We were never especially close. Clashing personalities and all that. Ironic, since Mom and Dad gave me Oliver as a middle name. We used to be much more alike, but times are different now and so are we. He's grown to be a stubborn man, and at his age I don't see that changing."

Stubborn. Nora wondered if that's where her father had gotten it from. Or her brother. Or maybe even her. It was an odd thought, to have a genetic link to this strange man in the forest outside a town few knew existed.

"So you don't see him, but do other people visit him?" Nora asked, remembering Phil leaving the house. If there was something suspicious about the man in the woods, Phil's presence there would make sense.

"He and Patty have always been quite close. I think she goes out there a decent amount. Aunt Dorothy goes on occasion, and Phil brings him supplies when he starts running low. Otherwise he lives a pretty isolated life."

Charles cracked four eggs into a patiently waiting frying pan and added the vegetables and meat they'd been chopping. The smell of food cooking immediately filled the small house, sending Nora's tummy rumbles into overdrive. Charles directed Nora to the cupboard with the dishes, and she set the table while he scooped two perfectly formed omelets onto plates. They sat down at the round wooden table by the kitchen window, and Nora threw all sense of propriety to the wind, her first eggy bite roughly the size and shape of an inflated puffer fish.

When Nora finally felt her hunger ease, a bigger void crept into its place. It was an empty space she hadn't expected to fill today, but she was already here, and the seal of secrecy had already been at least pierced if not yet entirely broken. She lowered her fork and wiped a rogue onion from her chin.

"Why did Dad leave?"

"Hmm?" Charles asked, chewing his own breakfast at a much more socially acceptable pace.

"I just don't get why anyone would choose to leave this place."

Charles swallowed his bite and gave Nora his full attention. His eyes were soft and filled with sympathy. "I wish I could answer that question. I wish I could understand. I've been trying to figure that out since long before you came along. Your father was never satisfied with life here. He always wanted more. I suppose he always wanted you, and your brother, and your mom, and his work, and everything else Virgo Bay just couldn't give him. We tried, for what it's worth. But I don't think he would ever have been truly happy here. It's just not the way he was built."

"But you're happy here?"

"I am," said Charles. "I love this place. Can't imagine ever wanting to leave for longer than a night or two at a stretch. But my brother and I always had different ideas of what life should be."

"I think I could be happy here too," said Nora.

This drew a gentle smile from Charles. "I don't doubt that. I see a lot of myself in you, Nora."

"You said Dad used to write to you. Do you still have any of those letters?" Nora asked, too intent on her own mission to acknowledge his words. Maybe there was something in those letters that could tell her why Martin Bird did what he did. Why he really left this place. Not that what her uncle said didn't make sense, but it didn't feel like the whole story. Nora couldn't imagine trading a life without fear for a job or even a family.

"Afraid not." Her uncle took a sip of water and began clearing the table. Nora trailed him as he continued. "I was still living at Mom and Dad's at the time. They would have thrown the letters out years ago." He put the dishes down and faced Nora square on, placing his hands on her shoulders. "But I'll tell you one thing: the past is an easy place to get lost in. It's tempting, isn't it? Hazy and imperfectly remembered so we can fill it in as we see fit. Spend too much time there, though, and you miss out on everything happening right now, and everything that could happen in the future. I think Martin understood that better than any of us. He'd want you to keep looking forward."

Nora forced a nod through the emotions swirling through her. "I'll try," she said.

"Good," said Charles. He let go of her shoulders and took a step back. "You know, for all the times I've wished he never left, I'm very glad he gave us you. As much as I see myself in you, your father's in there too. He lives on through you."

"Not as much as he does in Charlie," Nora said.

Charles gave a small laugh at that. "No, I'll grant you that. Charlie definitely inherited your father's fearlessness and ease with life. But just as Martin left to make his way in the world, you found your way home."

21

The little red house had been invaded. Nora returned to find Patty in the living room with Richard and Ruby. Her eyes ping-ponged from suspect to suspect, finally landing on the empty seat where her brother should have been.

"Where's Charlie?" she demanded.

"The girl has a catchphrase," Richard muttered.

"He's downstairs with a stomachache," said Patty. "I keep trying to check on him but he's locked the door."

Good, thought Nora. *He's finally using sense.*

"I thought you were bringing that to Vic," Nora said, jutting her chin towards the rope Patty held in her lap.

Patty looked down to the rope, then back up to Nora, her expression verging on sheepish. "I got a bit sidetracked."

Nora didn't bother dignifying that obvious lie with a response. Instead she hurried through the kitchen and down the stairs to the basement. She rapped on the bedroom door with one crooked finger.

"Charlie? It's me. You okay in there?"

The lock clicked and the door opened. Charlie stood in its

wake with Jessica perched on his shoulder. Both looked more disheveled than usual.

"Patty brought a rope," said Charlie.

"I saw."

"That's a fucking weird thing to bring to your parents' house, right?"

"It's not great."

Nora stepped inside the room and locked the door behind her. "How long has she been here?"

"She got here about ten minutes after you left."

Shit. Nora's gut was right. She should've come straight back.

"And you've been holed up in here since?"

Charlie nodded.

"Okay. Good. You did good, Charlie."

"It wasn't me," said Charlie. "I heard Jessica start flapping around and going nuts pretty much as soon as Patty got here. I had to stomp around a bunch and pretend my foot was asleep so Gram and Gramps wouldn't hear her. Then I made up some bullshit about having tummy troubles and got my ass back down here before anyone could ask any questions."

Nora looked at the bird, who looked back at her with nothing behind her eyes.

"Did you get anything out of Uncle Charles?" added Charlie.

Nora shook her head. "Not much. Apparently, Great-Grandpa Oliver is a bit of a hermit, but he wasn't always. No idea what changed, or why he'd need to be even more isolated than he already was in a place like this. I think . . ." Even as the words were coming out of her mouth, she regretted them. "I think I need to talk to him directly."

That stone house drowning in trees flashed into her mind's

eye, the hunched man with the bright white hair and dark eyes staring back at her.

"Cool," said Charlie. "I'll come with."

"Absolutely not," Nora said. "It isn't safe. We don't know the story with him yet."

"Nor, either I stay here with Lasso Patty and the world's sketchiest grandparents, or I come hang out with you and a guy old enough to remember the day the *Titanic* sank. Even if Great-Grandpa is evil, I feel like I could take him."

"What if he has a gun?"

"Then the reverberation is going to shatter him into a bunch of little old man shards. So, we going to Little Red Riding Hood this shit or what?"

A SOFT DRIZZLE HAD BLOWN IN DURING NORA'S TIME INSIDE, THE damp sinking down to her bones as they trudged through the forest. The twins had managed to sneak out the side door undetected while Charlie's possible would-be killers carried on chatting in the living room. Now they were up to their toes in mud, a ceiling of trees letting only choice raindrops through to splash on their faces at odd intervals. The path had mostly turned to a squelching sludge, which Nora was growing both accustomed to and more annoyed by with each soggy forest step.

"So, are we thinking this guy's in on it or what?" Charlie was shaking the rain from his hair like a dog.

"No," said Nora. "Well, maybe. I don't know. But I feel like he's connected to it all somehow. The town's just letting him rot out here in the middle of the woods alone. There must be a reason for that."

"And that reason's connected to why someone wants to kill me?"

"Could be. It's all I've got right now. Unless you have a better idea?"

"One time an ex wanted to kill me because I used all of her overpriced bodywash trying to loosen my phone when it got stuck in a storm drain."

"Did you waste all the bodywash of someone in Virgo Bay?" Nora asked.

"No, and I didn't waste Lexi's either. It worked. It also ruined my phone, but it worked."

Nora just sighed and kept walking. They reached the stone house a short while later, its gray facade poking discreetly through the trees. The air around it seemed heavier than normal, the sky a little darker. Nora's stomach filled with acid at the prospect of going back inside. Charlie, on the other hand, seemed to have no such misgivings. He strolled up to the front door with the confidence of a well-costumed kid on Halloween, secure in the knowledge of a full candy bar waiting on the other side. He gave the door a knock, paused for less than three seconds, and then plowed his way inside.

"You coming?" he asked Nora over his shoulder.

Regrettably, she was.

The interior was as dark and unwelcoming as Nora remembered it, the gloom of the day beyond reaching eerie hands inside, running fingers of bleak shadows into every corner.

"Maybe you should wait outside," Nora whispered. This only prompted Charlie to take another step inside. He scanned their surroundings, running his eyes over each dusty surface.

"Bet you this place is haunted as fuck," he whispered back.

Nora shook her head, despite the same thought having occurred to her when she'd first visited. "S.C.Y.T.H.E. has systems in place to minimize the creation of ghosts," she explained. "Besides, no one dies out here, remember?"

Charlie took another step into the belly of the house. "Where do you think the old guy's hiding?"

"He was upstairs last time I was here," said Nora. "We should—"

"Hello?" Charlie shouted, shattering the stillness of the house and Nora's nerves in one fell swoop.

"Charlie!" Nora snapped, giving his upper arm a hearty smack.

"What? We're here to see him, right? May as well get this party started."

The floor upstairs creaked. Nora knew that creak. The sound sent a chill rolling down her spine that landed somewhere around her knees. Her skin rose with the unbidden pattern of goose bumps. From somewhere upstairs came the step, shuffle, step, shuffle she'd heard while hiding inside the nursery closet. Her breath caught as the sound hit the top step and started its descent. Reflexively, she ducked behind Charlie. Then, remembering who was truly at risk here, stepped in front of him.

Step, shuffle, step, shuffle.

Nora thought her heart might burst through her ribs and start a new life on its own somewhere far away from here. Maybe Las Vegas. Finally the nearly fluorescent white hair emerged atop the dark eyes, sunken cheeks, and stooped back. Nora fought against herself to hold her nerve. She braced, scanning through a million sentences in her head, desperate to find the perfect one to make this exchange okay.

"Hey, Pops," Charlie said from behind her. She turned around to find him giving the old man a wave.

Oliver Bird narrowed his eyes at the twins. He cleared his throat, the rumble dry and wheezy.

"You're Martin's children, then," he said. His voice was what Nora imagined it would sound like if dust could speak. She nodded her reply.

The old man nodded back and walked to the rocking chair in the living room, lowering himself into it with a grunt. He faced away from the twins, his feet stretching out in search of the warmth from the healthy fire crackling in the belly of the fireplace. Nora had never seen anyone so unaffected by having their home invaded. Oliver picked a book up from the floor beside the rocking chair and opened it, flipping through weathered and dog-eared pages until he'd settled on a passage that intrigued him.

Nora gave Charlie a look that said, "He knows we're still here, right?"

Charlie shrugged and took a step forward. "Uh, so, nice place you got here."

The old man turned the page.

"Bit out of the way, but . . . nice."

"It's got good bones," Nora added awkwardly. "You built this yourself?"

Oliver didn't look up from his book, though his sigh was enough to tell Nora he could hear her.

"You kids staying long?"

"We didn't mean to bother you," Nora said.

"I mean in Virgo Bay."

"Oh," said Nora. "Maybe."

He turned another page.

"That's not why we're here though," Nora continued, still not quite sure how to speak to someone who so clearly didn't want to be spoken to. "We wanted to talk to you. And to meet you, of course."

"Of course," said Oliver. He turned another page.

"May we sit?"

"Don't see anyone stopping you."

Nora sat herself on the only other chair in the room. Charlie opted to crisscross himself onto the living room rug. Nobody spoke. Nora could hear the old man's breaths. The house settled around them, for real this time. Somewhere far away a clock ticked, or maybe that was in Nora's imagination.

"You wanted to talk to me," Oliver said at last.

"Yes," Nora said tentatively. She'd wanted to know the real reason why Oliver had separated himself from the rest of the town, but the more she was in his unpleasant company, the more apparent the answer seemed. "We were just wondering . . ." She looked to Charlie for assistance, but he seemed as mystified by the interaction as she was. Whatever fear she'd had upon entering the house had been promptly replaced by puzzlement tinged with a steadily growing seed of annoyance. She'd spent days trying to keep her brother alive while on limited sleep and more adrenaline than a skydiver after ten cups of coffee, and now, after facing the terror of returning to this place in the woods, she was being childishly ignored by someone who should have been buried a good decade before she was born. It was frankly absurd.

"We just wanted to find out who in Virgo Bay might be capable of taking a life," said Nora.

This forced both men's attention in her direction.

"What did you just say?" Oliver wheezed, laying his book open on his lap.

"You've lived here, in this town, on this planet, longer than anyone. You must know everything about everyone around here. It's a straightforward question. Who can we trust?"

"Why would you ask such a thing?"

"I just told you why," said Nora.

"No, you told me why you'd ask me, not why you'd ask it at all."

Nora chewed the inside of her cheek, contemplating the repercussions of telling Oliver the whole truth. If he was in league with Patty or Phil, who apparently were both frequent visitors, or with whoever else Charlie's would-be murderer might be, it would only be a matter of time before they came back out here and Oliver tipped them off that the twins were onto them. But as the person most removed from town, there was also a chance that he was the least involved of anyone in this whole murdery mess.

"Well," she said, carefully scanning each word before it left her mouth, "someone has been very unsubtly trying to cause us harm since we got here. If you have any idea who that might be, then I'd like to know too."

Oliver stared through her for a moment, dark eyes like bottomless wells pulling her into their depths. "You expect me to know the answer to that?"

"You do share DNA with three-quarters of the town," Nora tried.

"So do you," he said, his wispy voice somehow adding an unreadable weight to his words. "What are you doing all the way out here in Virgo Bay anyway?"

"Our dad—"

"Your father left," said Oliver. "Perhaps you ought to hurry up and do the same."

"I don't understand." Exasperation forced its way from Nora's throat. "Why won't you help us?"

Something in those dark eyes shifted. The apathy Nora had seen in them seemed to ebb into an out-of-place softness that unnerved her even more. Then he picked up his book with a shake of his head, burying his eyes in its pages. "You're mistaken. There's no one here who would wish to do you harm. The sooner you stop thinking as much, the better."

"I'm pretty sure I—"

"You're wrong," Oliver said, with the kind of finality that made Nora wonder for a very brief moment if she was. "And I can't help you."

"But—"

"I can't help you."

"Can't, or won't?" Nora said, but the words hung unanswered in the air, joined only by the crackling fire.

At this point Nora's seed of annoyance had fully bloomed. He must have at the very least had some thoughts on the subject, some hints or information or suspicions about the people he knew best. And yet, he was content to sit there dismissing Nora's fears, a feeling she knew all too well. But this time those fears had something very real to back them up, and yet she was still being patted on the head and told to calm down.

Not only was her investigation being actively stymied by this crotchety old guy, but she couldn't help but be a little offended by his utter lack of interest in his long-lost great-grandchildren. This could have been a touching introduction if nothing else, but instead he'd chosen to be an unapologetic ass. Just for that, Nora decided he was just as likely to be a murderer as the rest of this dysfunctional town, or at least that he made for a criminally bad host. She stomped up to her feet.

"Fine. We're leaving. Sorry to take up some of your endless time, you're clearly busy. Hope we get to have a proper family reunion one of these days, but if not, it's probably because we're dead and you could have prevented it." With that she marched indignantly out the door.

Back in the woods, the sky was doing something. There may have been rain, though it was just as likely sunny. Nora was too frustrated to notice. She had been so sure, so convinced that that sinister house in the woods held the answers to her brother's case, but instead all it held was a crabby old man with poor housekeeping skills and a complete unwillingness to help.

"So . . . wow," Charlie said as they shuffled across the muddy path, pulling Nora from her thoughts.

"What?"

"You really hated that guy, huh?"

"No," said Nora. "Well, yes. Maybe. It doesn't matter. We're no closer to figuring out who's trying to kill you, are we? That was a waste of time, and I don't know how much of that we have."

"Still," said Charlie. "It was pretty badass."

"Really?"

"Yeah. I mean, a bit weird and intense too, don't get me wrong, but you didn't take his cranky bullshit, so that was cool. And did you see his eyes?"

"What are you talking about?"

"When you dropped the bomb," said Charlie. "You know, 'who here could be a killer' or whatever. His eyes did this weird thing where they went all wide for a second and flicked off to the side. He definitely knows something."

Nora stopped walking for a moment. In truth she hadn't noticed. She had been too fired up, her fuel a steadily burning frustration, to catch the nuances of her great-grandfather's facial expressions. Which wasn't like her. But Charlie had caught them. Which wasn't like him. She would have plenty of time to overanalyze that later. But if Charlie was right in what he saw and his interpretation of it, then there was something Oliver knew that Nora needed to know too. She could have kicked herself if her hamstrings were more flexible and she wasn't worried about slipping in the mud. She had spent so much effort imagining the man in the hidden house was up to something almost otherworldly in her head. When she'd finally managed to work up the nerve to face him, she had quickly written Oliver off as a cranky old guy who had grown so derisive towards the world that he'd decided to shun it as soon as he could. To her he was now capable of nothing more than biting comments. But if he was hiding something, then that put him in the same category as everyone else in town: suspicious as fuck. She wasn't done with Oliver, Nora decided. She would just have to be smarter about it next time.

She was still half lost in the M. C. Escher drawing of her mind when the forest around her changed. It was a subtle shift at first, the air holding an almost-hollow quality, a small flock of birds fleeing a patch of the woods just visible from the path. Nothing that should have raised alarm, and nothing that likely would have raised alarm to anyone who wasn't already in a constant state of alarm. Then came the sound that a part of Nora had somehow known was coming. The blast tore out of the same patch of woods the birds had flown from. Nora's mind's eye flooded with visions of a bloody Charlie crumpled beside her. It all happened so quickly, she barely knew she was moving. Like her race to the cliff's edge, Nora was mostly a fast-moving body at this point, her thoughts somewhere a few seconds behind. They caught up just as she and Charlie hit the ground in a painful heap of sharp elbows and knees. Above them, the bark of a tree exploded, shards of sawdust raining down.

"Gun?" Charlie asked as soon as he'd regained the capacity to speak.

"Gun," Nora confirmed. Based on the destruction to the tree above them, very likely a hunting rifle built to take down prey. Which was exactly what the twins were now. But Nora didn't say any of that. Instead she dragged herself across the mud and fallen leaves on her elbows, leading them in an army crawl away from the shooter. Though, of course, that was of little use. Bullets, it turned out, were harder to avoid than falling tree limbs. And Nora hated the fact that she had the personal experience to make that comparison. The torrent of shots kept coming, each closer than the last, until one fired from right beside the twins.

Without thinking, Nora dove to cover her brother with her body and buried her head in her hands, waiting for the final bullet to strike, but the shot never came. She removed her ineffective hand shield and looked up to find Patty standing over them, rifle in hand, its smoking barrel pointed skyward.

"You kids okay?" She lowered a hand, offering it to Nora, who regarded it with the same level of disgust she'd view a rotting trout.

"The fuck?" was all Nora could manage.

"Sorry. Someone must've been out hunting and not realized there was anyone else out here."

"Someone, but not you," Nora said pointedly.

"I'm not much of a hunter," said Patty.

Nora pulled herself to her feet without the assistance of her aunt's hand. She wobbled, her legs weak with fear, and leaned on the shattered tree for support. When she looked over and spotted the bullet lodged in the bark, she weakened further and found herself caught under one arm by Charlie, who was somehow less affected by his tenure as a bull's-eye than Nora was. She eyed Patty with a knot in her stomach. Neither she nor Charlie had been particularly focused on anything but not dying during the barrage of gunshots. There was nothing to say Patty hadn't been the one doing the shooting, moving closer as they fled. Though that didn't explain why she didn't shoot them now, or when they were still on the ground. Nothing made sense. Again.

"Why do you have a gun if you don't hunt?" Nora said, voice trembling.

"You never know what you're going to run into when you live out in the middle of nowhere," Patty said simply. "Now, are either of you hurt?"

Nora scanned her body from top to bottom, finding none but the usual holes. She shook her head. Charlie, still propping her up, mimicked the gesture.

"Good," said Patty. "Good. Why don't you come back home with me and we'll get you cleaned up?"

Nora shook her head again.

"At least let me walk you back to Mom and Dad's," Patty tried again. She indicated her gun. "Like I said, you never know what you're going to run into out here."

Nora looked down at the weapon. It seemed to look back at her, regarding her with a smugness that said it knew exactly what it was capable of. Nora wasn't sure she or Charlie had much of a choice in the matter in regard to Patty's offer. She wasn't willing to risk what could happen if she said no. Instead she pressed herself firmly between Patty and Charlie as they resumed their walk back to the little red house.

"Phil said he saw you coming out here," Patty said, answering a question that hadn't been asked. Her voice was tight, almost defensive. "That's how I knew where to find you."

"You were trying to find us?" Nora said.

Patty didn't answer this. Instead she said, "Phil says he's likely got another few days to go on your car repairs, then you can get on your way."

"You suddenly seem to be in a hurry for us to leave," said Nora, a list of all the ways someone could fatally sabotage a car running through her mind.

"I'm sure you have things you want to get back to."

Nora realized Patty hadn't made eye contact with either of them once since she'd arrived. "I'm glad I found you out here," Patty continued, still focused straight ahead. "Charlie, I've been meaning to ask if I could borrow you for some help with a few things around the house. Nora mentioned you've done some odd jobs over the years. Not sure if any of those were particularly handy, but I'm sure you've got the knack."

"No," said Nora in Charlie's stead. The thought of Charlie alone in Patty's house—Patty, who was now confirmed to own a gun, and to be keeping tabs on their movement—made Nora feel like collapsing all over again. "Phil's handy," she said. "Why don't you ask him, since you two are so close?"

"Phil's helping out at the farm with his dad today," said Patty.

"The farm," Nora repeated. "Where you were bringing the rope?"

"That's right."

They emerged from the trees, the gloomy day brightening slightly without the cover of a foliage ceiling.

"You seem skeptical," Patty continued. "I know that incident in the woods must have been quite rattling. Are you sure you're okay?"

Nora didn't say anything. In truth there was nothing worth saying. Of course she wasn't okay, but there was no use explaining that to one of the main reasons for it.

"I'm actually heading back there now," said Patty. "Why don't you two come with me? You haven't been out there yet, have you? It might be a nice change of scenery after all of this, and I'm sure Vic could use some extra hands."

A farm was unappealing at the best of times: the smell, the rusty equipment, the animals who had no right being as big or trample-capable as they were. But the alternative was returning to the little red house to spend the rest of the day with Richard and Ruby who were, at minimum, accomplices in the attempts on Charlie's life. At least the farm offered witnesses. Witnesses who might also be involved, to be sure, but there was still a sliver of ever-unreliable hope that they would be on the twins' side.

"Okay," said Nora, surprising everyone, not least herself.

"Okay," said Patty. "Right this way."

And just like that, Nora and Charlie walked voluntarily into what was very likely a trap.

22

Wooden paddocks like patches in a quilt crisscrossed the rolling fields that pushed to the edges of Virgo Bay. Inside, livestock grazed and frolicked and occasionally pooped as Patty and the twins approached. A ramshackle barn and a compact farmhouse sat just back from the path, lined on either side by fences enclosing goats to the left and cows to the right. Nora kept herself firmly in the center.

Vic appeared from the barn at the sound of Patty's call, trailed by Phil and his father, the inexplicably nicknamed Pickles. Unlike his rugged son, Pickles was a primly dressed man with jowls and a permanent Eeyore-like expression. He had dirt in exactly one place on his slacks and kept moving his hand to cover it.

"You've brought the city slickers," Vic said in greeting, then fully took in the scene before him. "And a rifle."

Patty's eyes flicked to Phil, who brushed his nose with the back of his hand and looked away. Was he disappointed to see the twins standing there? Was Charlie the Snow White to Patty's Huntsman? Which would make Phil the evil queen, which Nora wasn't quite sure about. But regardless of what the look between them actually meant, she knew it wasn't anything good.

"It's hunting season," Patty replied to Vic, then quickly changed the subject. "We're here to help out. What do you need done?"

"Stalls need mucking, the rest of the horses still need turning out, and the pigs need feeding. Phil's working on repairing the riding lawn mower, and I've got Pickles pruning the hedges out back. Aside from those chores, you lot can take your pick."

There wasn't much picking to be taken, it turned out. Due to their inexperience with farm work, Patty suggested the twins take the stalls to start with. And, despite the smell, Nora was grateful for this. Pigs could break your toe just by stepping on it, and horses, well, they could break much more than that. At least a pile of feces mostly kept to itself. Nora soon found herself cleaning the stall of a horse called Wonderboy, Charlie half helping beside her.

"You still thinking it's Patty?" Charlie asked. He was making concentric poop circles with his shovel, which Nora decided was as productive as she could expect Charlie to be.

"I think it's a good possibility," said Nora. "You saw her out there with that gun. There's no reason she couldn't have been the one shooting it at us. And she gave Phil that weird look when we got here. *And* she wanted to have you at her house alone. I don't like any of it."

"It's not great," Charlie agreed. "But then why hasn't she killed me yet?"

Nora took a deep breath, then immediately regretted it as the odors of the stall flooded her nostrils. "That's what I've been trying to figure out. But we still don't know why she'd want you dead in the first place. Maybe she wants to make you suffer first."

"Damn, what the hell did I do to her?"

"If we knew that, we'd be halfway to getting this whole mess sorted," said Nora, heaving a particularly heavy plop into her neat pile.

"You know, Nor," said Charlie, swirling his shovel absently, "this has been kind of nice, huh?"

"What are you talking about?"

"We just haven't hung out in a really long time. It's been nice."

"Charlie, you've nearly been killed like seven times now."

"Yeah, but aside from that. It's hard to find time to catch up, you know? Especially now that I have Jessica. I mean, being a dad is a lot of responsibility, but I've missed my baby sis."

"You're three minutes older than me," Nora corrected. "And I still don't understand where Jessica even came from."

"I know, it's wild, right? One second I'm living the carefree bachelor life, the next she's on my doorstep with nothing but a cage and a note."

"A note? You never mentioned a note."

"It didn't seem like something worth mentioning," said Charlie. "I mean, Jessica's kind of the star of the show here, right?"

Nora propped her shovel against the wall of the stall and crossed her arms. Spontaneous parrot deliveries struck her as at least a little out of the ordinary, though with the way Charlie lived his life, she supposed it may have seemed a standard part of his day. Still, something bothered her, something she couldn't quite put a name to.

"What did the note say?"

Charlie shrugged. "Something about Jessica having a lot to say. Or, no, 'she'll tell you what you need to know,' I think it was. Or 'what you deserve to know,' something like that. Which was true; she told me where my favorite pair of boxer briefs was hiding like half an hour after I brought her inside. I thought I'd lost those things for good, but they were in an empty Cheetos bag under my bed. Go figure."

"Ew," said Nora as a first of all. "But also, that's kind of a weird note, don't you think?"

Charlie shrugged again. "I've had weirder. What, you aren't thinking she's connected to all this somehow, are you?"

"I don't know, Charlie, maybe. Isn't it just a little too odd to be a coincidence?"

"You and I have very different thresholds for odd."

"At least I have a threshold for odd," said Nora.

"Oh wait, the note said something else . . ." But before Charlie could finish his thought, chaos erupted outside the barn. Someone was shouting, which was promptly joined by the sound of thundering footsteps and more shouting voices. Nora froze. Those were never particularly positive noises. No less than eight possible horrors ran through her mind at once, each less welcome than the last and at least one involving an unexpected tornado.

Phil burst into the barn, his boots heavy on the hay-strewn stone floor. He looked from one twin to the other, face severe, and Nora braced for whatever was about to come.

"Leopold's escaped," he said.

Nora had not braced for that.

"Huh?"

"Uncle Vic's favorite goat. Sired three-quarters of the kids on this farm. Dad didn't secure his paddock properly and the bastard's practically uncatchable, apparently. Running all over the fields like a convict on the loose. We need more bodies to corner him. You coming?"

Nora pretended to consider this. "Oh, no, sorry, we have to finish in here," she said after what seemed like a reasonable length of time. There was no way in hell she was going to go chasing after a rogue goat. That sounded like a surefire way to end up with a horn in places horns had no business being.

"I'm in," said Charlie, dropping his shovel onto the soiled floor.

Nora tried to toss him a look that said, "Like hell you are," but he was already halfway out the barn. She threw her head back in exasperation and scampered out after him.

Despite her misgivings that this might have been some weird murder ploy by Phil, there was indeed a large black-and-white goat playing an aggressive game of red rover against a growing crowd of people. Which, in some ways, was worse than a murder ploy. Vic and Patty seemed to be approaching the animal from behind while it geared up to charge at Pickles and Charles, who must have shown up at some point during Nora's mucking and Charlie's dabbling in fecal art.

"You two go around that side," Phil directed as he went to fill in the other side of the circle.

Charlie and Nora did as instructed, heading off the goat from the side closest to them, which only served to take the creature's attention away from its initial target. Its great head swung in the twins' direction, horns locking on Nora, and before anyone could advise her otherwise, she was bolting away from Leopold at a full sprint. The goat was instantly on her heels, followed by a parade of frantic relatives rushing after them. She raced across the field and past the riding lawn mower Phil had been working on, engine on and tools strewn in front of it as though he'd been plucked from his duties by the renegade goat.

"Good, good," Patty called at Nora. "His paddock's a bit to your right, see if you can guide him there."

"I'm not doing this for his benefit," Nora shouted back. If they were planning on killing her as well as Charlie, she'd hoped for something more dignified than being used as goat bait. Still, she could see the upside of getting Leopold back into his enclosure. She veered left. Hoof steps followed, clopping with a small but mighty rage.

"You'll have to run him into the paddock and do a little U-turn back out, kiddo," Patty called.

Nora didn't even like doing a U-turn in a car, when the only horns she had to face were the kind that honked. She rushed in through the open gate, braving a look back to ensure Leopold was still on her tail, then looped through and back out of the paddock, slamming the gate with enough force to rattle the fence around her. The crowd trailing her stopped where they were, Patty offering a polite round of applause for her effort, which felt somewhat inadequate considering how very close Nora had come to having two extra holes in her bottom.

She scanned the field for Charlie, who was catching his breath at the base of the small hill the riding lawn mower sat on. He gave her a thumbs-up, doubled over from what was likely the first run he'd completed since high school gym class. The others had started to disappear from view as Nora struggled to regain whatever passed for her composure at this point. She sagged against the fence, trying to steady herself, before promptly springing upright again at the sound of Leopold's hooves trotting in her direction. When she turned her gaze back over to Charlie to give him a look that said, "This fucking guy," what she saw instead locked up her already-tense muscles.

The riding lawn mower on top of the small hill, the one Phil had just been working on, had begun to roll forward, picking up speed as it descended. Charlie was still doubled over, unaware of the vehicle plowing towards him. Nora could clearly see the mower making contact, turning her brother into mincemeat before he had the chance to fully realize what was going on. She was too far away to close the gap between them and push Charlie to safety in time, and calling out a warning with enough detail to get him out of danger would take too long. But maybe she didn't have to say as much as she thought.

Bubbie always hid the good snacks on the top shelf of the kitchen pantry. Whenever she went out back to garden, Nora and Charlie launched their contraband-retrieval system. Being the timid one, Nora played lookout and held a stool steady for Charlie while he scrambled up and snagged the Hostess snacks, the potato chips or, on one particularly blessed occasion, an entire chocolate babka. As soon as she heard the screen door creaking, her duty was to give the signal, a shout of "albatross," which would immediately send Charlie leaping off the stool and onto the kitchen rug before the inside door opened. This emergency operation had only been properly put into effect on two occasions, one of which ended with Charlie in a fluorescent orange cast, but they'd practiced so often that the leap at the code word had become a reflex for Charlie. Nora prayed that hadn't changed.

The mower rushed forward. There was no time for a plan B. The mower was at Charlie's heels, blades already primed to slash at the backs of his shoes. Nora cupped her hands around her mouth and shouted so hard she thought her lungs might pop out in conjunction with her voice. "Albatross!"

Charlie didn't even take the time to look up. At the sound of

Nora's code word he dove to the side, landing heavily in a patch of grass and rolling a few feet towards where Nora stood. The lawn mower, for its part, kept rolling into the open field, free from whatever burdens a working mower faced, ready to start a new, independent life. This time it was Vic alone who embarked on the chase, barreling after the machine and shouting obscenities as he ran. The rest of the crew was notably absent, not only from the mower wrangling but from the field itself. Patty made her way over to Charlie, presumably under the guise of ensuring his welfare, but Phil was nowhere to be seen.

Nora beat Patty to Charlie's side and immediately crouched beside him, looking him over for any signs of uninvited pruning.

"You kids ought to be put in Bubble Wrap," Patty said as she arrived. Her voice was measured, but her eyes had a frantic quality behind them; the disparity gave her the vibe of a woman possessed by the spirit of someone she would not have gotten along with in life. "I can't seem to turn my back on you for a minute without one or both of you ending up in harm's way."

Nora was a kneeling barrier between Patty and her brother. She could feel her nostrils flaring like a bull ready to charge. "Where's Phil?"

Patty cast her eyes around the fields. "Search me," she said. "He's not going to be too thrilled with whatever new damage that mower ends up with. It was giving him enough of a hard time already."

"It nearly gave Charlie a much harder time," said Nora through gritted teeth.

Patty unfolded her arms from where they'd been hugging her chest, appearing to try to soften her presence and failing miserably. She'd barely batted an eye at her nephew's second near-death experience of the day. Aside from a sarcastic quip, she'd hardly acknowledged it at all. And why would she, if she was the one or-chestrating it to begin with?

"You're right," said Patty. "Are you okay, Charlie? That must have been a harrowing thing to go through."

Charlie had propped himself on his elbows and was currently weaving his head around Nora to try to catch a glimpse of his aunt, but Nora was having none of it and remained firmly wedged between the two.

"No harm done," said Charlie, who clearly wasn't picking up Nora's simmering animosity or the charade of Patty's concern.

"And I intend to keep it that way," said Nora, her eyes locked on Patty's in challenge.

Patty nodded the nod of someone who didn't quite know why they were nodding but couldn't think of a better alternative. "Very good," she said tentatively.

"We're going," said Nora. She offered her hand to Charlie and hoisted him to his feet.

"Nora—" Patty started, then stopped herself. "I'm sure Mom and Dad would be glad to have some help with lunch," she said instead of whatever she'd actually wanted to say. "If you see Phil before I do, tell him I'm looking for him."

"What for?"

Patty feigned a smile. "Oh, just a little project we're working on. It hasn't been going very well so far, but I'm hoping we'll be changing that real soon."

They stood there holding eye contact, locked in a standoff neither of them dared name. Patty broke first. "And that car of yours," she said. "I'll make sure Phil has you behind the wheel again in no time. I'm sure we'd all like that, wouldn't we?"

23

Nora had carved an effective pacing route between the two beds. Up one side towards the back wall, pivot, back down to the door she'd locked and barricaded with a dresser. Charlie's and Jessica's heads followed her back and forth like the spectators of a slow-motion Ping-Pong match. Richard and Ruby were upstairs making lunch, just as Patty had predicted, but instead of helping, Nora had dragged her brother to their bedroom for the sake of general safety, a debrief, and to keep Charlie away from knives.

She chewed the inside of her cheek as she paced, stopping occasionally when an unexpectedly heavy step forced her jaw down too hard. This would usually be enough to stop the chewing altogether, but not today. Today the pain kept her alert.

"It's Patty," she said. "She's working with Phil. He's her stooge, the one doing the dirty work. That mower had Phil written all over it. Richard and Ruby are helping her too, or at least they aren't working against her. And then there's the old guy in the forest—"

"Forest house," Jessica squawked.

"Sure," said Nora. "He's close with Phil and Patty. He must

know what's up, though he keeps to himself too much to be an active participant in anything."

"Okay," said Charlie.

Nora paused her pacing and plucked Charlie's file off the floor by her bed. His cause of death was still a blur, its shape altered yet again. Also on the rug was Ruby's file. Somehow, Ruby's cause of death had completely vanished in the years since it had first appeared, but Nora didn't think she'd have much luck getting an explanation out of Ruby herself after what Nora had overheard that morning.

Nora could think of only one person who knew everything that went on in Virgo Bay but wasn't invested in any of it.

"I'm going back to see Oliver," Nora said.

"Okay," Charlie said again. "Why?"

"Because he has answers."

"Answers he clearly has no interest in sharing," said Charlie.

"Yeah, well, I had no interest in traveling to another country and getting stranded in a town full of sociopaths. We all have to make sacrifices from time to time."

"All right," said Charlie, standing up. "Let's give it a shot, I guess."

Nora shook her head. "I'm doing this alone, Charlie. You keep yourself locked down here, okay?"

"But—"

"Charlie . . ." Nora was instantly back in that forest, gunshots raining down around her, tree bark erupting into dust. The deafening blasts, the raw fear like a million thundering hearts racing in harmony in her ears. She could still taste the damp earth that had sprayed into her mouth as she'd scrambled across the ground on her elbows. It could all happen again. If whoever was after

Charlie wanted it to, it could all happen again. And this time there was no guarantee they'd both leave the woods in one piece. She didn't say anything else. She didn't have to. Charlie knew. One look at his sister's face and he knew exactly where she was.

"Be careful," was all he said.

"I always am," said Nora, but the longer she spent protecting Charlie from death, the less true that felt. She couldn't keep risking her life to save his. It wasn't how she was built. She needed this to end.

THE WOODS FELT SUFFOCATING. EYES LANDED WARM ON NORA'S back from behind every tree, from within every shrub. Each rustle of leaves sent her jumping, the crack of a twig beneath her feet summoning the reflex to duck for cover. Nora reminded herself she wasn't the target. Over and over again she repeated it like a mantra as she trudged deeper into the forest. But the more she said it, the less she believed it. Would that remain the case if she got too close to the truth? She had her doubts.

She made it to the stone house without incident, or at least without any physical harm. Her nerves were another matter. She was so worked up by the time she reached the front door that she could barely steady her hand long enough to turn the doorknob. When she finally managed it, she found something almost as shocking as a shooter in the woods. The door was locked. No door in Virgo Bay was ever locked. She tried again, thinking the anxiety filling her limbs like helium had made her grip too weak, but the knob simply wouldn't turn. Nora took a step back and examined the dark wooden door with a scowl. Interesting that Oliver would choose today, mere hours after his great-grandchildren visited him for the first time, to start locking his door. And by "interesting," she meant "infuriating."

Nora banged on the door. "Oliver," she called, but the house remained still and the door bolted. She knocked again. "Oliver, you open this door. I know you're in there. You're a hundred and twenty-seven. Don't pretend you've got somewhere else to be."

Still nothing.

Then, weakly, from somewhere inside: "Go away."

"I'm not going anywhere," Nora shouted. "This is a matter of life and death."

"We don't do that around here," Oliver called back.

Nora stopped knocking. This was beginning to feel as useless as it had that morning. The adrenaline in her veins eased. She lowered her forehead to the door, suddenly exhausted. "Please."

A few moments passed. Nora could feel herself melting deeper into the wood of the door. It was a good door, she decided. Sturdy and rugged without losing its elegance. She'd once wanted to design houses with doors like this. They kept the world out, kept you safe within. It struck her as exactly right that this was the kind of door Oliver would have built for himself. There was a part of Nora, a part she was somewhat reticent to acknowledge, that could see herself in Oliver, that could see a future much like this for herself. Just a little house all on her own in a pocket of the world where nothing could ever hurt her. And yet Oliver seemed deeply miserable. It was one of the many mysteries about this town and the people who called it home, but it wasn't the one she was here to solve.

Nora was so lost in her thoughts she barely noticed the vibrations of the door's lock clicking. Her forehead was still pressed against that sturdy wood when the door opened slowly, reluctantly.

"Oh," said Nora, stepping back. Oliver stood on the threshold, his expression as resolutely annoyed as it had been that morning. He gave Nora a grunt and shuffled back inside, leaving the door open behind him. Nora trailed him in, watching as he dropped himself back into the wooden rocking chair by the fireplace. She took her own prior spot in the other chair. The house was dimly lit, whatever natural light the clouds outside let through mostly denied entry by a notable lack of windows. Dust motes frolicked in the scant rays that had made it inside, and a single shelf of the bookcase and a few old picture frames were caught in the hazy spotlight.

"I need the truth about this place," said Nora.

"Here I thought you knew it," came Oliver's reply.

Nora had to snort at this. Virgo Bay had more secret layers than Bubbie's Super Bowl bean dip, and they made her just as gassy.

"Why do you choose to live out here all on your own?" she tried.

"To get away from annoying questions," said Oliver.

"You used to be an active part of this town. You *founded* this town. What changed?"

Oliver crossed his arms and curled into himself by way of reply.

Then it struck her, all at once. The one thing that happened to this town where everything and everyone lived on pause. "Dad died. That's what changed, isn't it?" But it wasn't a question, really. As the words formed and then left her mouth, she felt them with a conviction she only ever experienced when stating facts about all the different ways a person could die.

"You're a kid," said Oliver. "You barely know your head from your ass. You don't know what the hell you're talking about."

"I lost him too," Nora said, her mouth drying as Oliver's scorn sucked the moisture from the room. "And Mom. But I didn't hole myself up in the middle of nowhere about it." No matter how much she'd wanted to. Though she didn't say that part out loud.

"Do you know why I came to Virgo Bay?" Oliver spat. He shook his head with derision. "Forget it."

"Your wife died," said Nora, recounting what she'd learned from Richard and Ruby.

"Alice was *taken* from me," said Oliver. "I wouldn't let the same thing happen to our children. I wouldn't."

"You couldn't," Nora corrected. Her arms twitched. She knew that feeling. It had started nibbling at her the day her parents died, bit her hard after Bubbie passed, and since finding Charlie's file, it had fully consumed her. She couldn't let it happen again. It was simply not a possibility.

"I couldn't," Oliver relented.

"So you found a Blind Spot."

"It found me," said Oliver. "I could feel it, the moment we set foot here. It was different. It would all be different."

Nora nodded. In a way, she'd felt it too. And she wanted it, the sanctuary this place promised. She *craved* it. Whatever ire she felt towards this infuriating old man eased slightly in that moment. She would have stayed here too. She still would.

"Then Dad left," she offered gently.

"He was always a bold one. Could never be content with what was right in front of him."

"And then he died."

Oliver's dark eyes flicked to her, a sudden renewed sharpness behind them.

"He shouldn't have. It never should have happened."

"You mean if he'd stayed here he'd still be alive," said Nora.

Oliver evaded her gaze again. "There was no reason it had to end the way it did."

"Do you know how it happened?" Nora asked, suddenly realizing he probably knew a lot more than she and Charlie did about the accident that took their parents from them.

The old man seemed to wither in his chair. His face was a wrinkly knot of unspoken words.

"You do," said Nora. She was back on her feet, the revelation propelling her out of her chair.

Oliver said nothing.

"You do," Nora said again. "And whatever you know is the reason you let the forest grow in around you, the reason you left the town behind, isn't it?"

"Is that what you've come here to ask me?" Oliver said after a long, infuriating pause.

"Yes. Maybe. I have a million things I want to ask you," said Nora. "So Dad left and then he died and, what? You resented him so much for walking away from you and leaving the safety of this place that you locked yourself away in the woods?"

"You think that's it, do you? That I hated my grandson for leaving? And because I hated him I decided to live the rest of eternity alone out of spite? Is that what you think?"

"Well . . ."

"We all should've left this place," said Oliver, catching Nora firmly off guard. "It shouldn't exist to begin with. I regret coming here every day of my endless life. This town should be burned to the ground."

24

"Y ou're sure you heard him right?"

Nora had left the woods after only a few more words with Oliver, her mind somewhere far away from her body. She'd made it back to the little red house on muscle memory alone, every other sense numbed by a deluge of emotion. She still didn't fully understand how she'd gotten herself to where she now sat, sagging over the edge of her father's old bed, Charlie standing above her. He looked more concerned now, staring at the pale, clammy lump of a sister in front of him, than he had at any of his near-deaths.

Nora looked up at him, her head heavy on her neck. "Yeah, I'm sure."

"'Burned to the ground' is pretty dramatic. And he wouldn't say why?"

Nora shook her heavy head. "Not really. Just that this place shouldn't exist. And that Dad understood. And . . . Charlie, there's something else."

Charlie gave her a look that said, "Okay, hit me."

So Nora did. "He said Dad understood . . . and that's why he died."

They both sat in that revelation for a moment, breathing the words like salt water into their lungs.

"I don't get it," said Charlie at last.

"Ditto," said Nora. She flopped down onto the covers, unable to hold herself upright any longer. What Oliver had implied, that her father's death was somehow connected to this place, was too much for her mind to hold. It didn't make sense. How could the town he'd left possibly contribute to the accident that took his life? "I wish he was here," she said, her voice small. "And Mom. They both had lives before us, Charlie, whole lives we never got to hear about. It's like we never really knew them."

Charlie plopped himself down beside her, Jessica hopping off his shoulder to find a perch between their heads. "I know," he said. "But maybe that was on purpose. I mean, this place is fucking weird, Nora. Maybe Dad wanted to keep us away from that."

"I guess."

"There's gotta be a reason he never brought us here, or even really mentioned Virgo Bay to us much growing up."

Nora couldn't argue with that, which was a rarity in their relationship. "Oliver said Dad understood why this place shouldn't exist, but as soon as I tried to get an explanation out of him, he shut down. It's bullshit. And it's not like we can ask Dad about it, so we're right back at square one."

"Maybe not . . ." said Charlie, sitting up. "Charles told you Dad wrote him letters, right? We may not be able to talk to Dad, but that's kind of the next best thing."

"Charles also said Richard and Ruby probably got rid of them after he moved out."

"But what if they didn't?" said Charlie. "Look at this place. The basement is like a fucking shrine to Dad, Charles, and Patty. If they didn't throw out Dad's truly awful sketches, why would they throw out his letters?"

Nora blinked up at Charlie, bewildered by the sudden, uncharacteristic practicality in his words.

"Okay," said Nora. "Say you're right. I haven't come across them anywhere, so where would they be?"

"Only one way to find out," said Charlie. He held out his hand to her, and for longer than she was proud of, she seriously contemplated not taking it, and instead simply lying there on her father's old bed for the foreseeable future. She had been trying so hard for what felt like so long, and yet failure met her at every opportunity. She was on a steady diet of low sleep and high anxiety. It felt like she had risked her life more fervently than she'd ever avoided risks before, and yet she was no closer to saving Charlie. She looked up.

Charlie. There he was, all disheveled and hairy, his hand outstretched. There was never a choice, not really. She had given up on him in many ways over the years, but when it came down to it, she would always, always take his hand. And so she did.

"I'll check through the closet in here," said Charlie. "Why don't you look in that cupboard where you found Ruby's file?"

Nora nodded, relieved not to be the one making the decisions for once. She left Charlie in the bedroom and headed for the hall. Upstairs, someone was rattling around in the kitchen. Nora decided she didn't much care who it was; at this point they were all equally untrustworthy. She would need to be quick and quiet to avoid drawing attention to herself. Richard and Ruby had mostly left them alone since the morning, but if Martin's letters to Charles still existed, she wasn't keen for them to catch her searching.

The cardboard box of case files still sat on the floor of the linen closet. Nora stared at them, wondering if they held any other secrets she had yet to uncover. She quickly thumbed through them but turned up nothing of interest aside from a hit-and-run victim with the unfortunate name of Dick Cox.

She pushed the box back into place and examined the shelves, finding only frayed childhood linens, a photo album, and a stack of encyclopedias that, judging by the thick coating of dust, hadn't been touched in years. She quickly shook the photo album, but no letters fell from between the leaves. She closed the door and turned to make her way back into the bedroom, but someone was blocking her path.

Ruby. Her small but inexplicably intimidating form stood between Nora and the bedroom door. She observed her granddaughter with narrowed eyes, her face creased in a frown.

"What are you doing?" she demanded.

Nora tried to remember what nonchalance looked like. It was probably the opposite of the way she looked at the moment.

"Oh, I was, um—" But she didn't have time to lie badly before Ruby cut her off.

"Patty says you've been up to see Richard's father a number of times now."

Of course she did. Nora's jaw clenched. This further proved that Patty was keeping tabs on the twins. It was suddenly little wonder that Martin never wrote to his sister after he left. Was Patty always like this? Could she have been the real reason Martin left town? Or worse, the real reason he was dead, somehow?

"Oliver prefers his own company," Ruby continued. "I'm asking you on his behalf to leave him alone."

"On his behalf?" Nora spat. She knew she had to tread lightly with Ruby. She was still living in her grandparents' house, after all. Say too much and she'd be putting Charlie and even herself in further danger. But her nerves were too frayed to say nothing at all. "Really? Because he sure had a lot to say to me when I was over there."

Nora thought she caught Ruby's eyes widen before she regained her steely composure. "Did he? Well, you mustn't listen to him. He's been off on his own a very long time. These days he doesn't have anything of worth to say."

"Is that why you never visit him?" said Nora.

"I beg your pardon?"

"Patty and Phil do, though," said Nora. "Why would they visit him so often if he talks nonsense? Maybe he knows something you'd rather I didn't." The words tumbled out, her brain unable to catch up with her mouth. Now she'd really stepped in it, she was sure.

Ruby was radiating arctic temperatures. Nora took a step back from the small woman, bumping into the closet door. Ruby, for her part, took a step forward.

"You're playing a game you can't win," said Ruby. "What goes on in this town is none of your business."

"I—"

"For the last time, stay out of the forest, stay away from Oliver, and leave well enough alone."

"Is that a threat?"

"It's a warning," said Ruby. She eyed the closet behind Nora and shook her head, tutting at Nora's latest breach of town privacy. Then, just as quickly as she'd appeared, she left Nora standing alone in the wood-paneled basement, more confused and more resolute than ever.

"GRANDMA'S A BITCH," NORA DECLARED AS SHE SWEPT BACK INTO the bedroom.

"She really doesn't want you hanging out with Oliver, huh?" said Charlie.

"You listened at the door?"

"I listened at the door."

"What the hell is she hiding? What the hell are any of them hiding? Isn't a town where nobody dies enough of a secret? Why does there have to be more?" Nora had crossed through exasperation and was somewhere around the utterly irate mark.

"That's what we're trying to find out," Charlie reminded her.

Right. "Any luck in here?"

Charlie shook his head. "Nothing in Dad's closet, nothing in the desk or under the beds. Maybe Gram and Gramps really did throw them out in the end."

"Charles did seem pretty certain," Nora said, immediately losing hope again. It had always been a long shot, she reminded herself. Which brought them right back to the drawing board. Again. And Nora had never been particularly good at drawing. She took after her father in that regard. She looked at the misshapen sketch of a dog, maybe, or a horse, possibly, or potentially a human in need of a chiropractor that hung above her father's old bed; just one of the many masterpieces of visual nonsense that clung to the walls on thumbtacks. She flopped back down on the bed, facing defeat for the umpteenth time that day, but as she collapsed onto the mattress, she noticed something she hadn't before. The soft breeze brought about by her falling picked up the edges of the dog / horse / twisty human and revealed lines of scribbles across the back of the page.

Nora leapt back up.

"Charlie," she said, staring at the paper. This time she scrambled onto the bed and pulled herself to her feet on the mattress, plucking the drawing off the wall with a rip. She flipped it over. The blue pen scrawls were as recognizable to her as the art style of the creature on the other side. This was her father's handwriting; messy and impatient and too slow for his tumbling thoughts. "Charlie," she called again.

The bed squeaked and the mattress shifted as Charlie clambered up beside her. "What's up?"

Without a word, Nora handed her brother the letter. Charlie barely had to glance at it before he understood exactly what he was looking at. It was the same handwriting that had filled all their birthday cards and school lunch Post-it notes and letters from the tooth fairy. The twins knew it better than they'd had the chance to know their father.

"This is from Dad," said Charlie, though they both knew he didn't have to say it.

Nora spun around on the bed, taking in the drawings scattered around the room. She guessed ten, twelve, fifteen, maybe? Some were tacked on top of others, just blocking the ones beneath from full view. Others were folded oddly, as if they might be makeshift envelopes for even more. The half-decipherable sketches of unsteady lines and comically bad proportions that had been staring down at the twins since they arrived in Virgo Bay, only half-noticed and only for a bit of loving ridicule, now seemed to hold the key to a door bolted for most of their lives. Nora felt the room spin with her, the doodles on the walls acknowledging her as she properly acknowledged them for the first time.

25

The twins hovered over the pile of letters on the bedroom floor, their father's handwriting staring up at them with eyes of faded ink. The walls around them stood bare, the room almost seeming to shrink in embarrassment at its naked state.

"So, where do we start?" asked Charlie.

"Just grab one, I guess," said Nora.

Charlie bent to the pile and plucked out one of the pages, then crossed to his bed and made himself comfortable as he read. Nora took a deep breath and did the same, perching herself on the edge of her dad's old mattress, her body buzzing too much to strive for anything more reclined.

Hey Charlie Horse,

Nora traced the letters with her fingertips, trying to mimic the way her father's pen would have moved across the page. She could almost see him hunched over his desk, scribbling to his brother with the same enthusiastic intensity he'd always worn across his face while working on a new project. The light indents left in the page by the pen nib were soft against Nora's fingers. The words were slanted, pulling up to the right. There was no care taken in the penmanship, letters running into one another in a way that said he had no one to impress, that he was writing to someone he loved, that all he cared about was what he was sharing rather than how he was sharing it. Nora knew that hand well. She read on.

Hope you're good. Did you ever convince Mom about instant coffee? I still think she'd like it if she gave it a chance.

The twins are growing so fast. Nora's already trying to walk, the little daredevil. We ended up in the ER with Charlie last week after he shoved a pinto bean up his nose. Hannah said he takes after his father.

I know you're sick of me saying it, but I think you'd love it here, out in the world. We took the kids to the zoo a few months ago, did you know about those?

Give everyone my best. Or the ones who want it, anyway. Hope the rest will get over things eventually.

Later,
Mars Bar

Nora snorted slightly at the sign-off. The thought of her stoic bear of a dad referring to himself as Mars Bar struck her as hilarious. Though she supposed she didn't know the same Martin

Bird that Charles or the rest of them knew. Still, there was something about that nickname that rang a bell. She'd heard it somewhere before, she just couldn't quite place where. It certainly wouldn't have been from her mother. She'd only ever called her husband Martin or bunny, which was not Nora's preference. Nora couldn't think of who else in her life would have known her dad when he was still Mars Bar, but someone must have for her to have overheard it. Would Richard or Ruby have called him that? They didn't seem the type. It must have been Charles or Patty, though she was pretty sure she'd have noticed. She shook her head. Of all the things she had to worry about, that seemed by far the least important.

"This one's from when Dad and Mom first met," said Charlie, interrupting her thoughts. "Did you know Mom had 'legs like a gazelle and a voice you should have to dial an eight hundred number to hear'?"

"He clearly hadn't heard her sing yet," said Nora. "Anything relevant?"

Charlie shook his head. "Nada, other than the fact that Dad and Charles had the world's lamest nicknames. You?"

"No, though it looks like I've got the first time you were in the ER for shoving something up your nose, and it wasn't the Lego piece. Or my earring."

He cocked his head at her.

"Pinto bean," said Nora.

"Nice."

They both went for new letters and resumed scouring. Most of the notes seemed to be generic life updates about Martin's job and family. Nora knew she should scan past this, but she couldn't help losing herself in the mundane details of the life she'd all but forgotten: childhood milestones, family trips, and ballet recitals all told through the voice of her father. She could practically hear it, rich and soothing like warm milk. The anger she'd felt towards him for leaving this place and its promise of safety faded as she read. Martin Bird might have made a mistake keeping his family from eternal life in Virgo Bay, but he loved them with the ferocity and determination of the ink that still clung to the paper in her hands all these years later. That was a fact impossible to miss. It was the thesis of every letter; it made every period read like an exclamation mark, turned every sentence into a declaration.

But then the tone changed. In the more recent letters, the carefree exuberance of a new father shifted into something darker. The content became less about life outside of Virgo Bay and more about the little world within it. Not because Martin Bird was homesick; quite the opposite. It seemed the more he saw of the world, and life, and death, the more he saw his hometown as the enemy.

Nora sank to the floor and sifted through the remaining letters until she found the very last one, dated less than a week before her parents died. She curled up right there on the rug and let her eyes wash over the words.

Hey Charlie Horse,

Maybe you're right. You usually are. Tell them I'm sorry for what I have to do. But I do have to do it. I know you'll understand, even if the others won't. Life was never meant to be forever.

Virgo Bay is the town that death forgot. But without death there can be no life. I've watched Mom and Dad and Grandpa succumb to the monotony of an existence built on fear of the alternative. At least you leave town from time to time, but the rest of them are trapped in purgatory.

Hannah says it's the kind of place that destroys people. I can't help but agree. We have this neighbor . . . I know I promised not to tell anyone about Virgo Bay when I left, but I trust him, we both do. Anyway, when I did, he told us he works for this organization—I can't get too into it, but they deal with this kind of thing. Death, and what comes after. Remember those files we found in the linen closet when we were kids? I think Mom worked for them too, or something similar. All I know is Virgo Bay is wrong. It shouldn't exist. And the people at this organization, they can do something about it. I'm going to them. You can't tell anyone about this. Promise me you'll hide this letter once you've read it. Burn it if that's not too dramatic. I don't want anyone to die, I just want you all to live.

Later,
Mars Bar

Nora sucked in what she realized was her first breath since she'd started reading the letter. The room seemed to shift slightly, as if she were on a chair collapsing in slow motion. The secrets revealed in that letter exploded around her like glass, the shards piercing her reality until it shattered too. Someone had told Dad about S.C.Y.T.H.E., and he was going to report the Blind Spot to them. And then he and Mom died, only days after this letter was sent. He'd begged Charles not to let anyone read it, but someone must have. The question was who.

At some point during Nora's time reading the letter, Jessica had made her way from Charlie's bed to the floor and was slowly waddling towards Nora. Nora stared at Jessica. Jessica stared at Nora. Then Nora's eyes widened to saucers in her head, and this time she was the one squawking.

"You!"

Jessica blinked at her. Nora scrambled to her feet.

"You're the one!"

Charlie sat up on his bed, eyeing Nora with the same look of utter bafflement as the parrot. Nora's head was spinning. She needed revelations to hit her one at a time. This was frankly excessive.

"Fucking bird," she hollered at Charlie.

"You're a Bird too," said Charlie.

"No, *your bird*. Look." Nora shoved the letter she was holding into her brother's face and pointed to the sign-off. "Mars Bar—have you ever heard anyone call Dad that before?"

"No," said Charlie, still furrowing his brows.

"No," said Nora. "Well, I have. I just couldn't remember who'd said it. But it was her. It was Jessica."

"Jessica called Dad 'Mars Bar'?"

"Yes," Nora practically shouted. "And a neighbor told him about S.C.Y.T.H.E! And Dad wanted to report the town to them!"

"Huh," said Charlie. Then: "Did you get into my stash?"

Nora groaned and waggled the letter at him again, this time indicating he should actually read the whole thing. She waited until at last Charlie poked his head above it. His expression was enough to tell her he'd read the same words she had.

"Well, fuck."

"Yep," Nora agreed. "Sounds like a good motive to me."

"I bet it was Rachelle's dad."

"What?"

"The neighbor. That guy was definitely hiding something."

"Yeah, a second family. Don't you remember? His wife ended up divorcing him and running off with the other woman."

"Oh yeah. That was cool. But what does any of that have to do with Jessica?"

Nora looked at the parrot in question. "I have no idea, but she knew Dad's nickname. That means she must have known someone from Virgo Bay before she came here with us. You said the note you found with her said something else, right? That Jessica could tell us what we needed to know, and something else. What was that something else?"

"Oh yeah," said Charlie. "Just that whoever wrote the note regretted everything. Kinda vague, honestly."

Charlie's words ping-ponged back and forth between the walls of Nora's skull. They fit together somehow, likely with something Nora already knew, but how? Then the pieces fell into place.

"Oliver said he regretted ever coming here," Nora said slowly. Her mind's eye walked back through that old stone house on the first day she'd gone inside. The doused fireplace, the rickety staircase, the creaking from upstairs, the nursery. *The nursery.* Between the bed and the crib there had been an old birdcage collecting dust. Or had it been? Could it have been recently in use? Housing a selectively talkative African gray parrot?

"Forest house," Jessica squawked.

"She keeps saying that," said Nora. "That has to mean Oliver, right?"

"I guess. But wouldn't he have *wanted* Dad to tell S.C.Y.T.H.E. about this place?"

"Exactly," said Nora. "But Dad failed. Maybe Oliver brought you Jessica hoping you'd be the one to succeed."

"Why me? I mean, you're the grim reaper's secretary, why wouldn't he give her to *you*? And how would he have gotten Jessica all the way to my house, anyway? He's like a living cobweb at this point."

"All excellent questions," said Nora. She sighed, knowing exactly how they'd have to get them answered. "We're going to have to ask him."

"Oh yeah, he loves that," said Charlie. "And so does Grandma. You really think we'll make it out there under her nose? You heard what she said, Patty and Phil are keeping tabs on us. She warned us away from the woods, remember? I thought you were supposed to be the smart one."

"So did I," said Nora. "But I think we're going to have to do something a bit stupid here."

"Into it. What's the plan?"

WHOEVER WAS IN CHARGE OF FILLING THE HOURGLASS OF TIME seemed to have accidentally filled it with thick mud instead of sand. The hours crept by at an aching pace, filled with the emptiness of waiting. The twins joined the family upstairs for dinner at a rather forceful request from Ruby. Neither ate for fear of what the food might contain, though their growling stomachs seemed open to the idea of poison as long as it came in the shape of a potato. After the kitchen was clean, Charlie and Nora excused themselves and returned to their room, where they waited in varying degrees of impatience as the night crawled on.

Charlie lay face up on his bed, babbling nonsense at Jessica, which Nora tried to tune out from across the room. Jessica, for her part, had been restless since the conversation about Oliver that afternoon. She couldn't seem to settle, bobbing up and down and shuffling back and forth in a constant dance of, what? Excitement? Fear? Nora had a queasy feeling they'd be finding out soon enough. She dug her father's last letter out of her pocket and buried herself in the ink, tuning out the avian love fest across from her. It was only a page long, but an entire reality existed on that page, one that forever altered her own.

"Right, Nor?"

Nora dropped the letter to her chest and lolled her head in Charlie's direction.

"Huh?"

"It's weird, right? That we grew up next to someone working for the same supersecret death factory you do."

"Excuse me, not a death factory," said Nora. "We don't kill people. We just help those who've died get to whatever comes next. Or, *they* do, I guess. I'm, like, mega-fired at this point. If we weren't in a Blind Spot, they'd have torn me a new one by now."

"That's not so bad," said Charlie.

Nora gave him a look that said, "I'd rather stick with the one I've got, thanks."

"I just mean, it's not like that was your dream job anyway, right?"

"Oh right, you know me that well, do you?"

Charlie shrugged.

"It actually was my dream job, thanks very much," Nora said. "Being that close to death meant I could learn how to avoid it. How do you think I've managed to save your ass so many times?"

"I mean, sure," said Charlie, "it made your neuroses into a superpower, which is pretty cool and all, but it wasn't your *dream* job. It was your safe job, right? It was comfy cozy by the sound of it. But you always wanted to be an architect."

"Charlie, I'm not going to be an architect."

"Why not?"

"Because—"

"Because it's too risky," Charlie finished before she could.

"Fuck you," said Nora. "And no, it's not weird that we had a neighbor who worked for S.C.Y.T.H.E. It's a big company. What's weird is that he was willing to risk his job by telling Dad what he did. He must've really wanted to help, which meant they must've been close, but we can't even be sure who it was. That's how little we had the chance to get to know our own parents. I wish I knew so much more about them. They both had a whole life we barely got to see, and the more I learn about them, the more it feels like they were strangers."

"That's crazy," said Charlie, as if that could possibly help the tears pricking at the backs of Nora's eyes.

"What's crazy?" Nora practically spat.

"The strangers thing. We knew them. I mean, not all of them, duh. You can never know all of a person. We didn't know Martin Bird and Hannah Stein. And we definitely didn't know Mars Bar, thank god. But we knew Mom and Dad, right? Like, we knew Dad couldn't draw for shit, and made really corny jokes, and would always give us shoulder rides even when we were definitely too heavy for them. And Mom knew every word to *The Phantom of the Opera* even though she said she hated it, and she made up the best bedtime stories that almost always involved a character farting right when *she* had to. That was Mom and Dad."

Nora felt a hot tear land on her cheek in spite of herself. "Maybe you are the smart one after all," she said in a small voice.

"That's what I've been saying all this time," said Charlie. "Glad you're finally catching on."

MIDNIGHT ROLLED IN ON WOBBLY WHEELS, UNSTEADY AND SQUEAK-ing. This directly corresponded with Nora's state of mind. The footsteps emanating from the floor above had ceased hours ago, but Nora wanted to play it safe. She always wanted to play it safe.

The twins crept upstairs, leaving as little noise in their wake as they could manage. Charlie hefted his duffel bag on his shoulder, which made silently scooting out the back door a feat accomplished only by bodily contortions and a concerted effort to suck in his midsection.

Outside, the darkness was near absolute. Even the stars piercing the ceiling of black seemed to be shining less. This was good, Nora reminded herself as she locked eyes with the dark web of trees across the path. This was what she wanted. They crept through the darkest pools they could find, avoiding any hint of light that could touch them. Even if Patty or Phil were playing lookout, it would take some proper infrared spy tools to see the twins that night.

They made it into the woods in time for the eruption of a piercing shriek. Nora leapt back, nearly tripping over a twisted root. Charlie unzipped his duffel and Jessica's little gray head poked out to greet them.

"Fuck," said Nora.

"Fuck," Jessica squawked.

"Sorry," said Charlie.

"It's fine," said Nora.

"Not you." Charlie scooped the bird out of the bag and placed her on his shoulder. "You don't like the dark, do you, baby?"

Nora sucked her teeth. "Can we carry on, please? I don't like the dark much either."

They continued their trek, navigating half from memory and half by clawing their way from tree to tree.

"You think Jessica remembers this place?" asked Charlie.

"I don't know," Nora whispered back. Making any sound in that still wilderness felt wrong somehow. "Why don't you ask her?"

"Forest house," the bird answered without being asked.

"Forest house," Nora repeated. And Jessica was right. Just ahead of them, through the trees and the darkness, was the stone house in the woods. The twins exchanged a glance and headed for the door. It was locked again. Ruby said Oliver didn't want the twins to visit, but Nora couldn't help but wonder if it was the others who didn't want these visits taking place. If Oliver was caught in the middle and too afraid to say so.

As Nora lifted her fist to start banging on the door, she felt a flurry of wings at her side. Jessica took off from Charlie's shoulder and flew towards the back of the house, where she fluttered up to the nursery window. She hovered there, pecking at the glass with her beak as Nora and Charlie rounded the house behind her.

"What the hell is she doing?" Nora hissed.

"Beats me," said Charlie. "But if she's from here, maybe she's trying to go home."

The bird kept pecking at the window until it lifted open enough for her to get inside. In her place came a head topped by a shock of white hair. Oliver looked down at the twins with an unreadable expression. Nora could see anger in there, and annoyance, but there was something else. Something that scared her.

"You'd better get in here," the old man wheezed down at them.

Charlie and Nora trudged back to the front door just in time to hear it unbolt. Nora pushed it open and stepped inside. A lit candle flickered from its pewter holder in Oliver's hand, giving off an otherworldly glow. It was like a moment out of time. Which, Nora reasoned, so was Oliver in his way.

Jessica flew down from upstairs and perched herself on one of the old man's hunched shoulders. He tried to swat her off but relented as the parrot started rubbing her head against his chin.

"She's yours," Charlie said, half in awe and half-disappointed.

"She's no such thing," said Oliver, offended. "She was my children's, and then their children's. The thing just likes me because I used to share my hazelnuts. How'd you end up with her?"

"We came to ask you the same thing," said Nora.

"More questions," said Oliver. "Questions at midnight. Delightful. I suppose you want to sit down."

They each resumed what had become their usual seats by the fireplace: Oliver in his rocking chair, Nora in the chair across from him, Charlie on the floor. The fire was long dead, the room heavy with damp and must.

"You shouldn't be here," said Oliver by way of starting the conversation.

"We keep hearing that," said Nora.

"You should listen."

"We keep hearing that too," said Charlie.

"But you won't, of course." Oliver shook his head. "Because you're Martin's children."

"You said Dad was a bold one," said Nora. "Now I understand why. You knew he was going to S.C.Y.T.H.E. about the Blind Spot, didn't you." It was more a statement than a question.

A flicker of surprise appeared in the old man's dark eyes, his body jolting slightly. Nora watched him running though the options in his head. What to tell them, how much to tell them, if there was a point in holding anything back now.

"I knew," he said at last.

"It's what you wanted," Nora said. "But no one else did, right? It would mean putting Virgo Bay on Death's map. It would mean the town would have to face the same mortality as everyone else. And why the hell would anyone want that?"

"Because," Oliver said, hauling himself to his feet, Jessica wobbling on his shoulder. "A place like this, it's cursed. Oh, you'll think it's blessed at first, and by the time you realize the truth it's too late. What's the point of a life eternal if people have to die for it?"

"You're talking about Mom and Dad, right?" said Charlie.

"You know who killed them," said Nora.

"No," said Oliver, lowering himself back into his chair. "And that is another curse. I know their lives were taken by someone in this town, someone *in my family*, but Patty refuses to tell me who. She says the truth would destroy me, as if the act itself hasn't done that already. She says it's better for me to never know. That if I thought it could be any of them, then I would have no choice but to go on loving them all equally. In truth all it's done is make me loathe the lot of them. Gluttons for existence, like pigs rooting around for any scrap of trash in their sties without knowing or caring what real food tastes like."

Patty. So Patty was at the center of everything. She was withholding the full story from the twins and keeping Oliver in the dark as well. And by being the birdie in his ear, Patty was controlling the narrative. Especially when Oliver's only other visitor, Phil, was so clearly in Patty's pocket. But there was one more piece to the puzzle Nora kept forgetting, kept pushing to the back of her mind despite herself.

"Did you know that Ruby was on the run from a soul collection agency?" said Nora.

"A what?" said Oliver.

"Richard never told you what Ruby did before coming here?"

Oliver shook his head. "She was a kid when she came here; even younger than you. I just assumed she was a student like Richard. Never occurred to me to ask."

Everything suddenly clicked together. If Martin reported the town, Ruby would be at R.C.M.P.'s mercy again. And after decades in hiding, the thought of facing their wrath and her own imminent death—after years of postponing it—could have made her desperate. Nora relayed this to the others as quickly as she could.

"Hmm." Oliver shifted in his chair. "She always was something of an enigma, our Ruby. When Richard first brought her home I tried my best, gave her nothing but kindness, but she never warmed up, never dropped her guard. I suppose this could be the reason why."

The thought sent a tendril of chills crawling down Nora's

neck. She and Charlie had been sleeping only a few floors below Ruby all these nights. They'd shared meals, conversation, time. She was their *grandmother*. Their father's *mom*. And yet, it all added up too well to be a coincidence. She had the most to lose if Martin followed through with his plans. And of course Patty would help her mother. What lengths would Nora have gone to to save her own parents' lives?

What she didn't understand was Oliver. He knew. All this time he knew what had happened, and instead of doing anything about it he barricaded himself away from the world and allowed the family's secrets to fester. So why had he picked this little sliver of time to set the wheels back in motion?

"Why now?" she asked at last. "Why dredge it all back up now?"

"I don't understand the question," said Oliver.

"This all happened almost twenty years ago. You had twenty years to do something about it, to go to S.C.Y.T.H.E. or at least figure out who was to blame. Why bring Jessica to Charlie now, after all this time?"

The look on Oliver's face was one of genuine bafflement, tinged with a hint of offense. "What are you talking about? Who's Jessica?"

Nora indicated the bird on Oliver's shoulder. "You thought that Jessica would tell us what really happened to Mom and Dad, that's why you left her and the note at Charlie's."

Oliver studied the bird in question, his expression still bewildered. "I didn't leave her anywhere. And by the way, her name is Silver. *Jessica*. Like she's some kind of Hollywood starlet. Honestly."

"You didn't leave her at Charlie's?" Nora repeated.

"Of course not. I've not been out of Virgo Bay since we settled here. I don't even drive. How on earth do you expect me to track down two youths in another country?"

"Google Maps?" Charlie offered.

This drew an expression on Oliver's withered face that somehow managed to surpass bewilderment and end up somewhere around dismay.

"Or not," Charlie muttered.

"But if it wasn't you," Nora began. She was getting a little sick of being the one to have all the earth-shattering realizations, but she could feel another one coming on. Who in Virgo Bay had a car? Who often used it to go out of town? Who was brave enough to travel away from the safety of the Blind Spot? Who also had a birdcage, much cleaner and more recently used, in his home? Who would want the truth known about what happened to Martin Bird?

"Charles," she said at last.

"What about him?" asked Oliver.

"He must have been the one who left Jessic—Silver with Charlie. He wanted us to know the truth, for our dad's sake. They were close, even after Dad left. Charles never destroyed Dad's letter about going to S.C.Y.T.H.E. Ruby must have found it and did the only thing she could to stop Dad. And Charles had to live with that all these years. So he brought us Jessica, and she brought us home."

"Charles," squawked Jessica. Or Silver, Nora supposed, though she had no intention of calling her that again.

"And what do you intend to do about it?" asked Oliver.

"I don't know," said Nora. "But we have to do *something* or Ruby's going to kill Charlie."

"You've lost me again."

Nora took a deep breath. "I need you to keep a very open mind," she said. Then, as best she could without sounding like she was in need of a padded room, Nora explained the situation: her role at S.C.Y.T.H.E., finding Charlie's file, the world's worst road trip to keep him safe, the attempts on his life since they'd arrived in Virgo Bay. Oliver listened intently, saying nothing, his head bobbing almost as frequently as Jessica's. He seemed to take it all in stride, the revelations obviously less jarring to a century-old man who'd discovered immortality. When Nora finally finished speaking, Oliver's hands held firm to the armrests of his rocking chair.

"I came here because losing my Alice broke me. I thought the only way to be whole again was to keep myself and my loved ones safe, forever. But that's not the way it works; it only led to more pain in the end." He sighed, deep and mournful. "You realize, of course, there's only one thing to be done here."

This, in Nora's mind, was a factually incorrect statement. There were several things to do here. Just off the top of her head, there was having Charles drive the twins far, far away from this town, or there was staying way out here in the woods and hoping it worked just as well for them as it did for Oliver, or there was always crying in the fetal position, which Nora was particularly adept at. But Oliver's soft jaw was set, and Nora found herself deferring to him on the subject.

"What do we do?"

"You do what your father tried to do long ago," said Oliver. "Turn the town in to the authorities. Stop another attempt at killing for the sake of eternal life. It's the only way to end this. It's the only way to keep your brother alive."

26

The twins and Jessica left Oliver's house in the early hours of the morning, the blue light weak as the rising sun battled a thick cloud cover for ownership of the sky. Out of the forest, they made their way back to the little red house mostly out of reflex, only realizing the mistake they'd made as the bay came into view. They couldn't go back inside. If Nora's theory was correct, that would be like walking into a bear's cave dressed as a salmon. But they had nowhere else to go.

The wind had begun to pick up, rain spitting down on them in small but enthusiastic droplets. Nora's feet stopped beneath her on the beach, her shoes submerged in cold, soggy sand. She tossed her hood over her head and wrapped her coat tighter around her torso. Between the wind, the hour, and their distance from the house, they could speak freely, though Nora could barely dredge up the energy to say a thing. Unfortunately, Charlie didn't have the same problem.

"All right, so how do we do this?" he asked. His hands were shoved in his pockets, his face as keen and sober as Nora had seen it. "Do you, like, have to say S.C.Y.T.H.E. in the mirror three times to summon them or something?"

"They're not Beetlejuice," said Nora. "It's a corporation. You have to call them. Like, on the phone."

"Okay, cool, cool. And you have their number?"

Nora nodded and turned away, walking even farther up the beach. Charlie stumbled after her, Jessica in his arms.

"Okay, so, like—"

"Charlie." Nora stopped moving again. Or at least she stopped walking. The rest of her kicked into overdrive. Her hands began to shake, her eyes suddenly stinging with entirely unwelcome tears. "I can't."

"Right, because of the no phone thing. So we borrow a car and get you to a phone."

"No." The first tear tore loose and traced the soft contour of Nora's cheek. "I can't do this. I can't turn this place in."

"What are you talking about?"

Nora tried to steady her breathing, but hearing her own ragged inhale only made it worse. "I'm not like you, Charlie."

Charlie gave her a look that said, "Duh," but Nora shook her head.

"No, I mean . . . this place. Charlie. I need it."

"I don't get it."

"No, you don't, that's just it. You don't know what it's like to be afraid. Mom and Dad died and it was like you suddenly became fearless. You did everything. And everyone. But I . . . I'm not built like that. Losing them, it just made me see what a horrifying world we live in. But this place, it means I don't have to be afraid. I know what Oliver said, but he's bitter and lonely. It doesn't have to be like that. I could make a life here, Charlie, forever. I would never have to worry again."

Charlie stared at her for a moment, and for the second time in their lives she couldn't read his look. "Wow," he said. "That's . . . that's what you think?"

"I—"

"Nor, I'm not fearless. I'm terrified. Like, all the time."

"What?"

"Yeah."

"But the way you live . . ."

"I'm not scared of death, Nora," he clarified. "There's no point. It's always gonna happen in the end. But after Mom and Dad died, I became terrified of not living. Like, as far as I knew, Mom and Dad were these nice but boring people who just kinda settled down in the suburbs and that was that. Then the chance to be anything else was taken from them. Honestly, learning they had all these secrets made me feel a lot better about that. But I promised myself when it all happened that I wouldn't let myself go to the grave with regrets, and the only thing I ever seemed to regret was not trying something."

Nora swallowed hard. The wind swept her hood off her head, her hair back from her face, the cold pulling a flush of pink to her cheeks and nose. Charlie was as ruddy as his sister by this point, his bleached hair falling into his eyes, weighed down by the rain.

"I'm not . . . I can't . . ."

"I know." Charlie put a hand on her shoulder. "But I think you're braver than you think you are."

She shook her head. "I feel it, all the time." Nora was sobbing now. She didn't know when she'd properly started and didn't much care. "It's like this weight. Being afraid. It's like I carry it around on my back, and, Charlie, it's so heavy. Like if I don't stay one step ahead of life, it's going to catch up and take everything from me. Mom, Dad, Bubbie, you."

"But, Nor," said Charlie. "Then you're letting it take *you* instead."

Nora felt her feet sink deeper, the wet sand gripping her like quicksand. She could feel herself being swallowed as much by Charlie's words as by the hungry earth. He was right, which always came as a shock when it happened. She had spent so long trying to protect the lives of those around her, including her own, that she'd all but stopped living. In a sense, she had sacrificed life in exchange for existence.

Fuck. Maybe Charlie *was* the smart one.

"I have to do this, don't I?" Even as she said it, she knew it was true. Either live forever knowing she'd let her brother die, or save Charlie and return to the life she knew and feared and never properly gave a chance. That's what it boiled down to. Those were her only options now. "I have to do this."

Charlie smiled at her. "Yeah, you do."

Nora nodded. "We'll go to Charles's. He's the one who brought us here, the least he can do is give us a ride out."

"And then we call the Ghostbusters?"

Nora just rolled her eyes, but her insides twisted slightly at the thought of that call. Not only was she about to destroy the one place she knew Death couldn't touch, she had to call her old workplace to do it. The same workplace she'd been in hiding from for days. The same one that would be only too happy to punish her for taking Charlie's file. It was like sending yourself to detention, only much, much worse.

"God. It's all too much," she said. "I just want to scream."

"Okay," said Charlie. "Go for it."

"What?"

"Scream."

Nora looked around at the desolate beach, the rolling ocean merging into the heavy sky.

"Charlie, I'm not going to scream."

"Suit yourself," said Charlie. Then he turned to face the sea, took an exaggerated inhale, and shouted, "FUCK!"

"Charlie!" Nora shushed.

Charlie gave her a look that said, "What?"

Nora let the rain pummel her cheeks, blending with her tears. She faced the endless gray and squared her shoulders. "FUCK!" The sensation of such complete, feral abandon made her giggle. It shouldn't have, but the laughter bubbled up her throat, completely unbidden, and erupted in a girlish squeal, catching both of them off guard.

Charlie laughed right back. "What the hell was that? Did you snort?"

"Maybe," said Nora. She turned back to the sea and shouted again. "FUUUUCK!"

"FUCK!" Charlie joined.

"Fuck!" Jessica squawked.

This sent Nora into hysterics. She doubled over, her tears now exclusively from the laughter pouring out of her. "Fuck," she wheezed. She gathered herself enough to stand upright and undid her jacket so it flapped out behind her like a cape. A gust whipped at her, ready to carry her away, and she was almost willing to let it. She felt so light she was fairly certain she could fly. Her arms opened to the wind. "I AM NORA BIRD AND I'M SICK OF THIS SHIT," she screamed. Jessica flapped over and perched on her shoulder as Charlie stepped beside her. She could feel their warmth against the cold of the infant day, of loneliness, of life. An army of three against the world. Nora staggered through another gust. "I AM NORA BIRD AND I DON'T WANT TO BE AFRAID!" Jessica hopped up and down on her shoulder now, spurring her on. "I AM NORA BIRD AND I WANT TO LIVE!"

"I'm afraid you're making that very difficult for yourself, dear," said a sharp voice from just behind her. Nora whipped around to find Ruby and Richard standing there, faces pulled into caricatures of themselves. Her heart shot into rapid motion between her ribs.

"They've got Silver," Richard mumbled, tipping his head at Jessica. "Which means . . ."

"We'd wondered where she'd gotten off to," said Ruby. "You'd best give her here."

Nora pulled the parrot off her shoulder and instinctively clutched her tightly to her chest.

"You went out in the woods again last night," Ruby said. "After we warned you not to."

"They know too much," Richard said to Ruby as though the twins weren't there.

"We have to do something about them," said Ruby.

Nora's muscles were rigid. She had saved her brother from fires, lawn mowers, car accidents, and knives. Her gut was primed for tracking his safety, and right now it was signaling to her like a fire alarm.

"You took Mom and Dad away from me. I won't let you take Charlie too." She looked over at her brother and shouted, "Run."

Without a moment's hesitation, they took off down the beach and onto the grass, stumbling over their own harried feet as they raced. Nora led them onto the dirt path and into the heart of the strange little town, already out of breath but unwilling to break stride. Charlie, for his part, kept a few paces behind, his own breathing even more labored.

Behind them, Richard and Ruby maintained a pace no octogenarian had the right to keep, but still they lagged behind enough for the twins to gain a growing distance from them. As they turned the corner towards the town center, Richard and Ruby disappeared from sight.

Nora and Charlie stumbled down the main street of Virgo Bay, passing the still-shuttered general store and curtain-drawn houses as they ran. Across from the little church with no graves sat Charles's house, a beacon in the haze of panic, fear, and the early-morning light.

They bolted up the squat steps to the perpetually unlocked front door and spilled in. As soon as they were both inside, Nora slammed the door shut and twisted a lock that had clearly gone its whole life never serving its purpose. Inside, the house was dim; misty tendrils of weak dawn light playing in the gaps of closed shutters.

"Charles," Nora whispered into the space, the stillness echoing her voice back to her. Jessica grew restless in her arms, squirming for liberation. Nora obliged without much thought, her focus locked on the closed bedroom door at the other end of the little house. A clang of metal distracted her. She looked over to the source of the noise and saw Jessica perched on top of the metal birdcage Nora had noticed during her first visit. She was right; Jessica had brought the twins home. Nora called for Charles again.

This time the bedroom door opened and a very groggy Charles emerged, still in his blue-striped pajama set.

"Heavens, is everything all right?" he said through a yawn.

"We need your help," Nora said. From beyond the kitchen window she could see Richard and Ruby racing down the road, heading in the direction of Patty's house. Soon it would be too late for them to get away. Soon everyone involved in this sordid plot would be after them. "We're going to do what Dad tried to do," she continued quickly. "What you brought us here for."

Charles stopped yawning and straightened. "You are?"

Nora nodded, her eyes flicking between him and Patty's house. Charles followed her gaze. "Well, then, we ought to hurry," he said. "Or else I fear you'll no longer have a chance."

He led them back into the front hall, shoving his bare feet into a pair of sleek boots and tossing a coat over his pajamas. He grabbed the car keys from where they sat in the bowl by the door and held an arm out for Jessica, who took it with the swiftness of a bird who'd done so many times before.

They piled out of the house and raced to the driveway. "There's a pay phone at a gas station a few miles out of town," said Charles as he made his way over to the driver's-side door. Nora hopped into the passenger seat and Charlie climbed in behind them. Just as they were about to pull out of the driveway, Patty appeared at the front of the van, her hands on the hood. She gave a sharp look to Charles, then shifted her attention to the twins.

"Stop this. You need to come out of there," she shouted into the van. "Right now."

Nora just shook her head, unable to speak. Richard and Ruby were making their way over to the driveway, their faces as set and severe as their daughter's. From the rearview mirror, Nora could see the silhouette of someone with a rifle racing onto the scene.

Phil. She recognized the rugged shoulders immediately. They were all closing in around the van, trapping them like prey rounded up to be slaughtered. Nora's breath caught in her throat, her face tingling from the restricted oxygen supply. She could feel herself slipping, her fear gripping her, its hands around her neck, squeezing.

"Hey, Uncle Chuck," said Charlie from the back seat. "Any way you can swerve onto the grass and get us out of here?"

Charles looked across his perfectly manicured lawn with consideration, then seemed to come to a resolution.

"Nora," Patty called from the driveway. "Please. You don't know what you're doing. Charles!"

Charles set the van into drive and plowed onto the lawn, tires pulling up clumps of grass and mud as he peeled out, off his property and onto the grassy path out of town. Nora watched the crowd scramble in the rearview. Phil inexplicably seemed to be trying to chase after them, rifle raised. Richard and Ruby stared at each other with something heavy settling between them. Patty, meanwhile, had turned and begun to run in the opposite direction for reasons that didn't matter now. All that mattered was that they were on the road, or what passed for a road in this forgotten place. And soon this would all be over.

27

'm happy you kids came to me," Charles said as they reached the rickety old Virgo Bay welcome sign. "It's what Martin would have wanted. He was crazy about you kids, you know. Though I suppose you do know. You must have found the letters."

Nora nodded. "They were hanging up in your old room with Dad's sketches all over them."

A small smile brushed Charles's lips at this. "Martin never could get a handle on proportions. He'd always doodle something on the front of every note just to make me laugh. That was your father. I guess Mom and Dad must have hung them up after he died. I was so sure they'd have gotten rid of them."

"I don't get why Ruby would even want to display them after what she did," Nora said, her voice tight.

"People do difficult things when their backs are against the wall, I suppose," Charles said.

"And you knew, all this time?"

Charles shook his head. "I've been putting the pieces together very slowly, I'm afraid. I didn't know anything for certain until you confirmed it just now."

They passed the carcass of Nora's Honda Civic, though to her surprise it appeared some work had actually been done on it. The hood and bumper looked almost like they belonged to a car again, and the windshield had been fully removed, a tarp laid across it until a new one could take its place. Nora blinked as it passed. Why on earth would Phil waste his time working on her car if he was trying to cause her and Charlie harm? It was an odd move. She supposed he could have intended to keep the Civic for himself. That seemed like something a murderer's accomplice might do, though she had to admit she didn't know many offhand.

The road bent around, sending them deeper into the tunnel of boulders and trees. They should be back in civilization soon; the gas station and its pay phone must be coming up. She felt through the pockets of her pants and jacket, suddenly frantic at the realization that she didn't have any coins on her, and even if she did have one tucked away somewhere, it would be American. She didn't think a Canadian pay phone would take too kindly to that.

"Do you have change?" she asked her uncle, panic rising. Without money there was no way she could make the call she needed to make. The call Charlie needed her to make. She didn't even have her purse, which meant she couldn't get change from any cash she may have had on hand.

Charles kept his eyes on the road, but one hand left the wheel and fidgeted around in an empty cup holder between them. Nora could hear the telltale sound of coins jangling together. She exhaled her worry.

"I like to prepare for any eventuality," Charles said with a smile.

"Me too," said Nora. "Usually. Things have just been . . . unusual lately."

Charles's smile broadened. "It's nice to see you take after your old uncle. Your dad's in there too, of course, but I never thought I'd get to see myself in someone else like that. I never had a family, you know. Not the way Martin did. And that's fine, that was my choice. I chose Virgo Bay instead and I don't regret it. But still, I must admit, it's nice to find someone who sees the world as I do."

Now Nora smiled too. She couldn't help herself. Despite the utter terror of the day, and the days leading up to it, there was something calming in the sense of familiarity they shared. Charlie had never been like her, and Bubbie, though Nora loved her dearly, was from such a different generation, meaning they never had much in common. She knew she shared at least a few basic traits with her parents, but they were gone so soon she never really had the chance to experience that in person. But now, sitting there in the car next to her father's brother, and seeing so much of herself reflected back, she couldn't help but feel a little warmer, a little more at home. This, she thought, was what family felt like.

The boulders framing the van began to shrink, the sea suddenly undulating into view. It was rough that morning, a chaotic game of leapfrogging waves playing across its surface. Nora watched them roll, crashing recklessly into the rocky cliffs below. It was a sight that would have made her queasy only a few days ago; the thought of those salty fingers pulling her down into the hidden depths below, the restless wind, the spattering rain, even the slick road beneath the van's tires. But somehow it was all too familiar now to cause her much concern. She had grown accustomed to the turbulent life at the edge of the world, and part of her still imagined what a future here could look like, quiet and eternal.

"Will you miss it?" Nora asked.

"Virgo Bay?" said Charles. "It'll still be there. Just different than before."

A pair of booted feet appeared on the armrest between the two front seats, one ankle crossing over the other. Charlie stretched out, leaning back against his headrest. "Nora's not a fan of change," he said.

"That's rich coming from someone who'll go a weekend without changing their underwear," said Nora.

"I don't love change myself," Charles admitted. "If I had my way, everything would always be as it always was. But in the end, I guess everything changes. I know I have over the years."

Nora pulled at a crease in her pant leg. She wasn't quite so quick to admit it, but when she looked back at who she was only a few short days ago, there was no denying she had changed as well since coming to Virgo Bay. A previous Nora never would have risked her life as many times as this new Nora had; never would have had the guts to do what she was about to do. She couldn't decide which Nora she liked better, but she supposed she had no choice but to give the new version a chance.

"We're almost there." Charles indicated the road ahead, which seemed to branch off towards a paved driveway. The gas station came into view as they rounded the corner, its sign faded into illegible beige. The pumps were from a lost era, red paint worn to an uneven pink. Charles turned in to the driveway and parked near one of the run-down filling stations. From the looks of it, no one had filled much of anything here for years. Nora glanced around, clocking the pay phone near an outhouse around the side. This was it, then. One quick phone call and the Blind Spot of Virgo Bay would be erased. S.C.Y.T.H.E. would put it on the map, and Death would find it. People would die, Collections Agents—grim reapers—would come for their souls, and Nora would face repercussions from S.C.Y.T.H.E.

And Charlie would live.

With no one trying to murder him any longer, his case file would be updated, and he would live. Nora undid her seat belt.

"You kids go ahead," said Charles. "I'll be along in a moment."

The twins and the parrot left the van and hurried over to the pay phone.

"I hate phone calls," said Nora as they walked.

"Especially work calls when you know you're already in trouble," Charlie commiserated.

"Especially when those calls end in the destruction of immortality," Nora added.

"Especially those."

She glanced up at the bird circling just above them. "What do you think it was that Charles wanted her to tell us?"

"Huh?"

"You said in the note he left with Jessica, Charles wrote that she could tell us what we deserved to know, but most of what she says is 'fuck,' and I hear enough of that from you."

"Does it matter at this point?" Charlie shrugged. "I mean, you did a pretty solid job solving my almost murder all by yourself."

"I guess," said Nora. "I just . . ." She watched as Jessica landed on the pay phone and fluffed up her feathers, her eyes boring into Nora with the intensity of a scream. "When we were driving here . . . the reason I drove off the road . . . I asked Jessica about her life before you, and she screamed."

"Weird," said Charlie.

"Weird," Nora agreed. She reached out for the pay phone receiver and paused. "You don't think she was there when it happened, do you?"

"What do you mean?"

"When Mom and Dad . . . Nothing. Probably nothing. It's . . ." She looked back at the parrot. "Jessi—Silver, do you remember anything about Martin? Martin Bird?"

Jessica's little chest swelled with a deep breath before her lungs erupted in a soul-rattling shriek.

"Heavens," came a voice from behind them.

The twins turned around to find Charles walking in their direction. They could barely hear his footsteps over the sound of Jessica's scream. She raced back and forth across her perch, the scream beginning to form words.

"No! No!" she shouted. "I trusted you!"

Nora could almost hear her father's voice coming out of the parrot's mouth. She dropped the receiver and stepped back, heart lodged somewhere in her esophagus as she listened to the sounds of her dad dying.

"Please! Don't do this! Please! Charles!"

With one final, eardrum-shattering scream, Jessica plummeted from the top of the pay phone, diving straight towards the concrete. She caught herself just before colliding with the ground, swooping back into the air and landing on the shoulder of the man whose name she'd just called out.

28

Case # 73588
Charles Ezra Bird
Age: 26
Cause of Death: Struck by Vehicle /
Choking / Car Accident / Murder

Over the years Nora had sorted hundreds of case files, each filled with fear and curiosity and banal paperwork. Each etched on Nora's memory like a scar, a reminder of what not to do so she wouldn't end up in the next file. But Charlie's file was different. Charlie's file held only one thing: a promise that Nora couldn't hide from Death anymore. No, she would have to face it. And for the sake of her brother, she would have to win.

NORA FOLLOWED JESSICA'S MACABRE DANCE IN A DAZE, HER FOCUS finally, dizzily, landing on Charles just as Jessica did. Charlie had also spun to face their uncle, his face crumpled in the same shock and heartbreak that ran like a blade through Nora.

"You?" was all she could muster.

Charles shoved his hands sheepishly into his coat pockets. Nora thought she saw him blush, as if he were a teenager who'd just been caught shoplifting instead of a man who'd murdered his own brother.

"He didn't give me a choice," Charles said, almost meekly. "I tried to reason with him, but you know your father."

"No," said Charlie, more severely than Nora had ever heard him. "We don't. We never got the chance."

"He was stubborn," Charles continued. "When old Mars Bar got an idea in his head, he wouldn't let it go. He couldn't. He was like a man possessed."

"You tried to talk him out of going to S.C.Y.T.H.E.," said Nora. Her mouth felt as though it were filled with cotton. Her hands tingled. Beyond that, though, she wasn't entirely sure she was still in her body at all now.

"He wouldn't listen," Charles sniffed, as if he was about to cry. As if he had any right to be the one about to cry. "I swear I tried. I took them out to a nice dinner, him and Hannah, best restaurant I could afford. I was on one of my supply runs, it seemed like the perfect opportunity to talk things out, brother to brother. Letters can only do so much. But he said Virgo Bay wasn't right. It shouldn't exist. He had no choice. No choice, can you believe that? I told him if he did it, if he turned us in, it would cost us everything. Grandpa Oliver would die of old age. Mom would die of that long-ago heart attack, or worse once the authorities got a hold of her. And eventually, the rest of us would die too. But did he listen? No. Of course not. He scoffed at me. Said people die. That they had to die. Well, he was right about that."

Nora found herself leaning heavily against the pay phone for support, her limbs weak, her neck suddenly a dry noodle under the weight of her spinning head.

"You understand, of course," Charles continued, his attention squarely on his niece. "I know you do. We're the same, you and I. I've seen it in you for as long as you've been here. You understand things the way I do, the way Grandpa did before he went mad. Charlie, now, he's like your father. Stubborn. A wild card. I knew as soon as I was found out, as soon as Silver gave me away, I couldn't possibly trust him to understand the sacrifices it takes to keep death at bay. No, I couldn't risk him ruining everything. But you—you're just like me. You know what it's like. Sometimes you have to do things you don't want to do to keep yourself safe. It's unfortunate, but the best things in life will always come with a cost. And eternal life? Nora, that's priceless. I know you feel it too."

Nora could feel herself losing her grip on the pay phone and slipping slowly towards the pavement. She wanted to argue, but her tongue wouldn't let her. It knew it would only make her a liar. Because at the end of the day, he was right. She'd wanted what he had. From the moment she'd found out about the Blind Spot, she couldn't shake that want. It only seemed to grow.

"Your father never understood. It's why he left. And Patty . . . when she found out what had happened, she changed. Started spending more time with Oliver and buying into his ravings. She's the one who tried to bring the town down this time. Waited for me to leave on my supply run and brought Silver to Charlie behind my back. That bird knows all my secrets, and Patty figured it was only a matter of time before she revealed them. She was always too cowardly to do it herself. She even keeps Grandpa

Oliver in the dark. And yet, that coward still betrayed me. Well, you of all people must know how hard it is to count on your own siblings. But, Nora"—Charles's frustration turned to something soft and tantalizing—"this life, this safety we have here, it can be yours too. Forever. It's easy, really. All you have to do is leave the past in the past. The past is an easy place to get lost in, remember? Why not think about your future instead."

Nora's eyes flicked over to her brother.

"What about Charlie?"

"What about him?"

"You tried to kill him."

Charles shook his head. "I don't want to hurt anyone, Nora, I never did. I just needed to protect myself, my life."

"So you'll let Charlie live?"

"If he'll leave well enough alone, I see no reason why we can't all be one big happy family."

"Uh, because you murdered our parents," Charlie spat.

Nora clutched her temples, trying to stop the world from spinning.

"You could stay here, Nora," Charles continued. "We both know you want to."

A tear materialized on Nora's cheek. She hadn't felt it fall. How could she argue with Charles when what he said was true?

He extended a hand to her. "Here. It's okay. We'll go back to Virgo Bay and you can have the life you've always dreamed of. There's nothing to be afraid of anymore."

Nothing to be afraid of. The thought filled her with warmth like hot soup on a cold day. But the promise came from the man who'd started her cycle of fear to begin with. She finally felt herself land, the cold of the pavement seeping in through the bottom of her pants, though she barely noticed it. She wanted nothing more than to be back at the bay, screaming into the angry sea. No, what she really wanted was to go back to the moments before she ever found Charlie's file, to live there forever. No, what she really wanted was a life where Mom and Dad were never stolen from her. No, she no longer knew what she wanted. It was all a blur of promise and loss and pain and hope and she couldn't sift through any of it.

"Nora," came Charles's voice again, soft and saccharine. "Come along now. It's okay. I know how to make this all better. After all, you're just like me."

This drew a snort from somewhere above her. She looked up to find Charlie shaking his fluffy head. "Bullshit," he said.

"He's right," said Nora, voice barely a whisper.

"Bullshit," Charlie said again. "You're not going with him." It wasn't a demand, it was an observation.

"Charlie, I can't do this. You have too much faith in me."

"Bullshit," said Charlie again.

"Bullshit," Jessica echoed.

"You're not like this nasal douchefuck," said Charlie. "He sacrificed his own brother to save his ass, while you've been out here risking your ass to save your brother. That's, like, the literal opposite of this guy. Don't let him get in your head, Nor. He's a weak little sweater-vest-wearing weasel. If he was in your shoes, I'd be dead ten times over by now. Hell, if he had his way, I still would be. Can you really live for eternity with the guy who killed our parents? Can you really let him get away with that, just to not have to worry about, like, getting struck by lightning or whatever? Nah, I don't think you can. Actually, fuck it, I know you can't. I know you better than you do, and definitely better than he does; all I have to do is look at you and I know exactly what you're thinking. And right now you're thinking you're going to make that goddamn call."

Nora's eyes flitted between Charles's extended hand and the phone receiver dangling just above her. There had never been a choice between them. Not really. Charlie might see her with the rose-colored glasses of a brother who had no one else, but he was right about one thing: just like she was always going to sacrifice everything to save her brother, she was always going to make that call. For all the fear that ruled her, no matter what Charles said, she was her father's daughter first, and Martin Bird was a stubborn fuck. Nora, it turned out, had inherited more from him than she'd realized.

She dragged herself back to her feet by her own power, grabbing the phone as she pulled herself upright.

"This is disappointing," said Charles, voice even. He drew his other hand from his coat pocket, a knife in his fist. Nora knew that knife. It was the same one she had seen inches from Charlie's head on their first night in Virgo Bay. Part of her still struggled to reconcile the mild-mannered uncle she knew with the person who'd been constantly on the verge of causing Charlie's death. Though she didn't have much time for reconciling now—Charles lunged towards the twins, knife raised and poised to strike.

29

The knife shone silver against the colorless day, its tip sharp and gleaming. Nora buried herself behind her arms, already imagining the defensive wounds in her autopsy report. A cacophony of squawks and beating wings erupted. When the knife blade didn't strike her, Nora lowered her arms to find Jessica accosting Charles in a flurry of scratching talons. Charles ducked, swatting her away, aiming his knife at the bird.

"Nora!" Charlie hollered amid the feathered frenzy. He held the phone to her. "Call. Now. Please."

Nora looked back at the scuffle. Jessica had taken to the air to avoid the striking weapon, Charles's scratched face aflame with rage as he refocused his attention on the twins.

"But—" Nora started. She couldn't let this be the moment Charlie died. Not after everything.

"You've saved me enough," said Charlie. "I'm returning the favor. Now, call." He lifted a broken piece of metal pipe from among the assorted trash on the ground and swung it in front of him as Charles barreled towards him.

Nora's shaking hands punched in the number and held the

receiver to her ear, wrapping the cord around her so she could keep herself facing the unfolding battle.

"Hello and thank you for calling Secure Collection, Yielding, and Transportation of Human Essences," said a robotic voice on the other end. "If you know the extension you're trying to reach, please dial it now. To speak to an operator, please press zero."

Nora stabbed the zero with her index finger as Charles's knife plunged through the thick fabric of Charlie's jacket into his shoulder.

"Charlie!" Nora screamed.

"I'm okay," came the reply from between gritted teeth as Charlie swatted at his uncle with the pipe.

"Hello, you have reached the central offices of S.C.Y.T.H.E., this is Pranav speaking."

"I . . ." Nora's voice wavered. "I'm calling to report a Blind Spot."

Charles advanced on Charlie again, knife slashing at the arm holding the metal pipe. Charlie's grip weakened, the pipe dropping from his hand. He swung at their uncle, a right hook landing across Charles's cheek, sending the older man staggering backwards. Nora held her breath as Charlie advanced, fist still at the ready, but before he had the chance for a second strike, Charles lashed out, his knife embedding itself directly into Charlie's chest. Charlie lurched back, knees buckling. With an apologetic look at Nora, Charlie collapsed to the ground, sprawling on his back, the blade protruding from a chest that heaved twice more before falling achingly, permanently, still.

"Hello? Ma'am?" came Pranav's voice from the other end of the phone, but Nora had already dropped the receiver, time seeming to slow around her. Charles stood over her brother, his face stiff and somber. He wrenched the blade from where it stood and turned to Nora.

"I must apologize," he said. "I told you I don't want to do any of this." With that, he charged at her, the raised knife bearing the blood of her brother. For a moment she wanted nothing more than to let it strike her. For the first time in her life it wasn't death she feared, it was a life alone. Or maybe that's what she'd truly feared all along. If Charlie was dead, then what was the point of anything? Why bother fighting?

But then her sense of self-preservation kicked in, the same sense that kept her from eating foods high in cholesterol or wearing makeup with carcinogenic ingredients. But this time it didn't tell her to run from the dangerous thing. It told her to run towards it. As the knife swooped on her, she charged forward, torso hinged, and rammed herself at full force into Charles's stomach. The assault sent them both into the air and down hard onto the pavement, the knife flying out of Charles's hand and skidding across the driveway. They both scrambled after it on hands and knees as the sound of tires crunching on pavement grumbled from behind them. Charles looked back at the sound, but Nora kept after the knife, crawling until her fingertips brushed the hilt. Up close, her brother's blood was thick. A wave of nausea washed over her, dizzying and sweaty.

Car doors opened and feet tapped and Nora ignored them all. Charles had caught up with her now, grabbing her by the ankles, dragging her towards him. She kicked, trying to force him to release his grip, but his fists held too firm. She swung the knife at him impotently as he pulled himself to his feet above her. He'd found Charlie's discarded metal pipe and raised it now, primed to strike it against Nora's head with all the strength he possessed.

Nora kicked his shin, his flinch buying her just enough time to roll out of striking range. She lunged at him, something new and powerful propelling her forward, but before the knife in her hand had a chance to connect with Charles's flesh, he swung the pipe, the metal colliding hard with Nora's ribs.

She sank to the pavement in spite of herself, the air ripped from her lungs by the blow. She gasped, choked, tried to refill her lungs through the pain. Charles's sleek boots filled her vision. She looked up to find him hovering over her, metal pipe primed for one final strike across her head. She could have screamed. She could have begged. She could have done whatever it took to live, just as she always had. But this time, she didn't. Through the throbbing in her ribs, the stinging in her lungs, the threat that faced her from above, Nora did something she had never done before. She laughed. At the situation, at her uncle, at Death. Quietly at first, the pain of the laughter nearly causing her to throw up, but once she'd fought through the nausea, the laughter came out in long, high bursts. It was all so ridiculous. This is what she'd always been afraid of. The thing she'd been running from her whole life amounted to nothing more than a pathetic little man in a sweater-vest. It was absurd. It was hilarious.

Her laughter seemed to catch Charles off guard, and for a moment he appeared frozen by it. Without a second thought, Nora sobered up and plunged the knife in her hand through one of Charles's sleek boots, embedding it with enough force to send him screaming. With that, she collapsed on the ground, her last shred of strength lost in the knife hilt. Nora knew what this meant; she was a sitting duck now, but somehow it didn't matter. She flinched, waiting for the final blow from the metal pipe, but it never came. Instead a blur of neutral fabric whirled past her, toppling Charles to the ground beside her. Nora looked over from where she lay to find her uncle grappling with Patty's petite form. More footsteps sounded, the altercation quickly interrupted by the sound of a gun's safety clicking.

Phil walked over, rifle in hand, the barrel aimed at Charles. "Patty, move," he ordered.

Patty obediently rolled away from her brother and over to Nora, carefully helping her back to her feet.

"Right, we're done here, got it?" Phil shouted down at Charles. "We've put up with your shit for long enough."

"My *shit*?" Charles raised his arms in response to the gun in his face, but his expression was all hurt and innocence. "Everything I've done, I've done for our family."

"Bullshit," spat Nora. She dragged herself the rest of the way up off the pavement, palms scraped and stinging, torso aflame. Every part of her trembled from grief and fear and pain and anger and other emotions she couldn't yet put a name to. "You did it for you."

She shambled back to the dangling phone receiver, praying Pranav was still on the line. This was all she had left to do. The politely professional voice filtered through the speakers in reply to her words. She described their location, the gas station built between nothing and eternity, then promptly hung up the phone as a flurry of questions tumbled down the line. There would be time to answer them later.

When she turned back around, she found Patty waiting just behind her, her face an apology. Nora wasn't ready to accept it. Charles was still on the ground, held at gunpoint. And Charlie . . .

Charlie was still there, too. Still sprawled on his back, limbs unnaturally akimbo. Eyes still shut. Chest still empty of oxygen.

Nora pushed past her aunt, stumbled past her cousin and her murderous uncle. None of them mattered. Her only real family was lying dead on the concrete. She was numb and feeling too much, a husk about to explode. She sank to the asphalt beside Charlie, knees hitting the pavement hard. The pain caused little more than a twitch.

Nora swept the springing threads of bleached hair off of her brother's brow, cupped his furry cheek in her hand. He was still warm, but that wouldn't last. Soon his body would stiffen and cool. The blood would leave his cheeks, his features would further slacken, and everything that made him Charlie would be an echo in his unmoving chest. A Collections Agent would arrive, and his soul would move on, and Nora would be truly alone.

For all she knew about death and what led to it and what came after, it always seemed to come as a surprise to her, the reality of it. How utterly unremarkable it was. How utterly, pointlessly final. But Charlie had lived. Nora knew that much for a fact. Now she would have to do the same, since he no longer could.

A sob escaped her, the reverberations drowned out by the bleat of sirens in the near distance. Unmarked black vans packed into the driveway, sleek and organized as ants. Others sailed past, racing towards Virgo Bay. S.C.Y.T.H.E. special forces leapt onto the pavement before the vehicles pulled to a stop, agents' boots heavy, the commotion rattling the earth. Somewhere behind her, Nora could hear Charles being apprehended by S.C.Y.T.H.E.'s team. She wouldn't have to worry about them doing the same to Charlie. Their uncle had taken his life for them.

Patty was beside her now, trying to lead her away. Nora couldn't grasp anything. Couldn't understand why she would ever be anywhere but here. When her efforts failed, Patty simply lowered herself to the ground and sat with Nora, saying nothing. There was nothing to say.

The leader of the task force approached Nora. She couldn't see them through her tears. Nora said things, some of them comprehensible, and eventually the team cleared out and she lost herself completely to the depths of her grief.

30

Three Months Later

The day was bright, which it had no business being. The sun sat comfortably nestled in a cloudless sky, the rich blue spilling into the sea, painting the bay in cartoonish primaries. It made the black fabric draped across Nora's waiflike form feel even more stark. The dress was Patty's, simple and elegant and only slightly ill-fitting. When her parents died, Bubbie had forced Nora into a dress with crinoline and she'd spent the whole funeral scratching at her legs. Today, she wanted to be comfortable.

The procession was small, which was exactly as it should have been. Nobody cried today. They'd already done enough of that. Once S.C.Y.T.H.E. had finally cleared out, after a drawn-out investigation, tears had flowed freely throughout Virgo Bay as the dust settled and reality eventually set in. This morning wasn't for crying, it was for saying a final goodbye.

The little church looked different as the mourners approached, the garden dug up, ready to fulfill its ultimate purpose as a graveyard for the first time. Nora's breath caught as she saw the earth peeled back, a hungry void in its place. She could still see Bubbie's coffin descending into the dirt where it would remain until there was nothing left of it or her or anything recognizable.

Patty looped an arm through Nora's, guiding her gently towards the church. They walked in silence, helming the procession. They hadn't bothered bringing in a priest to officiate the funeral. No religion in the world was equipped to understand what the people of Virgo Bay had experienced. Instead, Richard stood on the mound of upturned earth, ready to speak on behalf of the town.

As they crossed through the garden gate, Patty gave her niece a nod and they separated, finding their places among the small crowd. Patty gathered near Phil, Vic, Pickles, and the rest of the Birds Nora hardly knew. They were Patty's people, the ones her aunt knew how to be with in times of grief. Nora hovered under a nearby tree, at a distance from the funeral and the family. Richard spoke and the caskets were lowered.

She had never wanted to return to Virgo Bay after everything that happened. It was too painful. But for this, for today, she'd endure the pain. Jessica sailed overhead and came to land on her shoulder. Nora acknowledged the bird with a tip of the head, and together they watched the proceedings, a Bird and a bird at the edge of the world.

31

Less than twenty-four hours later, Nora was back on the doorstep of her home. She wasn't entirely sure she could even call it home yet; it was still mostly boxes and furniture and boxes doubling as furniture. She would need to unpack eventually, but she wasn't ready to just yet. She supposed she'd start feeling at home at some point. Maybe once she'd explored the neighborhood more. It wasn't really her scene from what she could tell, but the place could always surprise her. There were more bars and clubs than cafés, but after all this was a college town. She wasn't exactly the target demographic. She wouldn't be here forever. The architecture program was only two years long, and who knows, by the end she might actually find her place among the other postgrads.

She lowered Jessica's cage to the stoop and dug her key out of her purse, fiddling with the unfamiliar lock until she finally heard it click. Inside, she tossed her keys onto their designated hook and hung her coat on its own, flicking on the lights to illuminate bare white walls and the stack of boxes waiting for her by the living room door.

She could do this. She would do this.

Nora carted Jessica into the living room and opened the cage, letting the parrot fly free. Jessica took off, disappearing into the kitchen. Nora did her own version of making herself at home, sprawling out on the couch that sat on a diagonal across the room. At some point she needed to move that thing.

Footsteps padded in from the kitchen, and Nora pulled herself upright.

"You really need to branch out with your cheeses, Nor."

Charlie stood in the alcove between the kitchen and living room, Jessica settled comfortably on his shoulder.

"I left seven varieties in there," said Nora.

Charlie sat down beside her. "None are string," he argued.

That was a fair point.

"You do the grocery shopping next time, then."

"How was the world's most belated funeral?" Charlie pulled a hunk of Swiss out of his pocket and nibbled at the corner.

"Brutal," said Nora. "But nice. Oliver asked about you before he died, by the way. I think he was holding on to say one last goodbye. He called you a 'god-awful louse' for what you did, whatever that means. Though he agrees with me that you should look into becoming an actor."

"Hey, what choice did I have? It was either play dead or get stabbed again, and the shoulder was bad enough. Thank fuck those weird café people lent me a thick-ass jacket. Got a gnarly scar on my arm now, by the way. Wanna see?"

"Gross," said Nora. "Maybe later. Anyway, I might go back and check on everyone again in a few months. I think Ruby's heart attack took a big toll on the family, even though they knew it was coming. Though I still don't think Oliver would appreciate being buried next to her. They never really hit it off. But I'm still trying to convince Patty to visit us here. I think she might. Did I tell you they're installing phone lines out there soon?"

"Yep," said Charlie. "Glad they finally made it to the nineteenth century."

Nora gave Charlie a look that said, "I know, right?"

Charlie just smiled at her, with a look that said nothing. It didn't have to. She already knew what he was feeling, because she felt it too. After Charlie had his miraculous resurrection, revealing himself to have cheated Death once again not long after Charles was hauled off the scene, S.C.Y.T.H.E. turned the little red house upside down looking for his case file. With the Blind Spot cleared and the file no longer glitching, the ink cloud was gone. But the middle name had been replaced. Now the file belonged not to Charles Ezra Bird but to one Charles Oliver Bird, who was already in S.C.Y.T.H.E. custody far, far away. Charlie was free to live for as long as he was meant to live, and that was all Nora could ask for.

Meanwhile, S.C.Y.T.H.E. allowed Nora to walk free in exchange for her assistance in eliminating the Virgo Bay Blind Spot, under the condition that she promise to never interfere with the business of Death again. Which was just as well for Nora. She had no intention of living the life she had before. After everything she'd experienced since finding Charlie's file, she was ready for something new.

She met Charlie's smile with her own.

"So," Charlie said as he put his feet on the cardboard box in front of him, crossing one ankle over the other. "What's the plan? What now?"

"I guess," said Nora, "now we live."

ACKNOWLEDGMENTS

It takes a village to raise a child, and sometimes that child happens to be a book. This is a thank-you to my village. To my mom, first and foremost and forever, thanks for being the best Book Bubbie in the world. Thanks to my dad for always telling me to keep going, and my sister, Sam, for the heartfelt support. To Jess Clement and Rachelle Zalter, thank you for your friendship, your general existence, and your inspirational hypochondria. To Greg Solomon and Mike Bredin for being such tireless cheerleaders and amazing friends. To Cleo and Noodles for being the best nieces. To the good folks at the Dundas Starbucks (and specifically Kieran) for letting me hunch gremlin-style over my manuscript for hours on end, and for always being an absolute delight whenever I come up for air. To Tracy Bernstein, my editing fairy godmother, thank you for believing in my words and putting up with my shenanigans. To Melissa Edwards, my incredible agent, for always being in my corner. To Natasha Tsakiris, my amazing Canadian publicist and to Elisha Katz, Yazmine Hassan, and the team in NYC, you're truly the dream team. To Jaime Lamchick for bringing my words to life in audio form, to Laurène Boglio for her gorgeous cover design, to my amazing copyeditor Angelina Krahn, and to every graphic designer, assistant, and intern who helped bring this book to the shelves.

And finally, but perhaps most importantly, to you, the reader, for being part of this story's story. If you followed me here from *A Grim Reaper's Guide to Catching a Killer*, an extra turbo-bonus thanks for hanging out with me again. I regret to inform you that we're best friends now.

On a serious note, this is a book about anxious people, for anxious people, by an anxious people. Sometimes the things that make our lives the hardest can also be our secret weapons when we figure out how to cope with them.

Photo by Madison Rose Photography

Maxie Dara is from a tiny, Hallmark-movie-style town in Ontario, Canada, where she works as a writer and actress, because rejection-heavy careers are her passion. She is also a two-time award-winning playwright. Maxie knew she wanted to be a writer at the age of seven, when she first fell in love with the written word. She also wanted to be a mermaid but has mostly focused on the writing side of things.